The Evolution of Elsa Kreiss

MICHELE E. GWYNN

An M.E. Gwynn Publication

Cover by Emeegee Graphics.

Editing by Emily A. Lawrence/Lawrence Editing and Michele E. Gwynn

First Edition, ISBN: 978-1-7324546-0-6

Contents

Chapter 1

Pskov, Russia

Present Day

The bells of the church rang informing one and all it was time to begin Supplication. Congregants dropped what they were doing and walked to their rooms. Inside, the rooms were all the same; a pallet for a bed, a small table next to it with a lantern sitting on top and a chest of drawers. The walls were cold concrete, and dull, drab gray. One window with a cracked pane faced north over the courtyard below. The chill in the air permeated the thin glass and wind whistled through the crack. Gregor closed his door and went to his pallet. Beneath, he pulled out a length of knotted rope. It was thick and frayed at the ends. The color had turned from white to reddish brown over the years. Oxidation of the blood that covered it created the ghastly stained hue.

He removed his robe and folded it neatly, placing it on his bed. Then, he kneeled on the gray stone floor and bowed his head. He began to pray. As he did, he lifted the rope in his hands and flung the knotted end over his shoulders one at a time, flagellating himself. Scars that had built up over the last ten years stood out stark white against his tanned back. With each prayer, he swung the rope. Skin split, and blood began to run in red rivulets down his backside soaking into his underwear. He knew he was supposed to clear his mind of all thoughts during Supplication. It was one of their rules pounded into his brain since he'd entered the Order of Rasputin at the tender age of sixteen by the will of his parents who could not afford to house and feed him anymore. The Order was an extremist offshoot of the Khlysty, a sect that practiced asceticism, or abstinence from worldly goods. It all bled from the Russian Orthodox Church, becoming more bizarre as it evolved into a close-minded, and sometimes brutal form of conservative Christianity. This Order revered Grigori Rasputin, the Holy man who was a favorite advisor to the Tsar and Tsarina of Russia during World War I. His death at the hands of those who viewed his influence over the Romanov monarchy as destructive was martyred in the inner-most sanctum of the Khlysty. Like Rasputin, all members of the Order were kept illiterate in his honor believing that worldly knowledge corrupted the otherwise sanctified vessels of God, his people. Religious teachings were handed down through verbal instructions and strict rituals. Questioning them was not allowed and doing so could end in a member's death by stoning.

Despite this, Gregor had difficulty clearing his mind and immersing himself in his prayers this day. Images of the young woman recently brought into the compound flooded his thoughts. She was the most beautiful creature he'd ever seen. Her flowing blonde hair and big blue eyes had pleaded with him for help as she was marched past him while he tended the garden. The two elevated members who each had hold of one of her arms barely looked in his direction as they forced the young woman through the doorway into the temple. One of them was Mikael, the guardian appointed by Holy Father Matteus. Mikael was beyond strict and seemed to revel in his role as guardian since it gave him the authority to administer punishment. Something he did on a regular basis and for the most minor of infractions. It boded badly for the lovely girl that she was in his hands.

Out of Gregor's sight, inside the temple, she'd been tied to a cross near the altar and stripped bare. They left her there during morning group prayer for all to see, stating her humiliation would help rid her of her worldly ways. She'd cried, and her tears caused a rush of heat to travel downward and settle into his groin.

Remembering this brought about the same reaction, and as Gregor continued to offer prayer on his lips, his hips bucked with each blow from the heavy rope. His erection strained against his dirty underwear, and the rub from the tightened material stimulated him. He swung harder, trying to cleanse his mind of lustful thoughts, but nothing helped, and on his last round of verses, he climaxed. Panting heavily, he bowed his head and cried. Over and over, he begged God to forgive him for being weak. His bloody rope lay on the cold stone floor next to him, and his back bled freely. Rising, he picked up his robe and walked out of his room toward the communal showers. Taking a deep breath, he turned on the cold spray and walked beneath feeling the sting. He clenched his teeth, and with both palms flat against the tiled wall, he cried once again. He didn't know how he would get her out of his mind, but he knew that after today, he was forever changed. He'd discovered pleasure, and knew that once discovered, he was now a corrupt vessel.

The only other thoughts he could entertain after this experience were how to have more of these feelings.

———◆———

That night inside the temple, Irina Bromovich hung by her limbs. Pain wracked her entire body as the stress from being stretched and tied pushed her in and out of consciousness. She'd pissed herself already having no other way to relieve her bladder. She felt water being sponged onto her body and struggled to open her eyes. A young man was cleaning her legs. She could see the top of his dark head kneeling by her feet. His hand shook as he lifted the sponge to her thighs and squeezed the water out allowing it to wash away the urine. She whimpered.

Looking up, the young man caught her eye. He gave her a look of such reverence and apology before dipping the sponge back into the bucket and lifting it once again to her body. This time, he reached between her spread legs and pressed his hand to her privates. He squeezed, and water gushed up and then ran down her legs. The feeling of being cleaner was cancelled out by the fact that a stranger, one who was an accomplice in her kidnapping, was touching her inappropriately.

"Please," she cried. "Please let me go." Her blue eyes pleaded with him.

The young man continued to wash her legs, then his eyes traveled up to her naked belly and breasts. He stood, and ignoring her cries for help, began washing her there, too. Irina struggled with her ropes and cried. The more she struggled, the more he touched her until he finally dropped the sponge and reached out with only his bare hands. Her cries grew louder. He clamped a large hand over her mouth. She couldn't get away. He parted his robe and stepped closer. Fearing the worst, she began to scream into his hand. He pushed harder on her face, covering her nose, too, as he pushed himself on her. Not quite knowing what he was doing, he pushed his groin up against hers, remembering a day long ago when he'd woken late in the night and had come upon his father on top of his mother. He didn't know then what was happening, but some part of his uneducated brain told him it was similar to this because his father seemed to enjoy it greatly. Her screams and struggles spurred him on and lasted only moments longer. Then, she went limp. Still, Gregor bucked until that feeling found him once again. He backed up and gave her a little shake. She didn't respond.

He shook her again, then slapped her face, but there were no signs of life. Her lips were blue and hung slack.

Eyes growing large, Gregor backed away looking around the temple. No one was inside at this hour. Still, he had to make sure. He searched every corner, and once satisfied no one had seen what he'd just done, he snuck quietly out of the side door. He knew he would have to leave. Staying was not an option. Tears stung his eyes as he realized he'd killed her. He'd killed the beautiful woman. He hadn't meant to, but her cries would have woken someone, and he would not have been able to touch her anymore, and he couldn't resist touching her. She was all he'd thought about all day, and the obsession to see her again, to feel her skin, and experience that pleasure was too much to resist, so he'd succumbed to his dark desires. Now, those desires had killed. Strangely, the only thing he was sorry about was that he would not get to touch her again.

He slipped into his room where he packed up the few belongings he owned. He'd have to find his way beyond the walls of the Order somehow. Staying meant certain death. He kept to the shadows until he reached the gate. There, he opened it wide enough only for him to fit through. He closed it behind him so no alarm would be raised. Down the road leading away from the compound, Gregor considered his options. He hadn't been outside in ten years. He didn't know if anything he knew back then might still be as it was. He had a cousin who lived five miles outside of Pskov, the town where he grew up, along the river Velikaya, in western Russia, and so he made his way in that direction. Ivan would help him. They'd once been close, before Gregor's parents had committed him to the Order. Ivan's parents ran a successful farm. Ridding themselves of their child had never crossed their minds. He was lucky, Ivan. His parents loved him enough to keep him. Gregor's parents, however, did not. If they had, then his father would've found a way to earn money or maybe given Gregor the chance to find a job and help contribute to the family. Why his father and mother had chosen, instead, to hide him away in a religious Order was beyond him. He had little memory of his early years. Those that he did retain were of hardships, no money for food, his father drunk, and his mother taking in dirty laundry to wash to earn a few coins. They weren't worth recalling.

The night air hung heavily, chilling his bones. It was at least ten miles to Ivan's home. He hoped he remembered how to get there. He kept himself company on his long journey with thoughts of the woman, how it had felt to touch a female for the first time. He knew he liked it, and he wanted more. But for now, he needed to secure his most basic needs, lodging, food, and a job. After that, he could figure out how to indulge his growing desire for the female flesh.

Chapter 2

Gregor did indeed remember his way to his cousin's home. It was nearly dawn when he arrived. He sat on the doorstep and waited. He was exhausted and cold, so he wrapped one of his extra robes around his shoulders. He would need new clothing, he thought. A stray cat wandered by on its way back to wherever it lived after a night of hunting mice, no doubt. He leaned on the handrail and curled in on himself. In an hour, the sun would be up, and he'd knock on Ivan's door. It would be rude to do so now. He thought about all that now lay before him. Life in the Order was the same every single day. He didn't have to worry about where he would sleep, when he would eat, or what he would wear. Members were assigned a room. Meals were provided through their own hard work gardening and raising cattle. Everyone wore the same robes made by the women of the group who wove the wool on looms after they sheered the sheep each spring. Then they would cut the cloth and sew the robes. Each member had five robes and was responsible for cleaning and maintaining their own clothing.

Now, he would need to secure a place to stay. He hoped Ivan would offer him lodging. It didn't matter if it was within the house or out back in the barn. He'd work to earn his keep. He was a good gardener and could do lots of heavy lifting and hauling. After ten years of self-flagellation, he was immune to pain. If he could just work the farm, anyone's farm, he could earn the money he would need to buy clothing. He wouldn't be able to continue wearing the scratchy woolen robes. He'd stick out like a sore thumb, and after what happened last night, he needed to blend in to be safe. His stomach growled reminding him he was very hungry after all the excitement of the night and the ten mile walk in the dark. Despite all the thoughts running through his head, Gregor fell asleep with his head leaning on the wooden rail. The sun on his face, and a rough shake of his shoulder woke him.

"Hey! Hey, you. Wake up. You need to move on, brother. You can't stay here on my stoop." A dark-haired, bearded man stood in front of him giving him an annoyed look. He wore a red checkered flannel shirt over a white T-shirt, jeans, boots, and a black coat.

"Did you hear me, monk?" He snapped his fingers in front of Gregor's face.

"Yes. I heard you, but I'm not a monk. Ivan, it's me." Gregor felt a smile begin to spread across his lips. His cousin had grown up in the last ten years. He was now a bear of a man, and not the same skinny boy he remembered.

"Do I know you?" Ivan asked, his eyes opening wider as he took in the stranger's face.

"Yes, cousin, you know me well. It's me, Gregor." Gregor started to stand but was stiff from the cold and sat back down immediately.

"Gregor? Little Gregor?" Recognition lit his eyes and Ivan smiled. "Cousin! Hello! Long time, no see!" He lifted his cousin up in a bear hug.

Gregor answered in kind, trying not to lose his footing. "Da. Too long. Kak Dela?" (*How are you doing?*)

"I am well. But you...you don't seem well. Let's get you inside and warmed up. Nina has just made hot porridge and bread. You can break your fast, and then tell me where you've been all these years. Your mother and father simply moved and told no one, not even papa." Ivan helped Gregor gain his feet and assisted him up the steps and through the door.

Gregor absorbed the news that his parents had moved without even telling him. Apparently, they left soon after committing him to the Order and told no one what they had done. Ivan had no idea. His cousin listened to the story Gregor told over his bowl of hot cereal. He perked up a little after eating, but his tale was one that could not be told in a few short sentences. As Ivan learned what his aunt and drunken uncle had done to his little cousin, he became angry. Ten years, Gregor rotted away inside the walls of that cult. That's what everyone in town thought of that place. They all knew it to be an extremist sect that most suspected was responsible for many a missing teenager; especially young girls.

"Those bastards!" Ivan's fist hit the tabletop causing everything sitting on it to rattle. Gregor jumped, as did Ivan's wife, Nina. Gregor stole looks at her, noting how lovely she was with her curly black hair and big brown eyes. His cousin was very lucky to have a woman of his own, one he could experience the pleasures of the flesh with as he pleased.

However, Gregor couldn't disagree. He'd long ago let go of any feelings he had for his parents, good or bad. He barely remembered them except for the odd memories of hard times. "It's in the past, cousin. What matters is now." He'd cleaned his bowl and consumed two hot rolls slathered in butter. Nina refilled his cup with the fresh milk collected from their dairy cow.

"Da, I know this, but I'm still angry. What they did to you was not right. Not right at all." He sighed. "Well, you've had one hell of a journey to get here. And I'm glad you did. I just wish you'd come to me sooner." Ivan stood, his chair scraping the floor as he pushed it backwards. "Let us just get you clean and into bed. Today, you rest. Tomorrow, I show you my farm, and we begin to build you a new life.

I can always use help here, and you are welcome for as long as you need me, cousin."

Gregor had to hold back the tears his cousin's words brought to his eyes. It had been a very long time since he felt the love of family. In fact, besides one or two very early memories of his mother, and summers with his cousin's family, he'd barely experienced it at all. "I'm ever grateful to hear that, Ivan. I won't let you down, and you'll not be sorry for taking me in. I'm a hard worker." Gregor stood, and followed Ivan as he led the way to the back of the house, and into a guest room.

"I'm sure you are, Gregor. You've grown into a strong and fine young man despite your circumstances. Here, let me get you some things to wear. They may be a bit large, but that should be okay until Nina and I can take you into town for a little shopping." Ivan left Gregor standing in the middle of the cheerful room. A large bed with a colorful quilt dominated the center space. A window with bright curtains let the morning sunshine in bouncing off the shiny wood surfaces of the dresser and chest of drawers. A rug ran along the side of the bed covering the wood floors. It was warm and inviting, and finer than anything he'd ever had before. A tear ran down his cheek.

"Here. Try these after your shower. It's right across the hall. You remember." Gregor thanked his cousin as he took the stack of clothes into his arms.

"Spasiba, Ivan." He could barely get the words out.

Ivan stood there and watched as his cousin, who used to spend summers with him here when his parents ran the farm, walked across the hall and looked around the bathroom like he'd never seen one before. He couldn't fathom parents who would put their child into some lunatic religious sect, giving him up. Why had they not simply sent Gregor to his parents? The life he must've led could not have been easy.

Gregor dropped the clothes onto the countertop and started pulling his robe up over his head. It was then that Ivan saw the macabre mapping of scars on his cousin's back. His mouth fell open in shock. Unaware, Gregor reached into the shower and found the handle to turn on the water. He shed his dirty underwear and stepped in. The offensive scars were no longer in view.

Rage bubbled up inside Ivan and he walked straight out into the kitchen and hugged his wife. He wanted to cry for his cousin, but grown men didn't cry. He wanted to punch something, anything, but that would not help. He vowed he would do everything he could to help him. Nina waited patiently for her usually happy husband to calm down, and when he told her what he'd seen, she wrapped her arms tightly around him and said, "We will help him, my darling. He's home now."

Ivan buried his face in his wife's hair and inhaled. He knew how lucky he was, but in that moment, he truly appreciated just how fortunate he'd been being his parents' son and being Nina's husband. Gregor never knew these things. Well, maybe briefly when he'd visit each summer as a kid. His parents loved him. Gregor's mother was his own father's only sister. She'd married a worthless man. Everyone in the family knew he was a drunkard, but Emily would not listen to reason. She thought herself in love back then. She suffered for her mistake in judgment thereafter. Boris Koslov was a no-good fool. His name should have given it away if his aunt Emily had been a little smarter; Koslov was Slavic for goat or goat herder. Hell, if only he'd even worked doing that instead of living life as an unskilled, lazy bastard, he would not have been so bad, even as a drunk. Being a drunkard could be forgiven if that man at least worked and took care of his family. Every summer they would come stay with Ivan's family and help work the fields. For this, his papa would give them some money and load his little sister down with vegetables and preserves she helped pick and prepare. He would slaughter a pig for his sister's family and offer a goat that they could keep for fresh milk, and to send to slaughter later in winter when the weather turned for the worse. Sadly, it was later learned that Boris, the selfish Slav, would sell the goat and the pig meat and then drink the money away. Emily had to take in laundry to make ends meet, and they still didn't. Sometimes, when Boris was really pissed, he would take Gregor into the village and make him beg for coins. If he refused or didn't collect enough, Boris would beat his son bloody. It really should not have been so surprising that he handed Gregor off to that damn sect. Ivan figured he probably sold the boy. Boris never 'gave' anything away.

He could not erase the past, but he was determined to help his cousin build a better future. No one should grow up feeling unloved. He hoped to set the proper example for his own children someday. He and Nina had been trying for the past six months, but nothing yet. He knew, though, that God would see his good deeds, offered out of love and duty, and would reward him soon with a son or daughter of his own. It was certainly no coincidence that Gregor had come to him, the one person in the world he remembered with love. So, it would be in love in which he would help him.

"I'll be back." Ivan let go of Nina and headed toward the front door.

"Where are you going, моя lyubovyu?" (*My love.*) She turned and inquired of his sudden departure.

"To the church to give thanks to God for sending Gregor home, and to light a candle and make an offering."

He grabbed his coat and threw it on as he walked out, closing the door behind him. Nina smiled. She was proud to be Ivan's wife, but at this moment, she wished she could shout it from the rooftops. He never hesitated to help someone in need, and family was a priority for him. He would make a wonderful father – very soon. She simply wished to wait a little while longer to tell him...just to be sure.

Ivan entered the church located three blocks from his home. Inside, it was far warmer, and a few faithful were kneeling in prayer in the pews closest to the altar. He walked to the side wall and the altar there where he placed a few coins in the offerings box. Feeling it wasn't quite adequate, he pulled some bills out and stuffed those in, too. Then he lit a candle and knelt in prayer. He thanked God for Gregor's homecoming, and also for the opportunity to do His work. He prayed for his parents who were now old and living in a small apartment in the center of town where they could get around easily. He thanked God for the harvest he brought in over the summer, and for Nina. He prayed she would finally conceive so that he might fulfill the Almighty's command to be fruitful and multiply. He remembered to also thank his heavenly father for everything he did not grant Ivan because it was not part of His plan for his faithful son. He made the sign of the cross, and stood, backing away from the mini altar respectfully before turning around and leaving the church.

Thinking of his parents, he decided to visit them and share the wonderful news about their nephew. He headed north toward the town's center, stopping along the way to pick up some bread and beef and cabbage stew from the Inn across the street. It was his mother's favorite, and he never came to visit empty-handed. He was so happy, he asked that they add a few slices of chocolate cake, and a bottle of Vodka—the cake for his mother (who had a sweet-tooth), and the Vodka for the men to make a toast to family. His spirits were high, and joy and gratitude occupied his gentle heart.

———————————◄◊►————————————

Gregor dressed in the clothes Ivan provided, feeling over-dressed after so many years of wearing nothing but the woolen robes. For the first time in as many years, he felt warm. The jeans were a bit big, but with the belt, were fine. The dungaree T-shirt and flannel shirt embraced him like a warm hug. They even smelled like his cousin making him smile. Socks on his feet were also a luxury he hadn't experienced since he was a child. The Order members wore work boots purchased from a second-hand shop near town, and socks were never part of their wardrobe. New underwear was not provided, either. The clean white cotton covering was the most valuable of gifts. He put on his old work boots since they were the only shoes he owned and walked out into the living room.

Nina was cleaning. He saw her bent over dusting the tabletops. That was why everything shone to a high gloss. She was a good homemaker. Her hips wiggled in her jeans as she hummed a tune to herself. Her rounded derriere swayed. Gregor felt the crotch of his jeans tighten as he grew hard. His eyes glazed over as he recalled the feeling of a woman's flesh against his own. He imagined her breasts bouncing around as she rubbed the tabletop in circular motions. The idea caused him to reach down and place a hand over his burgeoning tent. Bad idea. His hand there felt good. Feeling ashamed for reacting this way over his cousin's wife, he turned and walked swiftly to his room, shutting the door. Inside, he sat on the side of the bed trying to calm down. His cousin had been nothing but kind to him, and he would not reward that kindness by turning into an animal and harming Nina. He picked up one of his robes that was still folded from being packed and carried on his ten-mile journey and ripped it into strips. He braided them together and tied knots at the end. Then he removed his two new shirts, his pants, and even his nice new underwear and kneeled on the wood floors, careful to avoid the carpet runner, and wearing only his socks. He offered Supplication for his sins and began flagellating himself. The wool was not as heavy as his old rope, but if he swung hard enough, the scratchy material began to do its duty. Like before, he could not clear his mind, and like before, the more he beat his back, the more pleasure he experienced. He made a mess on Nina's clean floor. After using the rest of the ripped robe to mop up, he snuck across the hall and back into the shower. Afterwards, he stuffed the dirty robe and the evidence of his sin into the bathroom trash pushing it to the bottom. He decided to wait in his room until Ivan came to get him. That would be safest. And as soon as he could manage it, when he had enough money to begin a new life, he would leave.

He didn't want to leave his cousin, but until he could get himself under control, he realized he was a danger to Nina. Perhaps Ivan could help him get some kind of job where he would not have much contact with women, just until he could get it together. He lay back and thought about what kind of job that might be. Maybe as a sailor on a fishing boat. Women didn't go out on those, only men. Yes. That would work. He'd ask Ivan when he came to get him. Relieving his mind of worries for the moment, Gregor fell asleep, his back still bleeding, the red droplets staining his new dungaree T-shirt.

Chapter 3

Berlin, Germany

Rain poured down, washing the street clean along Tiergartenstrasse. Tourists ran for cover while native Berliners simply popped open umbrellas they carried with them, knowing how the weather faired in September. It was cold and wet, and Elsa Kreiss shivered inside her police-issue dark blue jacket. She was assigned to patrol the streets after two and a half years of law enforcement classes and on-the-job training. She was one of the oldest rookies in the group having entered this career path at the age of twenty-three. Most candidates began straight out of school, but Elsa had been busy caring for her younger brother, Anno, after the untimely death of their parents in an auto accident.

This meant providing for them both since there wasn't much in the way of savings in their parents' bank account, and funeral services weren't cheap. It was left to Elsa, who was almost nine years older than her brother, to find a way to pay rent, utilities, and put food on the table. There weren't many options open for a young girl of eighteen to make that kind of money, at least, not completely legally. Her friend, Hans, who graduated a year ahead of her, suggested she audition for the father of his lover at the time. He owned a club that catered to men who enjoyed bondage, games of dominance and submission. It wasn't technically prostitution, which was legal, but it did involve some sick shit sometimes. The owner, Herr Arnold Hausmann, a German Jew, took one look at Elsa and immediately said no.

"She's too young and inexperienced. I don't have time for that." He started to dismiss them, but Hans tugged at his lover's hand forcing David to speak up.

"Vader, look again. She's quite lovely. Surely there is something we can use her for. The women are always complaining about having to clean their equipment. Hans and I can show her how to use the auto-clave, and how to sterilize the instruments. It would get the dommes off your back about coming in on their days off to clean."

Herr Hausmann looked at his son. He sighed for the thousandth time thinking, *"Where did I go wrong to have such a woman for a son?"* He loved his child. He was, after all, physically fit, handsome, intelligent, and seemed to have a knack for business, which boded well for the future of his enterprise, but he would never have grandchildren from David. He glanced at Hans who stood off to the side. Hans was even more of a conundrum for Hausmann because the young man looked like some huge Gestapo agent until he opened his mouth, or walked, or even smiled. Then it was painfully obvious that he was a female trapped inside the body of a man. He could not, for the life of him understand the attraction men had for other men. In his day, gay people didn't exist. If they did, they hid it well for fear of being ostracized by family and friends, by society in general. Not so, today. Today, being gay was like some badge of honor. Supporting gays had become a near-global trend. Men married men. Women married women. Herr Hausmann wept for the decline of traditional marriages when a penis was a penis and it went only into a vagina, and no one even mentioned those words. Shaking his head, he sighed again.

He looked at Elsa. She was very pretty, and very young. Some men liked that. Still, he couldn't turn her loose on any of his highbrow clientele. She wouldn't know what she was doing, and it took a very strong level of confidence and knowledge to know how to inflict pain without harm. She'd be a liability as a dominatrix, but as a maid, she'd do. And the dommes would stop complaining to him all the time.

"All right. But she starts at the bottom, and you and Hans are responsible for her. She must learn to clean every single piece of equipment properly and quickly, and if she messes up, if even one of the dommes complains about her, that's it. No job!"

He walked out and left them standing there. After the door closed, Hans grabbed Elsa up in his muscular arms and swung her around. "You got the job! Fantastische, mein Liebling!"

Smiling hugely and feeling as if a weight had been lifted off her shoulders, Elsa laughed, then kissed Hans on his cheek. "Danke, mein Freund! Danke, David!" Hans set her down and she hugged David, too.

"Don't thank me yet. We must work hard to make you the best maid these dommes have ever seen. And in between, we're going to teach you the art of dominance and submission. It's really the only way you'll be able to make any real money to survive." Hans was so happy to hear his lover say this that he kissed him full on the lips. It turned a little sloppy as they momentarily forgot Elsa was in the room.

"Geez, guys. Cool it down!" She laughed at their antics. Her friend was so in love with David, and so happy to be working with him at Club Sexo as a ticket agent, and now his best girlfriend would be working there, too. Hans was over the moon.

That's how it began. She'd worked hard and listened to everything the guys taught her. David showed her how to hog-tie a man in a way that was painful and pleasurable but not permanently damaging. He also secured Mistress Lena's cooperation to allow Elsa to observe her work so she could learn how it's done firsthand. In two years, she'd gone from maid to dominatrix. In another year, she was a top-draw attraction at the club and in high demand. Two years after that, she'd quit at the top of her game in the BDSM business after a life-changing event. Her brother, who meant everything to her, had been kidnapped by a known sex trafficking criminal and taken out of Germany to Amsterdam at the whim of a sick pedophile named Peter Knudson.

Everything changed then. The true miracle, however, was that they got Anno back before any harm could come to him. That never happens, according to Kriminalkommissar Joseph Heinz who was the lead detective on the case. Heinz used his connections through Interpol to help get Anno back. They wouldn't have even known where to find him had it not been for new friends she'd made at the time, Sarah Brown and Paul Christiansen. Actually, it was because of the latter that Anno had been taken to begin with. The pedo was Paul's uncle who'd sexually abused him as a child. It turned out that Knudson had targeted Anno on a recruiting mission in Berlin, and he blamed his nephew for causing him to lose out on gaining Elsa as an employee, a ruse he invented to get his hands-on Anno.

Heinz brought her brother home safe and sound, and unharmed. Since that day, Elsa vowed to find a new career, one where she would be home at night to better keep an eye on Anno, and one in which she would be around a better quality of people. She really wasn't quite sure what that career might be, but she told Heinz and his partner, Birgitta Mahler, that somehow, she wanted to help others and maybe work in a field where she could stop people like Knudson. It became imperative she had a way to protect others, especially children. Mahler suggested law enforcement. She said they needed more strong women on the force. Heinz, feeling magnanimous after closing a child abduction case successfully offered to help her. He greased the wheels to get her into the program. She still had lunch with him once a month. He made a point of keeping tabs on her and Anno who was about to graduate Gymnasium and enter Technische Universitat Berlin.

Elsa smiled, remembering her journey from that moment to the present, while watching people go about their business as she patrolled the strasse with her partner, Hugo Beimer. They were Schutzpolizei, or more commonly, Schupo. Beimer had been a patrol officer now for nearly two years. He was large and friendly, and everyone along the Tiergartenstrasse knew him. She, however, was the new kid, the rookie. She would have to prove herself, and that took time, and more hours on foot than she cared to consider while standing in the rain.

The Tiergarten was nearly empty of tourists, so Beimer suggested they head east along Tiergartenstrasse. Their patrol took them to the end of the road, and they looped back around coming full circle on Corneliusstrasse. As they passed the Galerie George Nothelfer, they noticed a large truck parked in front while three men carried massive canvases removed from the back inside. Beimer threw a look at Elsa, indicating the vehicle, and he approached the gentleman standing on the sidewalk directing the other two in what to move and where to put the items.

"You can't have that truck parked here like that. It's obstructing traffic." Her partner was not one to mince words. He pointed at the cock-eyed way the truck's back end stuck out onto the thoroughfare.

The man turned, and his eyes briefly caught Elsa's before locking onto Beimer. "We're almost finished, officer. Our dock out back is flooded. A pipe broke last night, and maintenance is back there fixing it. We didn't really have any choice." He looked Beimer straight in the eye, which not many men could do since he was a tall man. But the gentleman was equal in height, and carried a pleasing amount of muscle, at least, so Elsa thought. His hazel eyes were outlined in dark brown lashes that matched his hair, which was cut short and gelled into messy spikes, a style fashionable among men lately. He had symmetrical features and a strong jaw softened by just a hint of well-maintained five-o-clock shadow, and nicely shaped lips.

"Not my problem. But traffic is stalled, so get this pulled off the road quickly." Beimer, for all his usual gentleness, could come off as one scary bear of a man sometimes. Maybe that's why he succeeded so well in the Schupo. His goal was to continue schooling and ascend into the upper echelons as a detective. Such took years and often had a great deal to do with who one knew. Elsa thought of Kommissar Heinz who'd become a pseudo-father figure over the last couple of years. Underneath his rough exterior, he had a heart of gold. He'd attended all of Anno's school programs and was there the day Elsa entered the academy, taking her and her brother out to dinner to celebrate when she completed it all and was inducted into the Schupo. Anno had really taken to him, too. Heinz was Elsa's "somebody" inside the force. She knew that some things had been easier for her than for others because the Kommissar was her benefactor. She knew it, and still she worked her ass off to prove herself. She was never one to get by on favors. She knew the value of hard work. She'd been a dominatrix, after all. But no one on the force knew this. Heinz told her it would be better for her to not mention it, ever.

"There's always a choice. It's called 'the right one'. Let's get this vehicle over, now." Beimer stood and waited as the man rolled his eyes and turned to one of the other two men coming out of the gallery.

"Otto, pull the truck up over there, so it's not on the street." He pointed a few feet up past the door onto the sidewalk.

"But we're almost finished, Lukas," the man, of mixed German and Turkish descent, whined.

"Doesn't matter. This officer here, and his lovely partner, will toss us all in jail if we don't." Lukas gave Beimer a none-too-friendly look, but the one he cast at Elsa was much warmer. Her eyebrow shot up at his cheekiness.

"Don't be a smartass." Elsa finally spoke, and although her words were meant to put the man in his place, instead, a smile broke out across his lips. It changed his handsome face to gorgeous in a split second.

"She speaks," he said with mock surprise.

Otto climbed into the driver's seat and proceeded to pull the truck further off the road as directed. Beimer walked over and circled the vehicle, eyeing it to make sure it was off the road enough to his satisfaction, and that oncoming traffic wouldn't have to go into the river across the street to get around. The man, Lukas, had pissed him off with his cocky attitude. Elsa, on the other hand, was intrigued. She was almost always attracted to cocky men. It was a sign of confidence.

"I speak when necessary, and your attitude made it necessary. Why make a simple situation so complicated? You only needed to move the truck, not run off at the mouth."

He continued to grin unashamedly. "Maybe I just don't like cops. Or authority of any kind, for that matter. But I could make an exception if they all looked like you." His direct gaze combined with the humor dancing in his eyes made Elsa chuckle.

"The incorrigible type, eh? What are you doing here, anyway? Delivering new art?" She inquired.

"No. They are delivering. I work here. I'm Lukas Trommler." He extended his hand to her. Elsa ignored it deliberately.

"What do you do here at the gallery?" He dropped his hand to his side and chuckled.

"I set up the exhibits for clients. Like the one we're having tomorrow night. It's a touring show of a new artist, the Paul Christiansen collection. He's come onto the radar in the last couple of years with his work, nightmarish imagery from his—"

"Did you say Paul Christiansen?" Elsa's attention was caught immediately.

"Yes, you know of his work?" Lukas asked.

"No. But I know Paul." She answered with blunt honesty.

"No shit! He'll be here tomorrow night for the opening. Do you know him well?" Lukas stepped closer to Elsa.

"You could say that." Her memories traveled back to those days when he visited her dungeon, shared lunch with her, Sarah, and Anno, and then to the nightmare of Paul's uncle kidnapping her brother.

"Oh, God, you didn't date him, did you? I hear he's a pretty-boy." Lukas asked the inappropriate question without an ounce of embarrassment.

"What? No! Nothing like that. We met a few years ago. He's a friend of a friend."

"Oh, good. Well, if you'd like, I can get you onto the guest list." He looked at her again with renewed interest.

"I don't know. It's tomorrow night. Isn't it too late for that?" Elsa wasn't at all sure she even wanted to see Paul again. Not because she disliked him, but because she didn't want to relive those bad memories.

"Not at all. You could be my plus-one." Lukas waited.

"As your date? Are you serious?" Elsa was taken aback. Here they were one step away from writing him a traffic citation, and this man was asking her on a date.

"I am very serious. So, what name should I put down..." He looked at her name tag. "Officer Kreiss? That would be a very weird way to introduce you around." A hint of a smile teased the corners of his lips.

"If that's your way of inquiring about my first name, it's not very original." She thought it over, leaving Lukas to sweat a bit. "Okay. I'll come. But I'm not telling you my name. If you're so smart, Mr. Cocky, you'll find a way to figure that out. What time?" She threw him a saucy look. Beimer watched the entire exchange and rolled his eyes.

Lukas grinned, accepting the challenge. "Half eight. I'll meet you here. It's our spot now, after all."

Elsa laughed. "Whatever. Half eight it is. Now, stay out of trouble until then, will you?"

She walked away and Beimer fell in step beside her. "That wasn't very professional, Kreiss."

"Neither was your Gestapo intimidation tactics, Beimer. But we're still here, eh?"

He sighed. He knew she was right, but he didn't like that the annoying gallery man had just asked his partner on a date. He liked Elsa. Not in a romantic way, but more like a younger sister. Beimer had grown up with three older sisters, so he was used to being around women. It was probably why he was as easy to get along with as he was, and why he never seemed to get the girl. They all thought of him as harmless. Hugo didn't think of himself as 'harmless' when it came to women, but women thought of him as a big teddy bear.

"So do you really know this artist Christiansen?" He asked, showing interest.

"I do, but he wasn't an artist then. Or, at least, he was undiscovered. No, back then he was just a... businessman."

"Well, then it will be nice for you to see him again and catch up." Hugo looked around in that way policemen do, ever watchful and on the lookout for crime.

"I suppose so." Elsa remained noncommittal. She wasn't sure, but she knew Sarah still kept in contact with him. It was one of the reasons her relationship with Anthony de Luca deteriorated over the last year. He just couldn't get past his jealousy despite the fact that Paul was no threat. Her friend had moved back to Texas after living with Anthony for over a year at his place in New York City. She talked often of coming to visit Elsa and Anno soon but hadn't yet made any travel plans. It would be nice to see her friend again.

For now, Elsa found herself with a date to a gallery exhibit opening tomorrow night with a man she'd just met. A very cocky man with a devilish smile. That part, at least, was interesting, even a little promising. It had been a long time since she'd dated anyone. Not since her brief attempt at a relationship with her ex-coworker, Nicolette. Nic wanted more than Elsa was willing to give in terms of commitment. She was okay with a dalliance with a woman, but she really didn't want to spend the rest of her life in a lesbian relationship. She realized she was definitely more on the heterosexual side of things.

Their breakup had been rough with Nic having a hard time letting go. It was messy. The hardest part was keeping it from Heinz. Somehow, she didn't want him to know she'd dated the woman. That 'father figure' feeling was very strong. It truly felt like hiding something from 'dad'. And no daughter ever wanted to disappoint her father.

Now she had to figure out what to wear for her date. As she mentally contemplated the contents of her closet, a young boy ran out of the corner Bakerei with a bag of bread. The owner ran out after him shouting "Stop! Thief!"

Beimer took off after the kid without hesitation, and Elsa had to run to catch up. *A bread theft. The kid was probably one of the many homeless runaways and was just hungry.* She hated having to arrest anyone down on their luck, but the law was the law, and no one was above it. She'd put in a call to Heinz. He had a contact that worked with homeless kids. Sometimes these bad moments were really blessings in disguise. The kid would get help, be homed somewhere and put through school until he was old enough to go out into the world. But at least he'd be prepared for it and able to take care of himself by then. Beimer caught up to the boy who looked no more than twelve or thirteen and grabbed him by the scruff of his shirt. Although he was a rather large brute, Hugo Beimer was firm but gentle with the boy. He still had to handcuff him, but he was nice about it. The store owner caught up, cursing and shouting.

"Calm down, sir. Here." Elsa pulled a few euro out of her own pocket and paid the man for the bread. "No harm, no foul. We'll take it from here."

He grumbled about no-good kids who were just a menace to society as he stomped back to his business.

"Now what am I to arrest him for if you paid for the stolen goods?" Beimer asked as he held the boy by the back of his shirt.

"You're not. I'm calling in a favor. We'll have someone down here shortly to take care of this young man." Elsa looked at the boy and immediately thought of her brother.

"You don't have a home, do you?" she asked. The boy hung his head and refused to speak. Elsa put her arm around his shoulders. "That's okay, son. I'm here to help you, not hurt you. You're just hungry, I take it. When's the last time you ate?" He was so skinny, her heart broke.

"Don't know, ma'am. A couple days, I guess." He whispered his answer, clearly ashamed and afraid.

Beimer looked at Elsa and shook his head, his expression full of concern. She gave the boy a gentle push in Hugo's direction, addressing her partner. "Hugo, take our friend over there to the bench. Have some of that bread. It smells good. I'll make the call and get some help here for our young man."

He walked the boy over to the bench telling him he'd take off the cuffs, but he mustn't run off. The boy promised, and Beimer removed the cuffs. They sat down, and Hugo handed over the bag of bread to the boy who tore into it, stuffing chunks into his hollow, dirty cheeks until they puffed out like a squirrel storing nuts.

Elsa called Heinz.

"You and your sensitive woman's heart" he said. "I'll have Mahler come pick him up and take him over to KinderHaus. Where are you now?" Elsa gave him the address.

"How's it going?" Heinz inquired about her patrol.

"It's going well, Kommissar. Nothing too out of the ordinary until now. But I did get asked on a date today." She waited to hear his surly reply knowing he'd have something to say.

"A date? And who is this individual? I want a name, an address...I'll need to run a background check!"

Heinz's protective side came out in force. Although she was already twenty-five, nearly twenty-six years old, he still treated her like she was eighteen. Well, he was forty-seven, an old man by her standards. His overreaction was one reason she'd grown attached to him despite her initial impression of him back when his abrasiveness stung during the circumstances of Anno's abduction. He'd grown on her, and it was just nice knowing someone really cared about what happened to her.

"Yes, a date. You should try it sometime, perhaps finally ask Birgitta out—" She had to slap her hand over her mouth to keep from giggling.

"Birgitta? My partner? Are you crazy, Elsa? What would ever give you such an idea?" Elsa had thought for a while now that the two would make a marvelous pair. It was obvious that Mahler was in love with Heinz, but he was too grouchy and too focused on his job to see it. She hadn't dated anyone in the entire time Elsa knew her, and Heinz may not realize it yet, but he'd come to depend upon her in ways that went just a little beyond the job. If he had to attend a function, or she did, they were each other's 'plus one'. It was really just a matter of time before he woke up. How he would react when he did was anyone's guess.

"He works at the Galerie Georg Nothelfer; sets up exhibits. But that's not the interesting part."

"No? Then what might that be? He's a career criminal? A smuggler? He has a nose piercing?" Heinz waited, knowing whatever it was, it wouldn't be good.

"You're crazy! No, the exhibit he invited me to tomorrow is for—wait for it—Paul Christiansen!" She watched Beimer talking to the boy while he ate a whole loaf of rye.

"Christiansen? Our Paul? Well, good for him! So, he's finally gone down a different career path, eh?" He thought about the last time he'd seen Paul. It was shortly after he'd finished giving a statement to the Dutch police about his uncle's criminal past. His newly deceased uncle. Paul was a mess. He really needed therapy and was happy to learn he'd begun seeing a counselor to work through all his issues of abuse as a young boy. That was the last he knew.

"Ja. It seems he's a hit in the art world. He paints his nightmares as a form of therapy," Elsa replied.

"So, you'll see him tomorrow night on your date? Well, tell him hello and if he has a chance, to stop by my office and visit." Heinz told her Mahler was three minutes out and would be pulling up shortly.

"Okay. I'll let him know. And thanks for helping this young boy. He looks so pathetic. It's breaking my heart." She saw just the smallest hint of a smile from the boy. Apparently, Hugo said something funny. Good old Beimer. He was such a teddy bear.

A car horn startled Elsa and she turned to see Mahler pull up to the curb. She stepped out and they walked over to the boy. As usual, Birgitta was dressed in police detective utilitarian clothing that did nothing to bring out how attractive she really was. Mahler's long, dark brown hair tended to curl so she twisted it up into a knot at her neck, and her black pantsuit with blue top seemed masculine on her petite frame. Despite her short stature, Mahler was very fit for a woman in her late thirties. She had a son named Jan who was the same age as Anno. His father lived in Italy now with his Italian paramour whom he'd left Birgitta for some ten years ago. Since then, the woman had devoted herself to her son and her career with little room for anything else. It was no wonder she found herself attracted to an older, rather crusty detective. He was pretty much the only man Mahler had any contact with in her life. But she didn't want to belittle the reason for her attraction to Heinz. She really liked the idea of the two of them together as a couple, and if she could help that along in any way, she would. Maybe Birgitta would let her work a little makeover magic. It was amazing what a little makeup and the right clothes could do for a person. Elsa made the introductions, and then Birgitta took the young boy by the hand and led him to her car.

"No more worries, young man. KinderHaus is a lovely place with other children your age, and a nice warm bed of your own. Frau Heffler is expecting you. She's very nice and bakes the best cookies..." Mahler had a good heart. Her mothering instincts were strong.

She buckled the boy into his seat and waved at Elsa and Hugo as she drove away. Just another day in the Schupo.

Chapter 4

Joseph Heinz was sound asleep when his mobile rang. He cursed, kicking his covers from his feet as he reached over for the offending object on his nightstand. "Zu sprechen?" His voice conveyed his irritation.

"Heinz, it's Faust." Herman Faust worked in the Landeskriminalamt (LKA) and had been both a friend and colleague of Heinz's for the past twenty years. "I'm sorry to wake you, but a case has come up—actually three cases—with the most recent one tonight."

Joseph sat up on the edge of his bed rubbing his face. "What has this got to do with me, Herman?" Heinz reined in his grouchiness.

"There are disturbing similarities in them, and it's your area of expertise. Missing girls. Two still unaccounted for, and the third one found dead tonight." Faust rattled off the information.

"Are they in my borough?" Anger laced Joseph's question as the memory of an old cold case reared its ugly head.

"No, not yours, but no one else has your personal level of knowledge on these types of cases, either. You're the go-to detective in Berlin for missing and abducted females, Heinz. Like it or not." Faust waited. He knew it would not be easy to convince his friend to come out in the middle of the night to view a dead girl.

Joseph placed a hand over his eyes and leaned onto his knees. He'd done his best to avoid missing and murdered female cases in the past couple of years, sticking instead with stolen property and fraud. No one went missing or got hurt in those situations and his peace of mind was not disturbed. He sighed. He knew he couldn't avoid it forever. "What do you need?"

Faust heard the resignation in his friend's voice, and he was sorry for being the cause of it. "I need you to come down to the coroner's office. Time is definitely not on our side, and the sooner we can gather some helpful information that will lead us to the abductor, the better. You know how it works, Joseph. We must act quickly. I'll tell you what we have so far when you get here, and then let's see what the medic can pull from the body."

"Scheisse," he grimaced. "I'll be there shortly." Heinz hung up and stood looking around his bedroom. It was dark save for the moonlight coming through a crack in the curtains. It was nights like this that he felt most alone; awakened when the world was sleeping and called out to investigate a crime. People generally felt safe locked away in their homes, tucked into bed, but the minute one must leave that warmth and security, and go out into the night, they immediately felt exposed to whatever lay hidden in the shadows beyond their front doors. Joseph knew all about those shadows. They took innocent people, mostly women and children, and never gave them back. If, by chance, they did release them, the shadows returned them, broken or dead. He hated the damn shadows. Now, he was being called out again. It had been a long time, and he dreaded stepping beyond his threshold.

He thought of calling Mahler, but unless he knew for sure he needed her, he decided she was safer undisturbed and tucked away in her bed. The thought of her still sleeping peacefully made him smile. At least he could protect one person. He'd make sure to share all the information in the morning. He considered bringing coffee and donuts. He knew her usual calm demeanor and extraordinary listening skills would help him sort through all the evidence. When the whole world was falling apart, Birgitta remained unfazed. It was what he liked most about her. Their partnership in the Kripo had been a godsend for him. She'd been assigned when he was falling apart nearly five years ago. At first, he gave her a hard time, not wanting to be around anyone, intent on self-destruction. But she would not budge. He would push, and she would stand stalwart. He would huff and puff, and Mahler would look the other way and simply bend in the breeze like a willow, never breaking. Eventually, the storm raging inside him died down. Between his partner's patience and sticking to cases that didn't involve murder or missing children, he'd found a place of peace. The tide turned when he successfully helped rescue Elsa's brother. That kind of ending, a happy one, was rare, and it seemed a good idea to quit while he was ahead. His superior understood, although he hated losing one of his best detectives in missing person's cases. He worked lighter case files, kept close to Elsa and Anno, and spent his days in a blissful tedium. He was okay with that, but now, Faust was pulling him back in. He promised himself it would only be as a consultant. As he went out the front door, Heinz made a mental note to pick up coffee and a couple of crullers afterwards. They were Mahler's favorites.

The morgue was quiet except for the annoying hum of fluorescent lights overhead. The dingy green walls and chipped white tile flooring smelled of antiseptic and formaldehyde. Faust greeted Heinz at the coroner's desk and introduced him to Doctor Menghala—a short man with brown hair that receded at the temples leaving a stark point at the center of his forehead. His wire-rimmed glasses were so thick, Joseph wondered how he saw the bodies he was cutting into. *Good thing*

they're already dead, he thought. He shook the man's hand noting a strength his stature belied.

Heinz looked at his friend. Faust stood by casually sipping a cup of coffee from a vending machine. His faded blond hair was liberally mixed with gray, and his jowls had begun to sag a bit. He looked rumpled in his tweed jacket and dark slacks, but his posture was all cop.

"The doc already performed the autopsy a couple of hours ago. Tell him what you've got so far." He turned the floor over to Menghala.

"Well," he said as he led them all over to the stainless-steel table, "there are abrasions around both wrists and both ankles. She'd been tied with rope. I retrieved a couple of fibers on her skin for analysis, but that will take a few more hours. The cause of death was asphyxiation, but the murderer would have you think she drowned." The doctor slipped on a pair of rubber gloves and lifted the sheet off the body revealing an open torso with several organs removed including the lungs, which lay in a large metal pan.

Heinz's lip curled in distaste. He never understood how anyone could be so coldly clinical about a human body. To him, this was someone's daughter. To the coroner, it was a specimen. To Faust, it was a mystery that needed solving quickly.

"Why do you say that?" Heinz looked over at the doctor who was lifting the lungs displaying them.

"There was no water in them despite the fact that the body was found submerged in the river. Had she died from drowning, her lungs would be filled with river water. They were not."

"Then how was the asphyxiation accomplished?"

Faust watched as Heinz began asking the questions he hoped would lead to a suspect.

"Her airway was cut off. Since there are no strangulation marks on her neck, and no river water in her lungs, the point of cutoff would have to be the nose and mouth. I've found no fibers on her face indicating the use of a cloth or pillow, so I surmise he simply used his hand to cover the airways."

"He?" Heinz interjected. "What makes you sure the suspect is a he?"

The doctor continued. "The size of the hand that could cover her airways and still leave a free hand to hold her down would have to be male. Also, she was raped."

Heinz blinked. This kind of information was why he hated these cases so much. Steeling himself, he waited for the doctor to finish.

"Semen was collected from the vagina. There was also vaginal tearing. The girl was a virgin. Shocking, I know. But we've since identified her from her fingerprints, and she matches up with the third missing young lady, Anna Popovich, age seventeen. Tomorrow would have been her eighteenth birthday."

Faust spoke. "Her parents are Russian immigrants. They've been here in Germany for the last four years. Middle class. Her father works for a solar panel company, on the line. Her mother teaches Sunday school at a local Orthodox church. No ties to Russian mafia. We already checked. The thing is, all three missing females are Russian. Also, they all pretty much look alike. All are blonde and blue-eyed. All disappeared in the last three weeks, but only this one has shown up dead. No other bodies reported found. Now, I know that doesn't mean they're alive. The suspect could have buried them somewhere and we've yet to find them, but it could also mean he still has them. If he does, we have a chance. It's a longshot, but it's all we've got."

Joseph looked at the girl's face. She would have been just getting out of Gymnasium and going on to some career or other. Her whole life was ahead of her. "A virgin, you said?"

"Yes. Her hymen was ripped, but not completely. Part of it was still intact, as if the assailant was either clumsy or maybe interrupted. And it could only have been one man, because more than one would have ripped it completely away, and I might not have had enough evidence to verify her chaste status."

"You said you collected semen, too. You'll be able to tell for sure if there was more than one attacker. Maybe if we're lucky he'll match up to someone in the database. Still, if he was unable to complete the rape—"

Menghala jumped in. "Some of the semen, well, most of it was spilled outside of her womb. It was on her legs, and the outside of the vagina. Really, that's why I surmised the rape as clumsy. It's like he didn't know what he was doing."

"If that's the case, he may not have meant to kill her. A girl who's a virgin will fight an attacker for all she's worth. Well, any woman being raped will, but he may have been trying to keep her quiet. Is there anything under her fingernails?" Heinz was working through all the possibilities in his mind. A young lady fighting off a man intent on raping her would kick, scratch, scream, and more. Her screams would prompt him to try to silence her. Putting that together with how the body was found submerged showed shame. It was as if the suspect didn't want anyone to know what he'd done. He made the attempt to hide his crime instead of leaving her out in the open or even leaving her alive. It wasn't just a rape.

"What are the circumstances of all three abductions? How were they taken? When? From where? I need a timeline, Herman. And doctor, you need to call me with the results of those tests as soon as you get them."

Faust could see the old Joseph at work. This was the man who went after child abductors and murderers like a pit bull. He had no mercy. Once he got the scent, he could hunt anyone down. "I'll give you copies of the files. All the interviews and information are there along with pictures of the missing and pertinent details. If we've missed anything, I'd be surprised, but that's why we brought you in. Because it's not adding up."

"I'll be sure to call you, Kommissar." Doctor Menghala covered the body with the sheet. "And yes, there was trace evidence under the nail beds, and a couple of missing fingernails. She fought hard. It's all being analyzed."

With the body once again covered, Heinz's heart rate began to calm. All he could think about was Marlessa Schubert. She was fifteen, and his daughter's best friend. Blonde-haired and blue-eyed. She and Ingrid did everything together, except on Marlessa's last day. The girl left school with an unknown boy. No one seemed to know who he was since he didn't attend school with them. The three teens who'd seen her take off with him said he was older, probably about nineteen. They walked away from the school together and were never seen again. The Schuberts were family friends, and knowing Joseph was a detective, they turned to him for help. He nearly killed himself trying to chase down leads, but they led nowhere. Marlessa disappeared into thin air. They never found her or the mystery boy with whom she left campus. One lead still haunted him. A woman who worked on the docks in Hamburg swore she saw a young girl fitting Marlessa's description being carried onto a ship by a sailor. But all inquiries about the ship itself turned up zip. There was no log for a ship of the description given by the witness on the harbor master's docket.

Failing to bring their daughter home, Marie Schubert raged at him, blaming him. As she pointed out, Heinz still had his daughter. Anton Schubert knew it wasn't Joseph's fault, knew he'd done everything he could, but he couldn't face him anymore. His wife's bitterness was too much to endure, so they moved back to Potsdam. Joseph was always secretly grateful that just that one time, Ingrid did not go with her friend. Still, his inability to solve the case, and blame being laid at his door by the parents, and even his own daughter who was so distraught she tried once to commit suicide, drove Joseph to drink. Those were the darkest of days. He stayed at work until all hours trying to find any lead. He wouldn't give up the case even though he'd been taken off it in the end. His neglect of his wife and his daughter eventually ended in divorce. Eva couldn't take it anymore. She'd tried to help him, but he pushed her away, and his drunken rages became too much. She had a daughter to think of, and so she left him and concentrated on Ingrid.

Both were doing very well today. Eva remarried just last year, and Ingrid was finishing up a master's degree in chemistry. Joseph, himself, was finally in a good place, and now old wounds were reopened with one phone call in the middle of the night. He'd go over the files with a fine-tooth comb first thing in the morning. He nodded to the doctor and turned to Faust who was already on his mobile ordering his staff to make copies for Kommissar Heinz.

"They'll be delivered to your house first thing in the morning." Faust looked at his watch. "Oh, well, in three hours." He shrugged.

Heinz glared at his friend. "I'll do all I can, Herman, but I won't let it swallow me up like before. I'm not willing to lose myself again. It cost too much the last time."

Faust offered a small nod, acknowledging the conditions. He appreciated his friend for willingly stepping into the dark void that all detectives dread, abduction and murder cases. "It's all I can ask, Joseph. If I don't make every effort, then why am I here?"

They left the morgue, both feeling like a massive weight was lifted from their shoulders the minute they were outside and breathing in the fresh, rain-soaked air.

"See you soon." Faust headed down the steps, making his way to his car. Heinz watched him drive off and wondered if he should even bother trying to get back to sleep this night. He headed home knowing that in three hours, a uniformed officer would arrive at his door with a stack of paperwork that would suck out his soul.

Chapter 5

"She's inside," Jan Mahler told Detective Heinz as he passed him coming out the front door of the flat where he lived with his mother, Heinz's partner, Detective Birgitta Mahler."

The Kommissar tossed a bag to Jan who'd grown tall over his last year in high school. "Enjoy." Mahler's son, like Elsa's brother Anno, was attending his first year of college. He was studying medicine and hoped to become a specialist in orthopedics. He wanted to treat athletes, a lofty goal. Jan looked inside the bag and smiled.

"You always remember!" He stuffed an apple streusel into his mouth and then waved as he ran down the street to catch the tube to school.

Heinz juggled his stack of files with the remaining paper bag containing two éclairs and two crullers, all while holding two hot cups of coffee in one of those flimsy cardboard drink carriers. He pushed open the door and walked inside Mahler's home. He set his load down on the kitchen table, and pulled one of the cups of coffee out, black with two sugars, and carried it back toward her room. Finding it to be the only one of two bedrooms with the door closed, he approached. Figuring she might still be asleep at this very early hour, he thought it only kind to have coffee in hand when waking her.

He reached out and opened her bedroom door. He was greeted not by Mahler still tucked away in bed but walking out of her bathroom... wet and naked.

"Joseph!" She screamed his name and ran back into the bathroom.

Shocked and unsure what to say, Heinz immediately backed out of her room spewing apologies.

"Sorry! So sorry, Mahler. I'll just, uh, I'll be out here." He beat a hasty retreat.

Out in the living room, Heinz set her coffee down and placed his hands on the table. Naked! He felt embarrassed for them both. Never had he seen Mahler in anything less than professional attire. This morning would have been the first time he'd ever even seen her in pajamas, but their relationship lately had relaxed so much that he hadn't really thought about the impropriety of waking her. It just felt natural. Now he felt like an ass. He'd blundered. But a wisp of memory of her wet and naked flashed through his mind. *Birgitta...* Heat suffused his cheeks, and he had to take several deep breaths. He didn't understand his reaction, the way his mind kept replaying the scene, even as part of him really wanted to run out of the house.

"What the hell, Heinz?" Mahler, dressed in her usual pantsuit, stood in the living room tucking a pin into her hair, now neatly twisted into a chignon.

"I'm so sorry, Mahler. I wasn't thinking. I have no excuse." Joseph could barely look her in the eye.

Birgitta noted the red flush on his cheeks. His usually direct gaze bounced everywhere but at her, as if she still stood naked. His hands didn't seem to know if they should be on his hips, at his sides, or in his jacket pockets. He shifted from foot to foot. He looked for all the world like a boy caught with his first pornographic magazine.

"He's nervous," she thought. Although she was still mad that he'd walked into her bedroom, part of her was pleased he did. She decided on a calm approach.

"Is that coffee for me?" She walked to the table and picked it up. Black with two sugars, just as she liked it.

"Yes, of course." He took two steps and picked up the bag containing the donuts. "I've brought you some crullers as well." He pulled them out, and grabbed a napkin from the bag, placing them on it, and handing them over.

"And what has brought you to my home so early with coffee and crullers?" She sat down at the table and began eating one of the treats.

Heinz pulled out a chair and reached for his own cup of coffee. He still had a hard time looking at her. He pushed the stack of files toward her. "I was called in last night on a case."

"Why didn't you call me?" She immediately reached for the top file.

"I didn't want to wake you until I knew all the details. It's not our borough. Faust called. It's a series of three cases. Two missing, abducted girls, and one murdered."

"Why would he call you for this? He knows you don't do these anymore."

Straight to the point and completely unfazed. This was what he appreciated about his partner. Rubbing the back of his neck, he leaned onto the table and explained.

"He knows, but things aren't adding up and time is running out. These were just delivered this morning, and I've brought them here so you can help me go through them. I need your keen sense of things."

His admission that he needed her made Mahler smile. Over the last few years, they had indeed grown to depend upon one another. The first few years were rocky, and she'd considered asking to be reassigned, but the more she got to know Joseph, the more she saw the man beneath the layers of cynicism. His grouchy exterior was his way of keeping people at bay, a way to mask his pain. To her, he'd become the wounded lion with a thorn in his paw. His roar scared everyone, but no one saw the reason for his aggression. No one but her. She saw it, and she'd hoped that one day, he might let her in close enough to pluck the pain away.

"It's about time you admit you need me." She said this as she stuffed a big bite of donut into her mouth and flipped open the file.

"I've always needed you," he muttered beneath his breath. Then louder, "Now let's go through these and see if we can't make some sense of it all. Faust is floundering." He pulled out an éclair and together they began reading through all the paperwork.

Birgitta made notes in her notebook, a habit that Heinz had grown to depend upon. She was thorough and logical, something he didn't often find in most people, let alone a woman. He glanced over at her, watching her chew as she read. Her hair was still wet, and up in its usual style. His memory flashed, recalling it down and curling only moments before. He hadn't realized how long it was. She shifted in her seat, pulling her leg up under her body. Her legs...toned, her breasts, alabaster, perfect. *Stop it! Focus, Joseph.*

Heinz shook himself and returned to reading his file. He shrugged off his jacket and tossed it onto the back of the chair next to him.

"So, all three of these girls were taken in the last month." Mahler spoke, startling Heinz out of his reverie.

"What? Yes. The first two are still unaccounted for, and the third, Anna Popovich, was found partially submerged in the river yesterday evening."

"They all look alike. Same hair color, eye color, and approximate height and weight. Our killer has a thing for blondes. He's trying to replace someone." Mahler, as usual, got right to the heart of the situation.

"Ja, but who? The coroner is supposed to call me as soon as the test results come back on the evidence he collected from the body."

"I don't see any similarities in the interviews with family on someone they knew in common. Perhaps we should conduct secondary interviews. These girls were targeted, and all within the same community. Our killer is either Russian, or he has a fixation for Russian girls." Mahler stood.

"That's a good idea," Joseph readily agreed. Anything to get them out of being in close quarters with each other right now would be good. He needed to distract himself because the picture in his mind of Mahler naked was doing funny things to him, things he hadn't felt in a very long time. Fresh air and a murder investigation were just what he needed.

She walked to her bedroom. "I'll be right out."

"Where are you going? You're already dressed." The moment the word 'dressed' left his lips, he wanted to smack himself.

"To put on some makeup." He could hear her talking from her room.

"What for?" He hadn't even noticed she wasn't wearing any. To him, she looked fine.

"Honestly, Joseph, do you not have eyes in your head? What kind of detective are you? You just saw me naked, and I'd swear you didn't even notice. We women must do all we can to look beautiful."

Heinz turned red again for the second time that morning. He tried not to smile but failed. He seemed to be doing a lot more of that particular facial contortion lately. "I noticed, Mahler, believe me."

Birgitta grinned. Reminding her partner that he'd seen more than he should have was a wicked ploy, but if it made him think of her as a woman for once, a nude woman and a sexual being, then all was fair.

Staring down the hall toward the bedrooms, Heinz sighed. To himself, he added, "and you're already beautiful." That epiphany surprised him.

Elsa arrived at the station house ready to tackle the day. Beimer was already there standing next to a vase of one dozen long-stem red roses.

"Hugo, you shouldn't have," she joked as she walked over to grab a cup of coffee from the vending machine.

"I didn't. But they're for you." He raised his eyebrow and gave her a look that said, "*and who did you sleep with last night?*"

"You're kidding! Who would be sending me roses?" Elsa carried her coffee over and set it down. She searched for the card. A tiny pink envelope was hidden among the greenery on a plastic pick.

"Well? Who sent them? Come on, Kreiss. Let's hear the damning evidence." Beimer leaned over onto his elbows while Elsa opened the card.

Officer ELSA Kreiss, Looking forward to seeing you tonight. LT. Her first name was underlined and in all caps.

Elsa laughed out loud. "Well, looks like he found out my name." She stuffed the card into her pocket and sniffed the roses.

"Who? That douche from yesterday? You're not going to let your head be turned by roses, are you?" Beimer continued to hound her all the way out the door as they made their way to their assigned patrol for the day.

"I did tell him he'd have to discover my name on his own, and he did. And Beimer, for your information, women like getting flowers. Maybe you should try it. You might get laid." She watched as Hugo began to sputter.

"I get laid plenty." He puffed out his chest and looked at Elsa from the corner of his eye.

"Sure you do, Hugo." She patted his arm.

"Women like me." His expression was indignant.

"Yes, they like you. But do they want to fuck you? That, my partner, is the question. I mean it. Try sending flowers next time after you meet someone you like. You'd be surprised what a bouquet will get you."

He looked dubious but remained quiet. Elsa knew he was thinking about what she'd said. She also knew he liked a certain clerical assistant to their captain. He'd been eyeing Sigrid for a couple of months now, but other than saying hello, he hadn't let his regard be known. Beimer needed help, but he was too stubborn to ask for it. So instead of outright telling him what he should do, she planted seeds. If he thought it was his own idea, he'd act. Men were easy that way. The same technique worked on her own brother. Untold numbers of times, Anno had come to her proudly showing off an accomplishment. It was always something Elsa had subtly suggested in the middle of idle conversation. Plant the seed and reap the rewards. She'd already done it to Heinz yesterday. She couldn't wait to see that one flower.

"Sometimes you're crass, Kreiss." Beimer turned right, patrolling on the north side of the Tiergarten.

"Why? Because I said fuck?"

"A lady doesn't use words like that." He swung his nightstick in his hand.

"Sure we do. A lady not only uses it, she knows when to say it, and when to do it." Elsa tried not to laugh. If Hugo knew what she used to do for a living, he'd probably piss himself. "And when your lady whispers in your ear," she leaned in close, "and says 'Fuck me, Hugo!' you'll be so turned on, you won't even notice she just said *fuck*."

Hugo felt her hot breath on his cold ear and something tightened. He tried to ignore it. He didn't want to have those kinds of thoughts about Elsa. But Sigrid... He suddenly imagined her saying this to him in a private moment where he could show her how he felt about her. That thought did not help him. He was glad his jacket was zipped and covering his instant semi-erection. He thanked God for the cold wind. It would soon shrink back to normal. He half-heartedly pushed Elsa away from him.

"Stop saying that or I'll begin to think you want me."

Hugo's attempt at a joke had Elsa cracking up. She shoved her hand inside her jacket pocket to keep it warm while her coffee cup warmed the other.

"Dream on, Beimer!"

They passed the gallery on their rounds. Lukas wasn't outside today, but a large black limousine was parked in front of the entry doors. As they approached, the door opened, and Paul Christiansen stepped out. He was still every bit as good-looking as Elsa remembered. He wore dark blue jeans, black boots, and an expensive black leather jacket. His hair was a little longer than she recalled, but in all, he still looked like a male model with his crystal blue eyes, perfect cheekbones, and strong jawline.

"I'm sorry, sir, but you'll have to place your hands on the vehicle." She handed Hugo her coffee and approached with her cap down over her eyes.

"What? What is the meaning of this, officer?" He turned in her direction, instantly annoyed.

"Hands on the roof of the car, please, and spread your legs." Elsa walked behind him, forcefully turned his face to the car, and kicked his feet apart, placing him in a spread-eagle position.

Paul complied, grudgingly, but repeatedly tried to see the officer over his shoulder and speak to her. "I've broken no laws, officer. What is this about? Do I need to call my attorney? I'm an artist, for God's sake. What am I charged with?" He was getting angry.

Elsa leaned in and patted him down, getting a little personal when she slid her hands over his legs and backside which she squeezed.

"Hey! Do you Schupos mind? When did the polizei start molesting innocent men?" He turned around and looked at the red-haired officer. He couldn't see her eyes, but she was laughing. Finally, she lifted her head and looked at him.

"Elsa? Elsa Kreiss? You crazy woman!" He wrapped her in his arms and hugged her tight.

"The look on your face, Paul! I almost lost it." She hugged him back, suddenly realizing she wasn't swamped with bad memories, only the good ones.

"And when did all this happen?" He gestured toward her uniform.

"In the last couple of years. I felt it was time to make a change."

He gave her an assessing look. "It suits you. But then, you were always good with the costumes."

Elsa gave him a slap on his arm and glanced sideways at her partner.

Paul understood. He turned to Hugo. "And who is this, Elsa?" He reached out a hand to shake Hugo's.

"This is my partner, Hugo Beimer. Hugo, this is Paul Christiansen."

"The artist? The one who's having the exhibit tonight?" Hugo felt like he was meeting royalty.

"Yes, Beimer. That Paul Christiansen." She rolled her eyes noting the look on Beimer's face.

"It's good to meet you, Hugo." He turned back to Elsa. "How did you know I'd be here?"

"I actually only found out yesterday on our rounds," she began to explain.

"But then she tried to give me a ticket and ended up being my date tonight." Lukas Trommler came up behind her and placed an arm around her shoulders. "Herr Christiansen, welcome." Lukas shook Paul's hand.

Paul glanced at Elsa, then looked at Lukas. His eyebrow quirked and he grinned. "Is that right? Well, she always did have a way with men. The meaner she is, the more they come back." Elsa flipped him off.

Lukas watched the byplay between them with interest. "That's pretty close to what captured my heart. But I'd say it was more her refusal to take any sh—crap from me." He censored himself.

"It's okay, you can say it. Kreiss isn't a lady," Beimer interjected. He waited for her to explode at him.

"Fuck off, Hugo." Green eyes glared at her partner.

"See?" Beimer withstood her scowl as long as he could, all of five seconds, before apologizing.

"That's the woman I asked out yesterday." Lukas looked at her proudly. Paul laughed.

"Well, this is wonderful. I'm so happy you're here and coming tonight, too."

"Yes. Hopefully we'll have a little time to catch up." She tried not to notice how good Lukas smelled. His body heat was comforting, and the way he walked right into this little reunion and staked his claim was kind of sexy.

"It's a gallery exhibit, not a lecture. There will be drinks, and oer d'oeuvres, and great company, it seems. Hell, Elsa, I was thinking I'd have no fun at all, but now it's looking up. No offense, Trommler." Paul patted the man on the shoulder.

"None taken. These things can be a bore. I'm happy my date puts you in good spirits. Looks like she's a good luck charm for us both." Lukas gazed into Elsa's eyes, sending a heated vibe her way.

Paul looked at Hugo, who seemed left out. "And what about you, Hugo? Will you be attending tonight?"

Hugo looked at a complete loss for words. Probably for the first time, too, Elsa thought. Lukas gave Beimer a dirty look. Hugo noticed and gave back stare for stare. "No, Herr Christiansen. It seems we're not all fortunate enough to be Trommler's *date*." He turned to Paul and stuck out his hand again in a gesture of courtesy. "But it was a real pleasure to meet you."

"Nonsense. You must come as my personal guest. And bring a date, too." Paul noticed the sour looks passing between the two men, and feeling like a pot-stirrer, decided to invite Elsa's partner, if for no other reason than to see what will happen if these two are around each other longer than a moment. He was desperate for some distraction and having an old friend present tonight with her two men facing off would be just the thing.

Hugo was caught off guard. "I'd be honored, sir."

"Hugo, call me Paul, please. Now, you should make a call to your lady friend and give her enough time to prepare. You know how women are, eh?" He clapped Hugo on the back.

Not wanting to look like a fool, Beimer agreed.

"Ja, Beimer, give Sigrid a call." Elsa, also a dyed-in-the-wool pot stirrer, egged her partner on.

He sent her a quelling look. She smothered the laugh bubbling up inside.

"Well, let's have a look at what you've got set up, Lukas, and then I can head back to my hotel for a bit." Paul pulled Elsa in for another hug. "I'll see you tonight, Red." He kissed the top of her head.

"Oh, Heinz wanted me to tell you hello, and if you had a chance, to stop by his office." She pulled out her wallet and found the detective's card. "This is his number. He can give you directions."

"And how is Joseph?" Paul looked at the card, smiling as he remembered the Kommissar.

"He's well. I'll tell you more tonight. Go. Do what must be done. I have rounds to make."

"All right then. Tonight!" He winked at her and waved at Beimer before heading inside.

Lukas caught Elsa's arm and pulled her close, kissing her cheek. "I, too, cannot wait for tonight," he said, his lips close to her ear.

Heat traveled into her cheeks causing her to blush. Lukas didn't wait for a reply but followed Paul inside. She turned to catch Beimer laughing at her.

"Cripes, Kreiss, you have them falling all over you." He resumed patrol.

She caught up. "So now you have no excuse. Call Sigrid."

"What? I can't. What would I say?" He looked panicked. Like a cow about to be slaughtered, all wild-eyed.

"Calm down, Hugo. It's very easy. Call her. Say hello. Tell her you've been invited to a gallery exhibit, by the artist himself, no less, and then say, 'I could think of no one else but you that I'd rather share this night with. Will you honor me by accompanying me tonight?'"

"That doesn't sound easy. That sounds like a speech." He pulled out his notepad. "Now, say that again, and slowly this time."

Elsa chuckled. "And after she accepts, we're stopping at the first florist and you're sending her roses."

"Roses, too?" He shook his head. "This is getting to be too much, Kreiss. Roses are expensive!" He jotted down his lines.

"Is she worth it, Hugo?" The question was simple.

Hugo thought about it, then a small smile sprouted on his lips. "Yeah, she's worth it."

"Then stop all your bitching. You've been handed a golden opportunity. Take it."

Beimer walked two more blocks before pulling out his mobile and dialing the station. Elsa knew better than to say any more. She'd already said enough. Now she waited patiently as her partner stumbled his way through a very awkward proposal. It was painful to witness, but in a way, quite charming. Any woman would recognize the outright fear in his voice, so she punched him in the arm hard to get him back on track.

He gave her a dirty look, but the instant pain brought out more confidence and a touch of aggression in his tone. "So, Sigrid, I could think of no one else but you to share such a grand night with. Would you honor me with your company?" He paraphrased Elsa's words.

Elsa waited, only hearing one side of the conversation. "Ja. Sure, I understand. Ja. Okay. I'll pick you up at the station house at half seven. See you then."

Once Elsa heard the last two sentences, she jumped on Hugo's back, nearly knocking him over. "You did it! I can't believe that worked!"

"What do you mean? I said what you told me to say?" He tried to remain upright while gently shaking her off.

"I know, but I still can't believe it worked." She was back on her own two feet again.

Hugo realized she'd set him up with no certainty he'd succeed. The idea was terrifying. Outrage bubbled to the surface. "If you weren't sure she'd say yes, why the hell would you tell me to do that? What the fuck, Kreiss?"

She reached out and patted his cheek. "Calm down, Beimer. It worked. And I told you to do that because you had to do something. You were getting nowhere doing nothing. So, this way, you'd either fail or succeed. It was a fifty-fifty chance. Well, maybe more like seventy-thirty, and not in your favor."

"Christiansen is right. You are a mean woman." He shook his head and remembered that Sigrid had said yes. Then he smiled.

"Come on, there's a florist two blocks down. Let's go impress your lady." She yanked at his hand.

"Wait. You threw me to the she-wolf a moment ago before knowing she wouldn't eat me. How do I know this will work?" He was hesitant after her admission to go along with her romantic schemes.

"Because, you fool, the roses do work. Look how happy I am that Lukas sent me such a lovely bouquet. He may even get lucky tonight. It has been a while, after all." She walked ahead of him.

"I take my earlier apology back. You're no lady, Kreiss. You're a man in women's clothing." He trudged along behind her, catching up. "Only a man would say such a thing."

"You have a lot to learn about women, Beimer." She shook a finger at her partner and dragged him to the florist where one dozen of their finest long-stem red roses was arranged and sent to Sigrid's desk at the station house.

Chapter 6

Charlottenburg was on the west side of the city center of Berlin. It happened to be one of the larger Russian communities in the area, and the place from where all three of the young women disappeared. Heinz and Mahler arrived at the home of what was thought to be the first victim, Liliya Avilova. The house was a two-story brick structure with black shutters and white trim. It sat between similar sized and shaped homes in a row. The yards were small, and space between them was barely enough to walk through. Still, the street was quaint, and mature trees lined the median down the center of the road providing green space and a place for residents to walk their dogs.

"Nice neighborhood."

Heinz looked around as he walked over to the curb waiting for Mahler to join him. The ride over had been awkward, at least, for him. Mahler didn't seem fazed at all by his seeing her naked that morning. In fact, she'd been quite comfortable in the car, chatting away, and reaching over to touch his arm during conversation. He'd noticed every touch. In fact, he'd looked at her hands for the first time noting long, slim fingers, and well-manicured nails kept simple with only a clear polish. Her gestures were graceful for hands that could handle all manners of firearms with deadly force. Her touch was warm and comforting. It was also distracting. Each time she'd made contact, he was reminded of her bare body probably still warm from her hot shower. Sweat beaded his forehead, and she'd taken notice, asking if he was feeling all right, which led to her applying that hand to his forehead, a natural gesture for a mother.

"Yes, yes. I'm fine. It's simply stuffy in here." He'd unrolled the window a few inches letting the cold air inside while pushing her hand away.

Now he was standing outside on a curb with the fall chill creeping in wherever it could, waiting patiently as she joined him. Usually, he would simply walk ahead. Now he found himself waiting, wanting to open her door, but she'd already done that herself. She arrived at his side and stopped.

"What are you waiting for?" She looked him in the eye, her expression curious.

The question reminded him he was being foolish, a feeling he did not appreciate.

"Nothing. Are you ready?" He walked ahead of her. At the door, he rang the bell and waited for the Avilovs to answer. He wished they'd hurry. He could smell Mahler's perfume, and the subtle fragrance was pleasant, teasing his senses. It seemed to be emanating from her hair, which he'd seen down, and wet, and curling over her bare breasts. Feeling annoyed, he rang the bell again earning a raised eyebrow from his partner, and an angry glare from the man who yanked the door open answering the insistent chime.

"What do you want?" An older gentleman with a hooked nose and heavy jowls stood facing Heinz.

Heinz raised his hand flashing his badge. "Petre Avilov?" The man nodded, his expression lessening in intensity upon viewing Heinz's badge. "I'm Kriminalkommissar Heinz, and this is my partner, Detective Mahler. We're here to ask you a few questions about your daughter."

Avilov backed up. "Certainly, Herr Kommissar. Please, come in, and forgive my rudeness." He gestured that they should enter. Heinz once again waited, looking awkwardly at Mahler. He swept his hand indicating she should go first.

Mahler gave him a strange look, unused to him being so courteous. She stepped into the foyer of the Avilov home. Heinz followed, and the door was closed behind them. A plump woman around age forty stood in the doorway of the kitchen with a questioning look at Avilov.

"This is my missus, Karina Avilova. My dear, this is Kriminalkommissar Heinz and Detective Mahler?" He looked at Birgitta stumbling over her name verifying he'd remembered correctly.

"That's right."

"They're here to ask us some more questions about Liliya."

Frau Avilova came right up to Mahler and took her hand, leading her into the dining room where they could all sit around the table. She immediately offered coffee, which Heinz accepted while Mahler declined.

"What can you tell me about your daughter's usual activities? I see she's enrolled in her first year of university?" Heinz was careful never to refer to a missing person in the past tense as it often put the loved ones on the defensive, and he needed them to be as open and at ease as possible.

"Da!" Frau Avilova's eyes brightened, beaming with pride. "Liliya is studying business management. She will one day take over the family business, three dry cleaners, from her father."

Avilov smiled and patted his wife's hand. "She is quite intelligent. Takes after her mother." Petre Avilov picked up the thread of conversation. "All she does is go to school, help out at work with me on the nights and weekends, and go to church, of course. Sometimes, she spends time with friends going to a movie maybe, but not much more. She's a good girl, our Liliya."

"And who are these friends?" Mahler opened her little notebook and began writing down names.

"Nina Belova and Oksana Zakrevskaya. They are school friends. They all grew up together. Nina lives two doors down, and Oksana lives on the next strasse over. I can give you their numbers and addresses." Frau Avilova leaned toward Mahler to make sure she wrote down the names and addresses correctly.

"You said she attends church. Which one?" Heinz directed his question to Avilov.

"Resurrection of Jesus in Wilmersdorf. The only Russian Orthodox Cathedral near us, of course," said Avilov.

"Of course," replied Heinz. He looked over to see if Mahler was writing this down. "And is Liliya active in any of the church's programs? Youth groups and such?"

"There's a singles group that meets on Saturday nights for Bible study. Sometimes they do community work, like helping the elderly at the hospital, reading to them and organizing activities, or volunteering with the children at the kindergarten. Recently, she was part of the elderly gardening project for the nursing home by the church." Frau Avilov was a veritable font of information. Information that hadn't made it into the report he and Mahler read just that morning. Faust was slipping.

"That's commendable of her. Did her two friends also participate?" Mahler asked, her pen poised.

"Oh, yes. They can tell you more. My husband and I did not attend, seeing as we're not singles." She reached out and placed her hand on her husband's arm, her affection for him obvious. Heinz noticed and instantly recalled Mahler touching his arm in a similar manner on the ride over. He blinked.

"Thank you. You've been very helpful." Heinz rose, and everyone stood.

"Do you have any news at all about where our Liliya might be?" Avilov's wife looked at Heinz, her eyes imploring.

"Not yet, ma'am. We're working on it, I assure you. As soon as we uncover anything, we'll let you know. In the meantime, please be sure to call us with anything else you can think of, anyone she may have recently begun to talk to or some new place she may have gone." He handed her his card.

Frau Avilova's blue eyes brimmed with unshed tears, and Herr Avilov placed a comforting arm around her shoulders. Heinz could see where their daughter got her fair looks. Karina Avilova was older now, but in her prime, she would have been as fresh and beautiful as the picture in the file.

They left intending to first question Liliya's two friends. It would be a long day interviewing the second and third families of the two other missing young women, one of which was no longer missing, but dead. Faust had informed them early that morning. Having a second pair of detectives knocking at their door while they mourned would be difficult. Their memories would be clouded by stress and grief.

It turned out that the second missing girl also attended Resurrection of Jesus, as did the third. Nina and Oksana were the most helpful that day sharing that on their last outing with the church, the girls met a very nice young man currently staying in Berlin visiting family. He'd shown them some planting techniques for winter vegetables, but he'd shown a marked interest in Liliya, ignoring the brunette Nina, and the redheaded Oksana. This could mean everything, or it could mean nothing, but one thing it absolutely did mean—he and Mahler would be going to church. Heinz looked up at the sky for signs of an impending storm.

———◆———

"Where are you going?" Anno walked into Elsa's room and threw himself across her bed. At eighteen, her little brother had grown quite tall. His boyhood beauty was metamorphosing into a handsomeness that caused the girls to flock to him like bees to honey. His shoulders were wide, his back straight, and muscles sprouted everywhere where before only stick-thin limbs existed. Even his voice had deepened, but to Elsa, he was still her little brother.

"Out." She stood looking at herself in the mirror trying to decide which dress to wear to Paul Christiansen's exhibit. She insisted on referring to it as that rather than a date. Lukas Trommler managed to maneuver her quite nicely into meeting him at the gallery. She was still undecided on how she would treat him, enemy combatant or possibly a new lover and cobweb cleaner. She enjoyed giving a cocky man a hard time, but it had been a ridiculously long time since she'd had sex. And he was very good looking. Her inner conflict was the source of her trouble at the moment in deciding what to wear.

"Looks like you're dressing for a date. I thought you said it was Paul's exhibit. You're not dating him, are you?" Anno's fair eyebrows came together above his blue eyes. Although he didn't dislike Paul, not after all they'd been through together, he still didn't want the man dating his sister.

"Of course not! He's not my type." Elsa pulled the green dress over her head and tossed it onto the floor.

"My eyes!" Anno covered his eyes and turned his head away. "You could warn me, you know. I don't need to see you naked."

Elsa laughed. "Then get out of my room." She reached for a red off-the-shoulder dress that clung to her body when she slid into it. The long sleeves would keep her arms warm, but the skirt hit mid-thigh, leaving her legs bare. She rummaged through her drawer and found a pair of nude nylons.

"Then why are you dressing like that?" Refusing to get up, much less leave, Anno continued to grill his older sister.

"Because I was invited by an employee of the gallery." She knew her non-answers were driving him insane. It was what he did to her every day. *Where are you going, Anno? Out. When will you be back? Soon. Who will you be with? Friends.* And on it went.

Anno stood and began to leave but stopped at the door. "So, it's a date. Is he nice at least? Because if he's not, I'll have to hurt him." He stood leaning on the door jamb; his expression serious.

"I think so. But thanks for having my back." The half-smile on Elsa's face was answered by her brother walking back in, wrapping his arms around her, and kissing the top of her head. Over the summer, he'd grown nearly a foot taller than her.

She pushed him off, laughing. "Stop kissing me!"

"But I love you so!" He picked her up and swung her around.

"Put me down, you boob!" He was laughing hard but finally set her on her feet.

"Be careful. And get home at a decent hour, young lady!" He wagged his finger at her, and then walked out heading for the kitchen. Anno was always hungry.

Elsa sat on the edge of her bed and inserted her feet into the silky nylons. They weren't much of a barrier to the cold, but they were better than nothing. After smoothing them up over her calves and thighs, she stood and began the process of yanking them up over her red thong. She decided to forego a brassiere since the dress was off the shoulders. The last decision would be shoes. She tried on two pairs, a classic black pump and red stilettos. The stilettos were sexier, but the three-inch heeled black pumps with a cute Mary Jane-style strap over the top arch of each foot screamed 'classy'. It was an art exhibit, after all. She would also be standing around most of the night, so she chose the black pumps.

With her red hair down in waves, and subtle makeup with a smoky eye effect causing her green eyes to look cat-like, she rouged her lips red and was ready to see what this night would bring. Elsa double-checked her Chanel bag, a larger-than-usual vintage clutch. Wallet. Compact. Lipstick. Badge. Discreet, police-issued handgun. Condoms. Everything a woman needed for a date.

"I'm leaving now." She walked out into the living room and headed toward the door. Anno poked his head out of the kitchen, a huge sandwich in hand, and mouth full.

"Good Lord! You're going out like that? I guess you're not planning on coming home." His expression was disapproving.

"Of course I'll be home. Leave the hall light on. And behave yourself while I'm out." She grabbed a classic black trench coat from the hall closet and put it on, tightening the belt around her slender waist.

"It's not me who's dressed for trouble. It's a first date, Elsa. Keep your gun in your purse." He tried to make light of it all, but he was clearly not happy about seeing his sister going out on a date. He'd not seen her date anyone since he could remember. She only had friends around like Nicolette who tended to stay overnight often.

"Shut it, Anno. I'll tell Paul you said hello."

"Yeah, do that. Is he still in contact with Sarah?" The boy could speak endlessly, even while chewing through a sandwich like a starved locust.

"Last I chatted with her, yes. He calls and texts. Why?" She eyed her brother curiously.

"No reason. Just wondered. We should call her tomorrow. She needs to visit again."

Elsa smiled. Her little brother carried a torch for her American friend ever since they first met. He was overly protective of her when it came to Paul Christiansen, and recently, when he was told Sarah and Anthony hadn't worked out, he was over the moon.

"I think so, too. Okay. We'll call her."

"She still owes me a date. And I'm eighteen now…" He headed off back into the kitchen with a smile on his face and a cocky swagger in his step.

"Oh, for goodness' sake, Anno!" She laughed as she headed out the door. Anno had no idea that she and Sarah shared a very steamy sexual experience together back then, nor would he ever. He also would never know the true nature of her relationship with Nicolette. It just wasn't something he needed to know.

The lifts were slow, and it took longer than usual to get downstairs. Frau Schmidt really needed to get them checked by maintenance. It was an old building on Köthener Straße, and things went wrong and broke down all the time. Still, it was home. She wouldn't trade it for the world. Outside, the cold night air slipped up under the hem of her coat, causing a chill. She passed Herr Schumaker out walking his dog as she headed for her old Peugeot. He waved and gave her a thumbs up noticing she was dressed up. It was too cold to take the tube tonight, and her attire wasn't ideal for a long walk. Plus, she would be arriving home late, and after years of working nights, and listening to Heinz, this taught her one important fact, danger lurked in the shadows.

Lukas surveyed the crowd assembled at the exhibit. Everything was set up perfectly. The Christiansen paintings were divided into two separate yet distinct themes, nightmares and wet dreams. On one side were the canvases that disturbed art appreciators with their dark and horrific imagery of a monster reaching out from various hidden corners to grab at a child with dark hair and tortured blue eyes. The drab colors denoting depression, fear, anxiety, and anger were relieved only now and again by red and bright blue. These were the paintings Paul Christiansen created over the years both before and after the death of his abuser, Peter Knudson. Knudson was Paul's uncle on his mother's side, and everyone in the world of art knew the story by now following the news of his death in Amsterdam nearly three years ago. There were clear differences between the paintings done before Knudson's death, and afterwards, when Christiansen began professional therapy to deal with his emotional issues. The pre-death paintings were far more disturbing and highly valued by collectors. The ones he created during and after his onset of therapy showed rays of hope for the child within.

On the other side of the gallery were the brighter, happier, and far more erotic paintings brought to life by the other side of Paul Christiansen and his love of the nude female form. Aptly titled *Wet Dreams*, these paintings would grace the private collections of erotisans, for lack of a better term. Christiansen liked to paint his women while they were still fresh from a good fuck. The blush on their cheeks, the glow of their skin, and the moisture still beading and pooling in humid places was so real in its authenticity that some patrons tried reaching out to touch the drops only to have Lukas step in and smack their hands away like naughty children. This did not interfere in the least with sales, which were going well as more red tags were being placed on pieces until only a few of the larger canvases remained.

Christiansen himself seemed to be holding court with a roundtable of lovely women, all of whom had arrived with a date, but seemed drawn to him. Lukas speculated they had dreams of becoming immortalized on canvas by the artist. Shallow women by his standards. He preferred the feisty, independent type that could give less than a damn about fame. With that thought in mind, he looked toward the front door for the umpteenth time in the last hour. His date wasn't late, but he was looking forward to seeing her and kept hoping she'd come early. The fact that she hadn't made him smile. Elsa Kreiss was not a woman to fall all over a man. She was the woman men trampled all over themselves trying to impress. At exactly half eight she walked through the door.

"Scheisse!" Lukas's harshly whispered expletive escaped his lips as Elsa stood a few steps inside the gallery casually removing her Trench coat and revealing the sexy, red dress beneath. As her eyes swept the room for a familiar face, Lukas watched, standing amid the Wet Dreams paintings and fantasizing a few of his own. His gaze traveled over her from head to toe taking in the fall of her red hair over white, smooth shoulders, to the clingy red dress that emphasized her breasts and tiny waist, to the end of the hemline over long, slender, yet athletic legs balanced on black heels with an adorable little girl quality to them. She was anything but. He began walking toward her before he even realized he was moving.

"You came." He reached out and gently grasped her upper arms as his lips sought her cheek, laying a warm kiss upon it.

"Did you think I wouldn't?" She tried for cheeky, but her voice came out breathy as heat lingered where his lips had briefly touched her skin.

Lukas smiled, still holding her arms, and keeping her close. His gaze skittered down over her face to the hint of cleavage above the scooped neck of her off-the-shoulder dress. He could see a sprinkling of light freckles right above the cloth, and his thoughts went to warm places where he pondered placing hot kisses on each freckle he found below that line.

"I knew you would." He looked into her eyes conveying that cocky confidence she was so drawn to. "You look very beautiful, officer." His low tone was intimate, and Elsa felt her body warm under the regard of this man.

"You look very handsome, yourself, Trommler." She took in his black suit and pin-striped, black shirt beneath, worn without a tie. He left a few buttons open at the neck, revealing just a hint of light chest hair. He smelled of sandalwood and soap, warm and clean.

"Lukas. Please...call me Lukas." He wanted to hear his name on her lovely lips. They were shaped in a Cupid's bow with the lower lip full and pouty.

"Lukas..." Watching her lips form his name caused a very strong reaction in his gut. He knew he needed to break this sensual spell between them that happened each time they were in close proximity, or he'd be conducting an exhibit with a massive hard-on. He stepped back and offered his arm.

"Let's get you a drink, and then maybe we can grab Mr. Popular over there and give you a tour." He indicated the other side of the gallery where Paul Christiansen stood head and shoulders above most men surrounded by four scantily clad women. Their dates stood a couple steps behind them looking quite put out.

Elsa smiled. *Same old Paul.*

"Looks like a full house. Lots of art lovers here, I see."

Lukas led them to the bar in the corner of the gallery where wait staff came and went filling trays with drink orders and delivering empties.

"And what would you like, Elsa?" He indicated the fully stocked wall behind the smiling bartender who waited patiently for her order.

"Scotch on the rocks." She waited as the man behind the bar pulled down a Chivas, but Lukas held up his hand.

"Not that one. The Johnny Walker Black Label." He looked at Elsa. "You seem like a Black Label woman."

"I am, actually. How did you know?" She raised one eyebrow, surprised at his intuitiveness.

"No nonsense, warm and spicy. That's you. That's a Johnny Walker." He put his arm around her shoulders as she received the drink from the bartender. Together, they headed toward Paul who'd already seen her. He disentangled himself from the bevy of hangers-on with a practiced skill.

"Kreiss! You made it." Paul pulled Elsa in for a hug, then stepped back holding her at arm's length. "Let's have a look at you." He spun her around with her free hand taking it all in. "Red suits you. It always has."

She gave him a look that said, *'Careful what you say!'* Lukas raised an eyebrow at Paul. He didn't like that Christiansen knew so much about his date. A hint of jealousy gripped him, and he stepped back in to claim his lady. "Yes, it does suit her. I was just telling her how amazing she looks tonight." Again, he let his voice drop and directed the compliment to her.

Elsa felt the heatwave he sent her way and tried to hide the smile threatening to spread across her face as she recognized Lukas's possessiveness in response to Paul's attention to her. She'd seen the same thing happen to Sarah when Anthony and Paul were in the same room with her American friend. The difference, of course, was that Paul did indeed want to steal Sarah from Anthony. She knew he had no such designs on her, nor she on him. Still, it was flattering, and she thought Paul was more than aware that he was needling Lukas. She didn't mind helping him in his effort just to keep her cocky date on his toes.

"Well, you do have many memories to pull from, Paul." She placed her hand on his arm, which he automatically offered without thought. Taking it, she stood at his side looking up at him leaving Lukas standing on his own for a moment as the two reminisced. After several comments of bygone times, Paul began to feel sorry for his host.

"But now you have a whole new career, and a very nice young man to treat you like a queen, Elsa." Paul handed her off to Lukas lifting his drink in salute to his very patient, probably seething, gallery host. "I'm so glad you're here, though. I was dying over there caught in the clutches of those fame-seeking gold-diggers. How boring they are. All they want to do is flatter in hopes I'll choose them for my next painting."

"Since when did you become so picky? I remember a time when you were all for fame-seeking, grasping women."

"Since Sarah." Paul's expression relaxed, and a smile tugged at the corners of his full lips. "If they could all be like her, I'd still be fucking my way through the continent. Hell, even if they were as interesting as you, Kreiss, I'd be happy." He tipped his drink in a jovial mock-salute

"Gee, thanks. I think?" Elsa laughed.

"Who is Sarah?" Lukas, who'd been trying to follow the conversation, asked.

"She's my friend from America. If you remember, she's the woman mentioned in the news that was with Paul all those years ago. She helped bring my little brother back to me." Her tone became serious as memories of the second darkest time in her life flooded back.

"Ah, I see. But wasn't she with another man?" Lukas hit a raw nerve for Paul who took a long swig from his drink.

"She was. But not anymore. It didn't work out." His eyes grew stormy.

"Then why do you look so angry? If she's available, and you obviously care for her—"

"Because she doesn't feel the same way. Her head was so full of Anthony there wasn't room for anyone else. Now, I'm stuck in the dreaded friend zone."

Lukas knew not to push it. When a man suffered pangs of the heart, he was like a lion with a thorn in his paw, best left alone.

"She texted me tonight, you know. Congratulated me on the exhibit. I told her you'd be here. She asked me to tell you to call her tomorrow." Paul rattled off the message to Elsa, perturbed that Sarah hadn't wanted him to call, too.

"Well, I was going to do just that. In fact, Anno insisted we should before I came here tonight." Elsa could sense Paul's pain. He really did carry a torch for her friend. She sought to change the subject. "What are all these red tags?" She reached out to touch one attached to a vertical canvas featuring a black figure poking a blue-eyed boy in the back with a lion's head cane.

Paul immediately brightened. "Those indicate that the paintings have sold. Looks like not many are left untagged."

"There are numbers on them. What do they mean?"

"They mean that I purchased them. Number twelve is my number."

A tall gentleman with silver hair and pale blue eyes spoke from behind. Elsa turned and looked at the man whose sharp features and long nose were set into an angular face. His mouth was a thin line, and his eyes emanated strength and cold detachment. His light gray suit had a patina to it, and the only color offsetting the gray palette was a light blue shirt. Even his tie was silvery gray.

Lukas reached out his hand in the age-old gesture of greeting. "Herr Ivchencko. Are you enjoying the evening so far?"

The Russian man refused the handshake and clapped Lukas on the arm, breaking their contact quickly. He was clearly uncomfortable with courtesies. "Yes, Trommler, I am." He eyed the canvas and then turned to Paul. "Truly amazing work, Christiansen. Would that all artists were so blessed with such talent." Again, his gaze returned to the painting completely unaware of the trace of offense that skittered through Paul's eyes. His 'talent' as the man referred to it was really a culmination, and exorcism of very bad experiences that no child should ever have to endure.

Ivchencko backed up from the painting, and his glance caught Elsa. He turned to look at her directly. "And what do you think, my dear? Is not this imagery disturbing? Does it impress upon you the deepest horror of a young boy forever lost inside a nightmare?" He waited; his cold blue eyes boring into hers.

Elsa didn't understand art, but she understood people, and this man barely hid what she knew was a love of pain.

"I think it's sad. While I'm very happy for Paul and his success, to know people are drawn to this kind of thing shows that there is a festering disease of sick minds out there. These paintings weren't meant to be *appreciated*, they were meant as a means to dispel demons." She knew she'd let her mouth fly off without her brain, but something about this Russian struck her all wrong.

Lukas coughed, then interjected quickly. "As you see, the art has struck quite a chord with our Elsa, a true sign of Christiansen's genius with a brush."

"Indeed." Ivchencko's eyes remained on Elsa longer than she was comfortable with, and she was glad when he turned back to Lukas. "I'll expect delivery to my home by tomorrow afternoon." He turned to Paul. "A pleasure, sir." He nodded his head, then walked away.

"I'm sorry, Paul. I didn't mean to belittle your art." Elsa's words were contrite.

Paul laughed. "Not at all, Kreiss. I couldn't have said it better myself." He reached out and tugged a lock of her hair in a brotherly manner. "That one there..." he watched Ivchencko's retreating form as he walked out the front door, "is a very familiar monster." His laughter ceased, and shadows darkened Paul's eyes.

"Who is he, Lukas?" Elsa asked as her date silently prayed that the sales would still go through.

"He's only one of the wealthiest businessmen out of Moscow. Yuri Ivchencko of Ivchencko Enterprises. He has multiple interests that include banks, mining, and shipping. He keeps a home here in Berlin, and another in Brussels. As you noticed, he's also a patron of the arts. He's supported several exhibits here over the years and often donates to galleries the treasures he acquires from around the world." Lukas recited the litany like a star-struck teenager. He obviously had a healthy respect for the man. Elsa just couldn't fathom why, what with the bad vibes she felt in just a few moments in the man's presence.

She was saved from answering when her partner joined them. Beimer was wearing a suit! It was dark brown and made him look like a giant chocolate bar, but he beamed like the brightest star in the sky because at his side was Sigrid.

"Well, well, Hugo! Look at you." She patted his shoulder, and then turned to give Sigrid a hug. "And don't you look lovely, Sigrid!" Sigrid, with her blonde hair and blue eyes looked like she and Hugo could be brother and sister. A sure sign they should marry and have lots of babies, she thought, since it always appeared that couples who stayed married for a long time looked alike.

"Danke, Elsa. You look gorgeous." Sigrid eyed Elsa's dress, a style her plump curves and fair coloring could not pull off, but she still looked beautiful in her lavender dress with chiffon skirt.

Beimer shook Paul's hand with enthusiasm. "Thank you, again, for inviting us, Herr Christiansen. This is my beautiful date, Sigrid Wiedner." He introduced her to Paul who proceeded to charm the socks off her. Tomorrow, the station house would be all abuzz with the retelling of Sigrid's encounter with a famous, handsome artist. Elsa smirked and rolled her eyes at Lukas.

Beimer looked at her date and gave only the most cursory of nods. "Trommler."

Lukas's eyes narrowed. He was not amused. He really didn't like her partner.

"If you'll excuse me, I need to make sure all is set for deliveries tomorrow. I'll be right back." He kissed Elsa's temple and left her there among her friends. She watched him walk to the other side of the gallery where he stopped to confer with a tall, black woman. She was stunning. Her ebony skin shone like polished mahogany, and her short haircut was combed in curling wisps around her lovely face. She was as graceful and regal as a runway model in her pale gold silk dress. The woman placed her hand on Lukas's arm as he spoke and smiled, her white teeth like the richest of pearls set in her perfect mouth. She leaned in and laughed. Lukas continued to point out various pieces of art on the walls, and she nodded, standing at his side, with her shoulder too close to his in Elsa's view. Her eyebrow shot up over an emerald-green eye. *And what is this?*

Imani Bishop watched Lukas Trommler speak as he pointed to a wall of canvases. She stared at his sensuous lips. They'd been working together for the past six months, and he hadn't asked her out despite the clear signals she'd put out. She wasn't used to men ignoring her once she set her sights on them. Lukas seemed to have at least noticed she was a woman, but so far, he had not taken the bait. This wasn't to be borne in her world. And tonight, he'd invited a date to the exhibit. She threw a sly look at the redhead who appeared chummy with the artist and was stealing Lukas's attention away. She would have to redouble her efforts.

"Take that block of four over there, and the two from the wet dreams collection on the south wall and get them prepared for delivery to Herr Ivchencko tomorrow by no later than three." Lukas gave the instructions as he looked around the room. He knew Imani would handle it. She always did, and with professional care. He had every confidence all would go smoothly. He mentally checked his 'to-do' list, eager to tie things up and get back to Elsa. He couldn't think of anything else imminent. He turned and looked at Imani.

"Do you think we've had a success here tonight or what?" He knew she would share in his joy over the outcome of the exhibit. Happy artist. Happy collectors. Happy gallery employees earning fantastic commissions.

She wrapped her hands around his arm and leaned in, smiling. "Of course. You've done it again, Lukas. Perfect, as usual." She laid it on thick, throwing the *'I'm available, take me'* vibe in his direction.

Lukas patted her hand and disengaged. "Thanks. I couldn't have done it without you. Can you handle locking up on your own?" He stepped away but waited for her reply.

Her face lost just a little of its joy. "Yes. Will you be leaving before it all ends?" She dug for information, feeling a pang in her gut.

"If luck is on my side, yes. I have a date," he said, looking over at Elsa, "and she's really something, Imani."

The look in his eyes as he watched the redhead brought forth the monster of jealousy within. She seethed. Still, she maintained an air of nonchalance. "Well, you have fun, and I'll see you tomorrow."

"You, too." He didn't even look at her again before walking with purpose back to the redhead. Rage simmered beneath the surface of Imani's burnished skin. On the outside, she smiled, but underneath, she promised herself that Lukas Trommler would be in her bed before the end of the week, redheaded bitch or not. She'd waited long enough. All she needed was the opportunity. Once she had him, he would see what he'd been missing.

Chapter 7

Paul was ready to ditch the exhibit, what was left of it, anyway. Most of the guests had come and gone already after either hob-knobbing or purchasing their pieces. With only drinks available for those in attendance, gastronomical needs began to arise in the form of grumbling stomachs.

"I'm ready for a steak, Lukas. I'm sure you've made arrangements. Where are we heading? I'm a starving artist, after all."

Lukas chuckled. He hadn't made any kind of dinner arrangement, figuring Christiansen would take care of himself, but he had contacts.

"Hold on." He pulled out his mobile and dialed. As it rang, he walked away from the group.

"What say you, Kreiss? Are you ready to dive into a juicy filet with me?" Paul put his arm around her shoulders and pulled her to his side. He was just this side of tipsy after many drinks, and no food to absorb them.

"I'm more of a chicken and vegetables girl, Paul, but yeah, I could eat." She watched Lukas gesture as he spoke to whoever was on the other end of that call.

"Well, no wonder you're so tiny. You need some red meat, Liebling. Now, Sarah would eat a steak with me!" He looked Elsa in the eye. She noted his gaze was slightly unfocused. "She's from Texas, you know.

They eat steaks in Texas. That's where cowboys live, and they have ranches just full of cows waiting to become juicy steaks."

Elsa laughed. Paul, despite the past few years, was still hooked on Sarah. She couldn't wait to share this with her friend tomorrow. "You'll have to make do with me and my chickens, Paul. I'm just a Berliner, you know. Not some calf-roping cowgirl."

His voice, which was overly loud because of the alcohol, carried when he suddenly said, "Yes, but you could give those cowgirls a real run for their money, Kreiss. No one can rope a man like you!"

Elsa quickly brought down her heel on Paul's foot causing him to yelp. Her narrowed eyes and facial expression screamed, "*Shut up, you drunken fool!*"

A few feet away, Imani looked on with interest at the byplay between Christiansen and the redhead as she spoke with a small group of attendees asking questions about the remaining pieces.

"What's this about roping? Did I hear that right?" Lukas walked back and looked between Paul and Elsa.

"It's nothing, Lukas. Paul just really needs to get some food in him. He's babbling like a baboon." She smiled and kept her cool.

"Well, I just got us reservations at Marco's. They have excellent chargrilled steaks, so if everyone is ready, we can head over. They're holding a table for us." He stepped between Paul and Elsa effectively prying Christiansen off his date.

"Excellent news. Hugo! Did you hear? We're all going over to Marco's for steaks. My treat!" Paul, feeling merry and magnanimous reached out to clap Beimer on the back. He then reached for Sigrid's hand, bending over to kiss it in a gentlemanly manner. "Sigrid, dear. Are you ready to join me for dinner?" In his tipsy state, his request came out far more intimate than he would otherwise intend. Sigrid blushed furiously. Beimer looked confused.

Under his breath, Lukas cursed. "For fuck's sake!" He looked at Elsa while Paul seemed to be flirting with Sigrid. "I didn't make reservations for them too. It was only for the three of us."

Sympathizing, Elsa patted Lukas's arm. "Well, sweetie, you'd better call your friend back and have him add two more chairs. It will be all right." She batted her eyelashes at him, leaning closer. She hoped it would diffuse the consternation she knew Lukas was feeling over suddenly having not only Paul, but her partner and his date foisted upon them. She figured he probably planned dinner to be just the two of them originally, and now, plans were changing in ways that were unpleasant for him.

He looked at her beautiful face imploring him to roll with it. He took a deep breath and hit redial. He would do anything to make this woman happy, even put up with a drunk artist who seemed to know far more about his date than he did, and her partner who got on his last nerve. Elsa took his free hand and held it. The contact made him smile as he rubbed his thumb over her fingers, enjoying the sparks. She was worth it.

Thankfully, his friend at Marco's was able to accommodate them, and they all headed out the door together. Paul and Lukas climbed into Elsa's Peugeot, and Beimer and Sigrid followed in his car. Elsa let Lukas drive since he was familiar with how to get there. Paul had to bend his tall frame to fit into her backseat, which made Lukas smirk with satisfaction. He liked Christiansen, but the intrusion on his date was not appreciated. Once everyone was buckled in, he took off, not really caring if Beimer kept up or not. Driving through the streets of Berlin with Elsa at his side felt good. He reached over to hold her hand once he got into gear. One good thing came out of this fiasco, he'd left his own car at the gallery and now Elsa would have to take him home. If luck was on his side, he'd convince her to stay.

———— ◄O► ————

The wait staff picked up trash and bagged it. Clean up was part of the gig. Imani had two low-level gallery employees take down all the canvases tagged and sort them by number. All the pieces marked with number twelve were placed in a special crate in the warehouse. Those would be delivered the next day. The remaining paintings were scheduled for pick up by their new owners. Imani watched as Otto closed the crate. He'd been one of their new delivery drivers for the past three months.

"What happened to Lukas?" He looked over at Imani as he taped up the crate with batting.

"He left with his date."

Otto nodded. Imani was not happy, and it showed.

"The Schupo?" He was surprised to see her there.

"She's police?" Imani's interest piqued.

"Ja, she was one of the two giving us shit the day before for parking out front. Still, she's a looker. I can see why Lukas is into her." He slapped a delivery tag on the now wrapped crate.

"They've only just met?" she asked.

"Ja. I just said so, didn't I?" Otto was oblivious to subtleties, which sometimes made him quite annoying to work with.

"That you did, Otto. Are you finished? I'd like to lock up and go home."

Otto nodded, looking around. "That should do it. I'll see you in the morning." He picked up his jacket and keys from the workbench and walked back out into the main gallery with his partner. Imani followed with coat and purse in hand. They left out the side door where she set the alarm before exiting. Once out, she checked the lock to be sure all was secured.

"Goodnight, Otto." He waved as she walked two blocks down to catch the tube. All the way home, she considered Lukas's date. He hated the police, despised authority, so he always said, and here he was dating a Schupo. The idea came that perhaps she could use that to drive a wedge between them before the redheaded bitch really got her claws into him. She would need more information. And for that, she needed to be stealthy. One place to begin might be with Christiansen since he seemed to know her quite well. It was time to change tactics, to act the friend with Lukas. With his guard down, he would tell her everything about this woman. And in the meantime, she'd work her wiles on the artist and weasel tidbits out of him. Then, surely, she would find out something that would put an end to his attraction to her. He'd be grateful in the long run. Lukas was hers. He just didn't know it yet.

⚬

Dinner was a long and drawn-out affair. Paul insisted they keep the drinks flowing. And much to Lukas's annoyance, he hadn't managed to ditch Beimer. He was forced to share Elsa with them through three courses. Christiansen became increasingly inebriated and laughed louder than necessary. Before long, he turned morose, and that was when Elsa deemed it time to wrap things up. *Thank the Lord!* Lukas wasn't sure how much more he could take with a fake smile plastered on his face.

"Seriously, Paul. Some of us have to work tomorrow. We'll drop you at your hotel," Elsa said firmly.

"No! It's early, Kreiss. Truly, you used to be more fun. What ever happened to that club—"

"Paul! Stop babbling. You're embarrassing Sigrid." Elsa jumped on Paul's words before he could reveal too much in front of her co-worker and her date. Sigrid looked surprised that Elsa would single her out. Hugo began getting up, ready to take his date and salvage what was left of the night.

Paul had the good grace to apologize, never one to offend a lady.

"Sigrid, my dear. Please forgive me." He reached out, and taking her hand, kissed it in a gentlemanly fashion. "I'm simply enjoying all of your company so much that I hate to see it end." He gave her his most devastating smile causing the poor woman to blush furiously. Beimer did not like this at all.

"Are you ready to go, Sigrid?" He stood at her side waiting as she tore herself away from the handsome artist.

Hugo's date rose and she offered her thanks to one and all for a lovely evening. Then she turned to Paul and said, "It was lovely to meet you, Herr Christiansen."

Paul stood on unsteady legs and leaned in to kiss Sigrid on both cheeks. He whispered something in her ear that caused her to turn beet red. "And please, call me Paul." He turned to Hugo and shook his hand. "Wonderful to meet you, Beimer. Good of you to join us. Next time I'm in town, we must all get together again."

Hugo gathered his date and bid everyone a good night. Paul settled with the waiter, and they exited Marco's.

Lukas went across the street to get the car, leaving Elsa on the sidewalk with Paul.

"You don't still have Nadia's number, do you?" He asked as he lit up a cigarette.

"No. And she wouldn't see you anyway. Not after the way you left things the last time." Elsa fanned the smoke away. "What did you say to Sigrid that made her so flustered?"

Paul's eyes crinkled as a devilish grin spread across his face. "I told her she has magnificent tits, and I'll be thinking of her tonight when I'm all alone and she's fucking Hugo."

"You didn't!" Elsa's mouth fell open at the audacity of the man.

"I did." He took a puff and flicked away the ashes.

"But why? She's not your type at all."

"And what is my type, Miss Kreiss? You think they all have to be as perfectly gorgeous as yourself?" He gave her an appraising look.

"Don't even try it." Elsa smacked him on the arm. "You know what I mean. And she's Hugo's date. What's the point?"

"Because, Miss Smarty Pants, he needed help. I could see she was more interested in me than Beimer, and now I've given her every reason to be completely naughty. Hugo will be thanking me in about an hour. If he's a smart man, he'll take full advantage and fuck her silly. Then she'll forget all about me...except in her private moments." He ribbed Elsa with an elbow.

"That's not something I want to know, Paul. And by the way..." Lukas pulled up to the curb, and Elsa walked to the passenger door. "Hugo isn't that smart."

Paul followed, flicking his cigarette into the gutter. "She is. If she's turned on enough, she'll take command. I can see that about her." He laughed.

"You're a sick man, Christiansen. Get in!" Elsa held the seat up so Paul could fold his tall frame into the backseat.

The ride to Paul's hotel lasted all of fifteen minutes.

Elsa said goodbye on the curb, returning his hug.

"And tell Sarah I'll call her tomorrow night when you speak with her." Paul leaned in and shook Lukas's hand. "First class evening, Trommler. Thank you for everything. Take care of our girl here."

Lukas was feeling more generous now that he was finally getting Elsa alone. "Anytime, Paul. Happy it went well. I'll get your paperwork to your rep this week showing the sales, and we'll get that check out to you right away."

Paul made his way into the hotel, and Elsa climbed back into the car. Lukas watched as she snapped her seatbelt in place. "Alone at last." His voice was low and sexy. Elsa turned and looked at him. He'd been very patient with her friends throughout the evening, despite his frustration. Now he was gazing at her in a way that warmed her from the toes up.

"I appreciate you putting up with everyone. I know it wasn't what you planned."

"And just what do you think I planned, officer?" He reached over and placed his hand on her knee, stroking her nylon-clad leg with his fingertips.

"To seduce me, of course." She relaxed and her knees parted a fraction. Lukas trailed his fingers a few inches higher, teasing her.

"You're very presumptuous. How do you know I didn't plan things exactly as they happened to keep you from seducing me?" He raised one eyebrow and smirked.

Elsa laughed. "So, this was your master plan to protect your virtue?" She reached down and took his hand in hers and inched it up a little higher under the hem of her short skirt.

Lukas inhaled sharply. His voice deepened. "A man has to do what a man has to do." He squeezed her thigh, and his caressing fingers met the barrier of her nylons.

Elsa felt heat blossom, causing her to become increasingly sensitive to his touch. "Well, a woman has to do what a woman has to do, too." She leaned closer, whispering her words. Her lips were so close to his, sparking passion like fireworks between them.

"And what must you do?" His fingers found her heat, and caressed through the thin material, teasing and tantalizing.

Her lips parted on a sigh as her eyes closed. "Have you inside of me. Drive!"

"Where to, beautiful?" Lukas whispered as he skimmed kisses around the corners of her lips.

"Your place." She lifted her hips against his probing fingers. It felt so good, but then he withdrew and put the car in gear.

"Your wish is my command." Lukas drove fast, exceeding the speed limit. He didn't care. He knew he wouldn't get a ticket with a Schupo in the car. He was eager to get her to his place and strip her down to see exactly what she was, or wasn't, wearing beneath that slip of a dress. He was so hard; he was sure he'd wreck the damn car from the pain. But it was exquisite torture, and he knew that soon, he'd be sliding between her warm, supple thighs.

Paul walked into the lobby of his hotel, a far more elegant and expensive one than the last time he was in Berlin, and stopped, looking for the bar. He wasn't quite ready to go up to his room, didn't want to be alone. He glanced around and noticed a tall ebony woman standing by the column near the elevators. She looked familiar. As that thought crossed his mind, she caught sight of him and sauntered his way. Her long legs reminded him of a runway model, and her slender hips swayed rhythmically with each step.

"Herr Christiansen, I was hoping to find you." She stopped a foot away, clearly inside his personal space.

"Well, my dear, you've found me." He smiled, giving her the full Paul Christiansen effect.

"I'm Imani Bishop, from the gallery." She looked up at him from beneath her long lashes.

"Ah, yes. I thought you looked familiar. Is there a problem?" He retreated to his professional behavior.

"No. No problem." She let her gaze slide down over his form. "No problem at all. I was simply hoping to catch you. Care to share a drink with me?"

Once Paul realized why she was there, he relaxed and extended his elbow in a gentlemanly manner. "I was just looking for the bar. How nice that I now have such a beautiful companion to accompany me.

Imani took his arm and together they walked toward the lounge, lured by the sound of soft jazz piano in the distance.

"So, you know Lukas's date?"

⏤◇⏤

Lukas lived in Mitte on the Hausvogteiplatz. The apartment was located in Meisterhaus. Quite luxurious by Elsa's standards as she lived now on a government servant's pay; considerably less than what she made as a dominatrix, but her job afforded her both credibility and the ability to be home to care for her brother.

Lukas parked in the underground garage. Her Peugeot stuck out like a sore thumb among the high-end automobiles parked there. It wouldn't be difficult to find her car later. The thought struck her that she promised Anno she would be coming home. He might worry. She certainly did whenever he was out. She pulled out her mobile.

"Who are you calling," Lukas asked as she began typing.

"I'm texting my brother." Her thumbs bounced over the keyboard.

"Now?" He was impatient to get her inside.

Elsa looked at him. "Yes. He'll worry if I'm not home. I'm letting him know I'm okay, and not to worry."

"How old is your brother?"

"He's eighteen." She finished her message and hit SEND.

"I've never known anyone who checks in with their younger brother." He got out and walked around to open her door.

Elsa stepped out and looked Lukas in the eye. "You've never known someone who almost lost the only family she has left before, either. It may seem silly to you, but Anno is everything to me. If that's a problem—"

Lukas wrapped his arms around her and kissed the top of her head. "It's not. And I'm sorry. I didn't mean to sound like such an ass. Forgive me?" He looked down at her face.

Elsa went quiet for a heartbeat. "I'll think about it. But you have work to do." Her serious expression was ruined by the twinkle in her green eyes.

Lukas grinned and leaned closer. "I'll make it up to you, officer." He kissed her, slowly at first, but then it sizzled and sparked, and threatened to get out of control fast. He pulled back. "Let's take this upstairs."

He took her hand and led them both to the elevator that took them up to the third floor. The apartment was as modern and contemporary on the inside as the exterior glass facing and concrete columns implied. Lukas decorated sparsely but tastefully. The high ceilings, wood floors, and fireplace were advantageously showcased with warm earth tones in the materials of the couch, chairs, and tables. Tall potted bamboo trees livened up corners, and abstract works of art were prominently displayed on the walls. Elsa didn't get a chance to take the house tour because once they were inside the door, Lukas lifted her in his arms and carried her to his bedroom. She caught only a glimpse as they passed through.

He set her down as he crossed over the threshold of his bedroom. "Now, what were you saying earlier about what a girl has to do?" He teased with his words as he shrugged out of his jacket and unbuttoned his shirt.

Elsa backed up a step, her eyes following his fingers as they freed tiny buttons in no time at all. He peeled the shirt off revealing a muscular torso and a vivid tribal-looking tattoo on his left shoulder that extended down his arm and onto his chest. "That's quite a work of art you have there, Herr Trommler."

Lukas took three slow steps toward her, stalking her like a jungle cat. "Thank you. Got it in Cairo on an art buying trip. What about you? Any body art I should be made aware of?" His eyes slid over her body making her heat up all over again.

"None, sorry to say." She smiled when he stopped only inches away.

"So, you're a blank canvas..." He reached out, slid his fingers under the lapel of her coat, and gently slipped it off her shoulders revealing the naked skin exposed by her strapless dress. The coat hit the floor.

"I suppose so." She touched the markings on his chest. "What does it mean?"

He sucked in a breath as her fingertip circled his left nipple. "Strength, wisdom, and endurance."

"Hmm." She was about to say something when Lukas captured her lips and proceeded to kiss her senseless. His tongue swept in, caressing the inside of her mouth and stealing any resistance she may have had. Her knees went weak. The man really could kiss!

His hands ran up and down her back pulling her close. She felt the heat of his naked chest through the thin material of her dress and longed to be naked too. It seemed like he read her mind as those large, warm hands tugged her dress down her arms, the material sliding, then pulling taut over her pert mounds. Finally, with one last tug, the dress dropped below and revealed her to his eyes. Lukas stared hard, loving what he saw. Perfectly shaped breasts sprinkled with freckles and topped by two cherry-pink nipples. His mouth literally watered, and he couldn't wait to kiss each freckle and taste those cherry peaks.

"Damn!" He leaned down, wasting no time, and took one into his mouth, sucking hard, and running his tongue over the rigid nub.

Elsa melted. She buried her fingers in his hair as she struggled to remain standing. Understanding her need, Lukas reached around and lifted her, his hands cupping her ass. Elsa wrapped her legs around his waist, and he carried her the few steps to his bed where he laid her down and switched to the other nipple giving it equal attention. She got wet fast under his ministrations growing needier with each nip, each lick. He worked his way back up where he claimed her lips again, kissing her until her body begged to be relieved of the tension he was creating. Clothes flew off, and before she knew it, they were both naked. Lukas rose above her sitting on his knees. He placed her legs on his shoulders and leaned forward. With one hand to guide himself, he found her slick opening and poised his tip at her entry.

Elsa wanted him so badly that she couldn't wait any longer. It had been ages, and she needed to feel him deep inside her. "Lukas. What are you waiting for? Fuck me!" She wiggled her hips forward trying to push his cock in.

He smiled. With his fingers, he began to caress her moist folds. He watched her close her big green eyes and sigh. He pressed further and found her clit, rubbing it in circular motions with his thumb. Still, he held back.

"Lukas, please!" Elsa clutched his arms, digging her nails in. He found her need so arousing that he couldn't hold back anymore. Without warning, he plunged deep. "Yes!" Elsa's head rolled back, and her spine arched as the pleasure swamped her.

Lukas reared back and thrust hard again, and again, finding a furious rhythm. Elsa matched him and they fucked hard, bodies gleaming as they broke a sweat. He allowed her legs to spread out and wrap around his waist. The action brought them closer, and he cradled her head in his hands, kissing her with desperate passion. There was no finesse this first time, only hard and fast sex. Tension built, and Elsa dug her heels into his tight ass, forcing him deeper. Her nails scraped his back and sweat pooled between her breasts causing their chests to form a weird suction that made a wet sound when they parted. She knew she was about to orgasm.

"Fuck me, Lukas!" Hearing the need in her voice, he propped himself up on his hands and plowed her into the mattress. Each stroke brought her closer, and with the next, she let go and her climax exploded.

"Oh, my God. Yes!" The spasms wracked her body like warm, wet waves.

Lukas felt each one gripping his cock, and they brought him to the edge and sent him flying. He reared back, shuddering hard before falling forward onto her. They lay entwined, panting and trying to catch their breath.

"You are an amazing woman, Elsa Kreiss." He caressed her cheek.

Elsa laughed. "And you are one lusty lover, Lukas Trommler."

"I was inspired." He smiled; eyes closed.

Elsa waited a moment and then pushed him off and sat up. "Where are you going?" He watched her, wondering what she was doing.

"I'm going to use your toilet." She stood up and walked naked to the bathroom, picking up her clothes along the way. "And then I'm going home."

"What?" Lukas sat up, fighting the lethargy. "Why?"

"Because I have to work in the morning, and I also have a brother to care for." She made her way down the hall and entered the bathroom, closing the door.

Lukas sat in his bed, confused. He'd often left women immediately after having sex, but he was also usually at their place. He rarely brought a woman home, and even then, they didn't stay long since he would gently talk them around to leaving. But he wasn't ready for Elsa to leave. He wanted her to stay, and here she was leaving him like a cheap one-night stand. He didn't like it. He waited until she came back out, fully dressed.

"I get that you have to work, but can't you stay a little while longer?" He walked over to her, still naked, and visibly ready for round two.

"No. It's nearly two in the morning. As it is, I'll get maybe three hours of sleep if I'm lucky."

He enfolded her in his arms and kissed her softly. "Who needs sleep?" His teeth nipped her lower lip.

Elsa giggled. "I do. I have bad guys to catch."

Lukas ran his hands over her lower back, buttocks, and thighs while sucking on her earlobe. "I'm right here. Catch me."

Feeling wicked, she reached down and gripped his penis, gently pumping it. He stopped kissing her, and she heard the guttural intake of a sharp breath. She teased him with her fingertips. "I already caught you. Now, I'm setting you free." Releasing him, she backed away and spun toward the doorway.

"You're just going to leave me like this? That's police brutality, Kreiss." He followed her down the hall, cock bobbing like a divining rod seeking moisture.

Elsa reached the front door, and stopped, laughing as she turned around. "I'm sorry, sweetheart. We'll do this again. I promise." She opened the door.

"Soon!" he said as she walked out. "I'd walk you down, but..." He pointed at the engorged cock that seemed to be following her movement as she walked to the elevator.

"It's okay. I carry a gun." She winked at him and then stepped inside the elevator.

Chapter 8

Joseph Heinz rose early, as was his custom on workdays. But today was Sunday, and he was putting on a suit and tie, combing his graying brown hair into some semblance of order, and even splashing on a bit of cologne. After checking his choice of dark gray coat and slacks against a white button-down shirt and blue tie with flecks of green and silver, he grabbed his wallet, keys, and his service firearm and put each item where they belonged, back pocket, side-arm holster, and palm of his hand. Heinz whistled a tune as he walked to his car. He was on his way to pick up Birgitta for church. Sure, it wasn't a date. He knew that. This was all part of the investigation. Still, there was a spring in his step, and a song in his otherwise guarded, curmudgeonly heart making its way past his whistling lips.

Thick, gray clouds hung heavily in the sky, and the forecast called for rain with the temperature set to plummet. Traffic was light, and Heinz made it to Mahler's residence in less than twenty minutes. There would be no going inside to wake her up today. For that, he was thankful. Sort of. On one hand, he wouldn't make a fool of himself again, but on the other hand, he wouldn't get to see what he saw the other day, probably never again after his thoughtless action of walking into her bedroom unannounced. As he pulled up to the curb, she walked out the front door. For a moment, he once again saw her in his mind's eye naked, wet, and with her long, dark hair hanging in curls over her shoulders and across her breasts. He unrolled his window and let the cold air hit him in the face. Mahler opened the passenger door and slid in.

"Good grief, Joseph! Close your window. It's cold out here." She slammed the door shut and reached for the seatbelt.

He rolled the window back up, irritated now. "And good morning to you too." He put the car in gear and pulled out into the lane.

"What's wrong with you? Hot flashes?" she joked.

"I contacted the Avilovs and witnesses this morning. We'll be sitting with them. Both girls will be in attendance and can point out the young man if he's there."

"That helps." She shifted in her seat, and he caught a whiff of her perfume.

Heinz glanced her way and finally noticed her outfit. Not her usual business attire at all. Instead, she was wearing a black patterned dress with a red sash around her tiny waist. He'd never really noticed her waist size before since she wore suit jackets most of the time, but he noticed now, and he remembered the forbidden glimpse he'd caught of her in her bedroom. Her legs were covered with smoky-colored nylons, and she wore classic black pumps. Instead of her usual tight twist, her hair was pinned up loosely, and a few curls framed her face around her ears. She even seemed to be wearing makeup, which made her dark eyes appear wider, and her lips redder.

He cleared his throat. "You look different."

She looked down at her dress. Even wearing a dark overcoat, which, at the moment, was open, she did look quite a bit different than usual. She'd chosen her clothing with care this day.

"Well, it is church, Joseph. I see you also went the extra mile. Not bad." She lifted an eyebrow, her red lips twitching.

Heinz turned his head away to look briefly out the driver's side window and smiled. The rest of the ride was completed in a comfortable silence as they made their way into Wilmersdorf. The parking lot at Resurrection of Christ was full, and it took Joseph a few minutes longer than he cared for to find a spot. He really wanted to put his police parking badge on the windshield and just park up front, but that would give them away. They parked half a block down and then made their way to the front steps.

The Avilovs waited there along with Nina and Oksana.

"Kommissar Heinz, Guten morgen. Detective Mahler." Mr. Avilov addressed them as they approached.

Heinz was quick to remind him not to use their official titles. "Ah, yes. My apologies," he replied, contrite.

"Under the circumstances, it's best to simply use our names, Joseph and Birgitta. In fact, it may help to introduce us as a married couple to put people at ease." Heinz reached out and took Mahler's hand, holding it.

Birgitta kept a straight face, but a small tick at the corner of her red lips gave away her thoughts on the subterfuge to the observant. She liked the idea. Karina Avilova noticed, and she couldn't quite hide her smile. She understood a woman's heart, and she sent a meaningful look her way. Fortunately, the men weren't quite so attuned.

"Come. We need to get inside and grab our seats before someone else does. We always sit on the right. It's easier to get out at the end of service, and we can see everyone from our pew." Karina Avilova ushered everyone inside like a mother hen with a mess of chicks.

Birgitta spoke to Nina and Oksana. "If you see him, don't be obvious. Just touch my hand and look in the direction where he is, but don't stare. We don't want to alarm him in any way. We just need to speak with him, see if he knows anything. Do you usually talk with him after services?"

"Sometimes, but only briefly. Without Liliya, he doesn't pay much attention to me and Oksana." Nina's face was set in a pout.

Mahler chose to ignore the girl's interest in the young man for now. They didn't know yet whether he was even a person of interest, and until they did, she would say nothing. However, she decided that if he piqued even a hint of suspicion, she'd warn the girls off him immediately. She wouldn't be able to live with herself if either girl went missing. She glanced to her left. Heinz still had hold of her hand. It was warm and comforting. She tried not to smile, but it wasn't easy to maintain indifference.

***

The sermon was long-winded in Heinz's view, but he was sitting next to Mahler in church on a Sunday morning. He'd finally had to relinquish her hand because he couldn't justify holding it any longer. Her skin was soft, and her hand felt small in his. It was a perfect fit. He would have held it throughout the entire service if he could, but it was perhaps best that didn't happen. It was all he could do to stop himself from caressing each finger and drawing circles on her palm. And he couldn't wipe away the image still burned in his mind from the morning before.

The Avilovs had introduced them to a few couples sitting close by as their cousin and his wife visiting from Frankfurt. Mrs. Avilov seemed to be getting too into her role as accomplice and invented an elaborate fiction about how he'd met Birgitta only a few years ago and fallen deeply in love. "Just look at them! Still the lovebirds. He can barely keep himself away from her. Still thinks she's the most beautiful woman on Earth, don't you, Joseph?"

Playing along, he'd looked at Mahler, and noting the blush on her cheeks from the embarrassing scene, found himself charmed and unable to stop his own words from spilling forth. "That she is, cousin."

The low tone of his voice, and the look in his brown eyes made Birgitta's breath catch in her throat, and she started coughing uncontrollably, which led to Heinz patting her awkwardly on her back until it subsided. Mrs. Avilov smiled to herself, proud of her accomplishment. It occurred to her that sometimes men needed a little nudge to see what was right in front of them.

Oksana suddenly reached over and lightly touched Mahler's hand. Birgitta looked at the girl and followed her line of sight to a young man with dark hair sitting a few rows up on the opposite side. He wore a gray suit jacket with dark pants, and a white shirt. His thick hair was slicked back, and at first, he seemed focused on the mass, but then he began looking around. Finally, his gaze locked onto a young woman with blonde hair sitting toward the front.

Mahler turned to catch Joseph's eye, but he was already watching the young man. They exchanged a quick look and waited.

The service ended and Mrs. Avilov once again ushered everyone out in a hurry so the detectives and the girls could be in position to both see, and to engage the young man when he left. He wasn't difficult to spot. He followed the blonde-haired girl out, hard on her heels. As he began to speak to get her attention, Nina Belova stepped in his path.

"Hello, Greg. Nice service today, eh?" Oksana stepped in close beside her friend, effectively cutting him off from the other girl who continued, unaware, with her parents.

Hiding his frustration, Greg responded in a courteous manner. "It was quite uplifting, Miss Belova. And how are you, Oksana?" He clasped his hands behind his back and took a casual stance.

"I'm well, thank you."

Birgitta stepped forward next to the girls. "And who is this nice young man?" She smiled and played her role.

"This is Greg Koslov. Greg, this is Liliya's cousin's wife, Birgitta." Nina performed the introductions.

At the mention of her name, Greg's face stilled, and the smallest twitch of his lips ticked once before he extended his hand in greeting. "Very nice to meet you." He turned to Nina. "Any word on Liliya yet? It's been a few weeks now, hasn't it?"

Heinz joined them, placing his arm around Mahler. "Hello, I'm Joseph, her other half," he joked, grinning as if nothing were amiss.

"Yes, we're all very worried. It's not like her to just run off. Did you know her well?" Birgitta asked.

"No, not really. I only met her once."

"And where was that?" Heinz stared at the shorter man.

Koslov looked at the girls. "It was that gardening event we did at the nursing home, wasn't it?"

Oksana nodded, but said nothing else.

"Did you happen to notice if she spoke to anyone?" Again, Heinz took the lead.

"No, I can't say that I did."

"But you spoke with her, Greg. For quite some time." Nina said this innocently enough, but her statement was anything but.

"Oh, and what did you talk to my little cousin about?" Birgitta suspected he was feeling cornered, so she smiled and kept her tone light.

"Not much, just gardening. I believe she mentioned something about Belgium, maybe that she wished to go there. Has anyone checked? Maybe she had a boyfriend and ran off."

"We are checking everywhere." Mr. Avilov stepped in. "So far, nothing. And I can tell you that if we find out someone harmed Liliya, there won't be a place where that villain can hide where I won't find him." Avilov's voice dropped low, and his face contorted in anger. "I will kill him with my bare hands."

Heinz placed a hand on Avilov's shoulder. "No killing, cousin. We'll find her, and if she was harmed, the law will handle it." His words held a double meaning.

"So, what is it you do, Greg?" Heinz went back into subtle interrogation.

"I'm a sailor by trade."

"You're quite a way from a port here in Berlin," Heinz pointed out.

"Yes, well, I'm visiting my uncle right now. I'll be leaving soon to get back to work."

"Well, it was nice meeting you." Birgitta brought the strange conversation to an end.

"And yourselves. Nina. Oksana. It's always a pleasure." He shook Heinz's hand and then walked away quickly.

Mahler looked at Heinz. "He knows something."

"I'll get the car." Heinz moved quickly. He pulled up to the curb where Mahler was being waylaid by Mrs. Avilov.

"What do you think he knows? Do you think he hurt our girl?" She was getting hysterical.

Nina and Oksana stepped in. "We'll take care of her. Just go and find out what you can. Hurry."

Mahler thanked them and told Mrs. Avilov she'd call her later if they found out any new information.

Heinz drove quickly to catch up to the young man who had walked three blocks down and got into a dark sedan, quite a fancy car for a sailor.

"Something about him doesn't strike me right," Birgitta stated as she held onto the bar above her head.

"Nervous ticks."

"What?" She looked at Heinz.

"Nervous ticks. He has nervous ticks. Whenever we mentioned Liliya's name, his lip twitched at the corner, and I know you couldn't see it from where you stood, but I could see him twisting his hands behind his back. And his palm was sweaty."

"How do you know that?"

"When he shook my hand, it was wet." He looked over at her.

"So, you can pick up on all these small things, but see me naked and you see nothing?" She threw it out there, emboldened by their unusual morning of church and handholding.

Heinz went from cocky and superior to embarrassed in a split second. He looked back at the road. "Now is not the time, Birgitta." He ran a red light but tried to stay two cars back as he followed. He noticed that his own palms were now sweating.

———— ◆O◆ ————

Imani rode in the delivery truck with Otto and Bruce, the gallery's weekend crew. She was tired and a little hung over, but she felt satisfied that she'd uncovered some very juicy information about the redheaded bitch. Once Paul Christiansen was drunk, he was a blabber mouth. He spilled a lot of details about his infamous incident nearly three years ago, including why he came to Berlin in the first place, to recruit a certain dominatrix for his uncle's sex club, a certain redheaded dominatrix. After that, it was easy to shake him off and leave him at his door. He was, thankfully, too drunk to get it up, so she didn't have to worry about that. Christiansen was very handsome, but somehow, not her type. Perhaps because he was too easy, or maybe because she viewed him as weak. Either way, it wasn't going to happen no matter how hard he'd tried to charm her.

Still, she had very little sleep after she arrived home because she went online digging around until she found an old link to Elsa's page on Club Sexo. Not even a very original name, but that nugget of evidence was going to get her what she wanted—Lukas. She couldn't wait to trip the bitch up. She just needed to figure out how she would do it without making herself look bad. She pondered this all the way to Yuri Ivchencko's home.

Once they arrived and were given permission to drive up to the house from the gate guard, work took over. It was all about delivering the artwork and getting it hung where Ivchencko wanted it. Otto and Bruce did all the heavy lifting. It was simply up to Imani to supervise and make sure the client was happy. The tall Russian met them inside the house. Even his Sunday casual clothing was formal. He wore gray slacks, a Navy-blue sweater over a white collared shirt, and expensive gray slippers, the kind that cost upwards of eight hundred euro per pair. When he saw Imani walk through the door, his eyes narrowed, and his face froze.

He led the way first to his gallery where the *Wet Dreams* canvases were then hung on the far end of a long wall. The hallway already contained masterpieces by artists such as Chagall, Picasso, Rubens, Harlamov, and more. As Otto and Bruce completed the first four, Ivchencko escorted Imani to his library.

"This is where the other two will hang." He indicated the blank space on the wall opposite two wingback chairs near the vast marble fireplace.

Imani put her hands up in the shape of a frame and squinted her eye as she pictured how they should be hung, side by side or positioned with one high and one low.

"And where is Herr Trommler today? I thought he would be here overseeing this himself." The somber expression on his face did not seem to reflect the irritation in his voice.

"Lukas has entrusted me to handle this for you." She turned away trying not to let the anger show on her face at his condescension. His tone seemed to imply no one else could hang pictures but Lukas. Ridiculous.

"I'm sure you are very good at your job, Ms. Bishop. However, I'm not one to tolerate new people well. I know Lukas. I expected Lukas." He lit a cigarette and puffed as he sat down in his chair.

"Then I apologize for what is obviously a miscommunication. Lukas informed me last night that I was to handle delivery of your items to your home. He never said anything about needing to be here himself. I'm sure had he thought that the case, he would be here now." Imani defended her boss, mostly because Ivchencko had already offended her.

"Then what *did* he say?"

"Pardon?" This caught her off guard and she turned to face him.

"What – did – he – say?" His sarcasm, although subtle, came through loud and clear.

"He said he had a date, and then asked me to ensure that your items were delivered on time." She noted the gleam in his eyes but couldn't tell by his expression if he was amused or angry.

"The redhead." He pulled a drag on the cigarette fixed between his long, slender fingers.

Imani's eyebrows rose. "Yes, the redhead." She turned back to the wall.

"What was her name again..." He spoke as if to himself, trying to remember.

"Elsa. Her name is Elsa." This time, a little bit of her displeasure trickled through.

Ivchencko noticed. "You don't like her? Why is that?" Imani didn't answer. "I see." He stated this simply, but it came across as mocking.

She turned back again, standing defiantly. "You see what?"

He stared at her with his cold gray eyes. "Elsa has what you want." His voice held a cruel glee. His expression showed clearly that he enjoyed her pain.

Her anger spiked. "Elsa has nothing. She won't last long. And it's none of your business!"

Yuri Ivchencko let out a loud laugh. It went on too long and Imani stomped angrily over to stand in front of the man. Leaning down and pointing her finger, she let loose.

"I know your type. You get off on hurting others. Well, it won't work with me. I put up with no man's shit, so you can stow your inquiries. I don't give a damn what you think or what some two-bit sex-worker thinks. She won't have him. I'll see to it. And you," She narrowed her eyes, "you are simply a man with too much money and time on your hands. You wouldn't know a real woman if she spanked your old ass! You sit around looking at your masterpieces in this mausoleum of a home all alone, and you dare to question anything about me? You have no right. And I won't apologize for my outburst since you seem to have instigated it from the moment I walked through the door!" She straightened her spine, stepped back and waited. She knew she'd gone too far, but Ivchencko had pissed her off.

Yuri Ivchencko stood. His height topped her own, and the look in his eyes promised retribution, but it didn't come. Instead, opportunity knocked. "Did you say *sex worker*?"

It was like she hadn't said anything else. He locked in on only those two words, two words about Elsa. Damn it! "Yes. Apparently, she used to be quite the in-demand dominatrix. That's how Christiansen knew her."

A rare smile spread across his face, but it didn't sit well there. Where a smile usually makes most people appear approachable, his smile emanated pure evil, sure to send anyone on the receiving end of it running.

"That's quite a story. Ah, Christiansen. He's a twisted one. I knew he and I were kindred souls. That's what drew me to his art." He walked to a side bar and poured himself a drink. "So, is this enticing redhead still in the business?"

His curiosity about Elsa felt out of place, but if it kept the man happy after her tirade, she'd play along. She really didn't want to lose her job despite her lapse in decorum. "No. She's Schupo now."

He nearly spit out his drink laughing. "You don't say! Why, that's the most contradictory change in career I've ever heard. How did she accomplish that one, I wonder?"

"I have no idea. All I know is she's a cop."

He regarded Imani. "You're no sexy redhead, Ms. Bishop, but you have qualities that may appeal to lesser men." His gaze traveled over her body leaving her feeling dirty. "I wouldn't worry. I'm sure you'll get your turn."

Otto and Bruce knocked as they came through the door hauling the last two large canvases from the *Nightmares* collection. "Where do you want these," Otto asked.

"Ms. Bishop will guide you. I have a call to make." Ivchencko walked out without a second glance.

Imani watched him go, angry at his insults and glad he was taking his bad energy with him. She shook herself as if she could rid her body of the last fifteen minutes. "The blank wall over here. Let's set one high, and one low, and then get the hell out of here."

Sunday traffic was heavier in the afternoon than expected as Heinz and Mahler followed the dark sedan. It finally turned off into Charlottenburg. After driving through the denser neighborhoods, they made it further to the less populated area where larger homes stood. The sedan slowed down up ahead and turned into a long driveway that ended at a gate. Heinz pulled past the driveway and U-turned coming back around to park on the opposite side of the road a block down. He reached in the backseat for his binoculars.

The sedan stopped at the guard gate, a moment passed, and the gate opened. It continued up the cobblestone drive and parked in front of the large gray manor house behind a delivery truck that said Galerie George Nothelfer on the side.

"I know that gallery." Heinz made the statement as he tried to remember where he'd heard the name recently.

"You're into art? I had no idea." Mahler's tone sounded innocent enough, but he knew she was being sarcastic.

He looked over at her. "It was mentioned to me the other day. Where?" He thought a moment, and then it came to him. "Elsa. Elsa's date. He works there."

"Elsa had a date? She didn't tell me. Is he nice?"

Heinz eyed his partner. "I don't know. I haven't received all the intel back on him yet." He returned to the binoculars.

"You didn't! You ran his name?" Mahler was shocked he would do this.

"I did, and I'm not sorry about it. Elsa's past bad choices show she needs help in picking and choosing who she befriends."

"Her choices were those of a young woman trying to survive and care for her brother, not because she was looking to run with a bad crowd."

"She's my responsibility, her and Anno—"

"Elsa and Anno are fully grown. You can dial it back, *Papa*. She's a smart woman. Hasn't she already proven it?" Mahler felt the need to defend Elsa in the very same way Heinz felt the need to protect her.

He turned to her. "And yet here her boyfriend's delivery truck sits at the home of an unknown family member of a possible kidnapper and killer of young girls." His eyebrow was up as if to say, "*You were saying?*"

Mahler blew out a frustrated breath. There was just no arguing with him. He was set in his ways, and he was dogged about Elsa and Anno. He even treated her own son, Jan, to this same level of ...care? Once that word skipped through her mind, she lost her anger. He cared. That care extended to her son, and it probably even extended to herself to a degree.

"Well, let's run the address." She typed it into the computer and waited for the police database to spit out the name of the owner.

"Hmm, this just got stranger." Mahler read the real estate listing and then cross-checked the name with Interpol.

"What? Who lives here?" Heinz waited.

"Yuri Ivchencko." Her expression grew serious.

"You don't say..."

Heinz bit his lip, and his memories flew back to Hamburg eight years ago. A woman reported seeing a young girl fitting the description of Marlessa Schubert being carried onto a ship there, but when he investigated, no such ship had been on the docket. There were, however, several ships in port both during the time he was there, and the weeks prior, all under the same company name, Ivchencko Enterprises. The business damn near owned that port, and yet no one knew anything about that particular ship on that particular night. The harbor master's docket was suspiciously clear that evening despite ships coming in and out of port regularly. And a representative for IE claimed no knowledge of any women on any of their ships. When he tried to push it, an attorney had contacted his superior threatening to file a complaint against Heinz personally if he didn't cease harassing their employees. Already in hot water, he was ordered off the case.

"Anything come back on him?"

"Not that I see." She read the brief information on the screen finding only the expected: name, date of birth, country of origin, etc.

"Run his business through the database. Ivchencko Enterprises."

"What is it? What do you know?" Mahler asked, curious.

"Nothing yet. Run Koslov's name too. See what you come up with." As he waited, the delivery truck began to pull out of the driveway and back to the main street. "Damn it. I didn't see who came out. Did you?"

"No. I was on the computer."

The truck exited the gate and turned onto the street pulling away from them. A clear view of the driver wasn't possible.

"I'm not coming up with anything on a Greg Koslov. No relatives of Ivchencko, anyway."

"Cast a wider net. Put his name out on Interpol. Include variations on the name with his physical description. He's Russian. There may be a criminal record on file with the Politsiya at the Kremlin." Heinz started the car. Unless he had a clear link between Greg and the girls, and a warrant, there was nothing more he could do here.

He pulled out his cell phone and hit dial. Mahler looked up. "Who are you calling?"

"I need to speak to Elsa."

Chapter 9

It had been one long day on patrol with Beimer and Elsa's feet were killing her. Worse, she was tired and cranky, and her partner noticed.

"You've been worse than a grouchy bear all day, Kreiss." He was not enjoying her irritability. He was in a joyful mood, and wanted to share it with her, but she was not herself, and her sour disposition was starting to wear on him.

"I'm sorry, Hugo. I just need some sleep. Thank God it's my day off tomorrow. I'll be better by Tuesday." She plodded along, huddling into her dark blue police jacket. Her body was feeling every bit of the cold today as the temperature fell. She looked up at the sky. Clouds gathered and rain would begin to fall soon. "Good thing our shift is over in ten minutes. Otherwise, we'd get soaked. I don't envy second shift."

Beimer nodded. "We should head back now." They turned and walked through the near-empty park on their way to their patrol car parked on the far end. "Did I tell you Sigrid is cooking me dinner?" His grin was even more ridiculously goofy today.

'Yes, Hugo, you did." She held up her fingers. "Three times." Elsa couldn't quite feel the enthusiasm necessary for Beimer. She was happy for him, but at the moment, all she could think about was a warm bed. She'd even turned Lukas down for dinner. He'd been texting her throughout the day trying to convince her to come by after work. She politely and delicately declined. She knew where that would lead, and her body simply wanted rest more than it wanted Lukas.

Her phone vibrated in her coat pocket. She didn't even bother to look at it this time. She knew Lukas would be trying again to convince her to come by. He could wait. It would be good for him. Besides, she wasn't at her best, and she wanted to be at her best when they went for round two. They passed second shift's car as they drove out of the tourist area. Hoff and Haecker waved at them. The looks on their faces showed they were not looking forward to patrolling in a downpour.

The drive back to the station was short and quiet. Beimer had given up talking with Elsa about his budding romance with Sigrid, and Elsa was thankful. Her energy tanked at least three hours earlier, and she couldn't muster enough interest to be sufficiently thrilled for him. She was looking forward to a quick ride home on the tube, and bed. Inside the station house, she signed out and checked her mailbox one last time in case any memos had come down the wire. Inside was an envelope. It was addressed simply to *Elsa*.

It looked like it was some kind of invitation, so she shoved it into her coat pocket. "See you Tuesday, Hugo. Enjoy your dinner and tell Sigrid I said hello." She pulled a rain scarf out of her backpack and tied it around her hat and under her chin.

"Any last advice?" Hugo picked up his umbrella from the bench. He looked both extremely happy, and completely terrified.

Elsa smiled, but it was a tired smile. "Just be yourself." She patted him on the shoulder and walked out into the rain.

<hr />

The UBahn was crowded as people who usually might walk the extra blocks opted to ride because of the weather. A gentleman wearing a tweed jacket sat to her right. He smelled like a wet dog. Tweed never fared well in the rain, and he'd obviously gotten caught in the downpour. Elsa shoved her hands in her pockets to warm them up, and her right hand encountered the envelope. She pulled it out and tore it open.

My dear lady,

You were right. There is, indeed, a world of 'festering diseased minds', those that quite enjoy the pleasure of inflicting pain. You and your sharp observation skills saw a side of me I rarely share with outsiders. But you're not that much of an outsider, are you? You, too, understand the 'art' of inflicting pain. Yes, Mistress Elsa, I know your secret. I am expecting your company tonight at my home. Please see yourself here at the address listed below as soon as you leave work. Don't think to decline my invitation. It would be unwise as your secret might just find its way to the ears of those you care about, Lukas Trommler to start, and then, I believe your career in law enforcement would be in jeopardy should this information find its way to your captain's desk. I expect to see you soon.

Yuri Ivchencko.

1211 Baumgartenstrasse

Elsa stared at the short missive, horrified. With each word, her anger rose, and her heart pounded. How? Why? What the fuck just happened? How in the world could this man know about her past? And why was he fixated on her? What was this about? Did he expect she would simply drop everything and come running? She was never the submissive type. She was dominant, and damned proud of it. But he seemed to know what only three others knew; that she'd once been a very successful dominatrix. Only Heinz, Mahler, and Paul Christiansen knew that. Well, and Sarah, of course, but she wasn't here. And Paul was back in Holland already as far as she knew. He should have left this morning. So how did this man, whom she only met briefly last night, suddenly know about this, and what in the hell did he want with her?

Elsa's stop was next. She stood and looked around, desperate. If she continued home, he said he would start telling people her secret, the one Heinz warned her never to reveal lest it kill her new career. Despite Germany's liberal ways in the eyes of the world, the police force was still very patriarchal, and word arriving at her captain's desk of her past would surely sink her. She wasn't sure how Lukas would take it, but it wasn't the image she wanted him to have of her. One of the finest qualities of any sex worker was discretion. It protected both the dommes, and the clients. As the tube slowed, she had only seconds in which to make her decision; get off and go home, risking Ivchencko making good on his threat, or continue, switch trains, and then head into Charlottenburg, and then find out exactly what this creep wanted. She didn't like her options. Still, she was used to handling men like him. It may have been a while, but she figured it was like riding a bike. She could get into character if need be and tell this Russian bastard to fuck off. No one manipulated Mistress Elsa. She was the one in control. He was probably looking for someone to tie him up or beat him. She'd recommend Nadia or Nicolette and then go home—after she chewed him out for daring to threaten her.

⬥

"She's not answering." Heinz waited through the voicemail greeting, then left a message. "Elsa, it's Joseph. I need you to call me as soon as possible." He hit END and stared at the dashboard, frustrated. Outside, rain began to fall in fat drops.

"Let's head back to your office. I think we must be missing something in these reports." Mahler's instincts kept telling her that there was more to Greg Koslov than he cared to reveal, something in his manner that was nagging at her.

"I suppose until we get toxicology and analysis back on Anna Popovich from Dr. Menghala, that's all we can do. And you're right. We're missing something."

He flipped on the windshield wipers, put the car in gear, and merged into traffic. As they drove out of the neighborhood, they passed a church. It was much older than the surrounding buildings, rather gothic. A Lutheran church, perhaps one of the originals that survived the decades and a world war. It had an add-on that appeared modern, but the integrity of the main building stood the test of time. Mahler blinked. "Why church?"

Heinz was lost in his own thoughts. "Hmm?"

Birgitta continued to gaze out the window. "Church. Why the church? All three girls went to that church. Koslov is a visitor here, so he claims, yet he has been attending that church. This morning, I noticed his mannerisms. He was focused during the mass, almost in rapture."

"You think these missing girls are related to religion in some way?"

"You saw the Popovich girl. Were there any marks on her body, any religious symbols?"

"None. She was raped, but there didn't seem to be any ritual to it. In fact, Dr. Menghala mentioned he thought it was a rather clumsy attempt."

"Clumsy, how?" Mahler was intrigued.

"Well, he said the girl's hymen wasn't completely torn, and that most of the semen was spilled outside of the body. He mentioned that the rapist was either terribly clumsy or didn't know what he was doing. He also said that the manner in which the body was partially submerged into the river water showed haste, a desperation to hide the original crime."

"Shame," she muttered.

"That's what I said." He glanced briefly at his partner admiring her quick mind. "The perpetrator exhibited shame with that act."

"Those raised in some religious order might harbor that type of shame. It's what they teach, isn't it? That the body and its desires are shameful?" Her mind was spinning like a top.

He remembered his own response to seeing her nakedness and shook his head. "And you just said he seemed enraptured during services."

"Yes. And all three girls came from that church." She pulled out the computer and began typing.

"What are you doing now?" He tried to see what she was typing while keeping an eye on the road at the same time.

"I'm casting the wider net. I'm adding a search tag to Koslov's inquiry. We should be looking for someone who belongs to a Russian Orthodox Church or religious order, someone who recently left the area."

"Good thinking. But what we also may need to be thinking about is what would cause someone raised in an Orthodox Order to suddenly begin kidnapping girls. Let's add to that search. See if we can find any recent missing girls of the same description around any Orthodox communities in Germany, and Eastern Europe to Russia. Popovich was not his first."

Mahler's fingers tap-danced over the keys. "This may wield more than we can filter through."

Heinz nodded. "Or it may narrow it down to one."

They drove past the entry to the UBahn, continuing to the office where they might once again pour over the files provided to them by Faust.

Elsa climbed the steps up from the tube station onto the busy street. According to her phone's GPS, she needed to go left and walk three blocks before turning left again onto Baumgartenstrasse. By the time she arrived at the address, she was cold, wet, and miserably tired. The trek up the long driveway to the guard gate tripped her up twice as she slipped on the wet gravel, almost falling.

The older man inside the gatehouse didn't seem surprised to see a woman walking up on foot.

"Officer Kreiss here to see Herr Ivchencko." Her teeth chattered from the cold.

"He is expecting you." The bald man looked more like a Russian KGB agent than a gate guard. A loud click signaled that the gate was unlocking. It swung open automatically, and Elsa slipped through, walking up to the large gray manor house. It reminded her of a mausoleum from the outside. She stopped at the door as her phone vibrated again. She pulled it out and glanced at the screen. It was a text from Anno asking when she'd be home. She quickly typed in a short message. *Running an errand. Should be home within the hour. E.*

As she raised her hand to knock, the door opened. Standing before her was a short, round gentleman in a butler's uniform.

"Please come in, madam. Herr Ivchencko is expecting you." He backed up and swept his arm out, indicating she should enter and proceed in that direction. "May I take your coat?" He stood waiting.

"Nein. I won't be here that long. Which way?"

He smiled at her terse reply, but it was an odd little grin. "As you wish. This way, please."

She followed him down a long hallway that seemed more an art gallery. On all sides were paintings from throughout the centuries, some she recognized, others she didn't. He was a collector, that much was obvious. The butler led her into a library where a fire roared, offering the only warmth in the room.

"He'll join you shortly. Please make yourself comfortable." The butler left, closing the double doors behind him.

Elsa walked up to the fire and put her hands out trying to warm them. She glanced around the room, and then looked up, noting the two canvases adorning the space above the fireplace. They were Paul's paintings from the exhibit the night before. Lukas's gallery had delivered them. That meant Lukas might have been here earlier. She wasn't sure, though, as she hadn't asked about his plans for the day. He hadn't mentioned going on a delivery today when he texted her all morning. By his own words on the day they first met, he didn't do deliveries. He set up exhibitions and sometimes helped procure art for the gallery. Still, the thought of him brought a smile to her lips.

"I see you're admiring my Christiansens."

Elsa jumped. The Russian was suddenly a few feet behind her, and she hadn't heard him come in.

"Herr Ivchencko, you startled me." She turned to face him.

"My apologies. I didn't mean to interrupt your appreciation for my artwork."

"I wasn't appreciating it, actually." She stuck her hands in her pockets.

He walked nearer, standing a mere two feet away, a little closer than she cared for. He was inside her personal space without her invitation. "You were smiling." He looked at her with his cold gray eyes.

"I was thinking about something else. Why did you send me this message?" She pulled it out and tossed it at his feet.

"Right to the point, I see." He clasped his hands behind his back and turned to gaze at the paintings, ignoring the wadded-up missive.

"I'm always right to the point when someone threatens me. What is the meaning of this? What secret do you think you have knowledge of that you can infer threats?"

Ivchencko noted the defiance in her voice and stance. He smiled, then said, "One which you obviously responded to. You're here, after all. If you didn't have a secret, you would be home, da?"

Elsa drew in a steadying breath. "I don't know what game you're playing, but I'm tired, and this has gone far enough already. What is it you want?"

"You're quite the spitfire, aren't you?" He walked over and sat down in one of the two wingback chairs facing her. "Very well. It's simple, really. You, yourself, noted it last night at the gallery. I have a diseased mind."

"Herr Ivchencko, I've no interest in your mind, diseased or otherwise—"

"Mistress Elsa! I am a man who tolerates very little, and I will not tolerate being interrupted." He held up a hand.

"I don't give a flying fuck what you tolerate. State your business, and let's be done with this. I'm tired and wish to go home." She quickly went through a mental checklist. Her gun was still holstered on her left side, but her jacket was zipped. She slowly reached to unzip it, talking as she did to keep him distracted.

"Do you know how those paintings arrived today?" His question threw her.

"I imagine someone delivered them, why?" Her jacket now unzipped, allowed her easy access to her firearm should this situation escalate out of control. She had a queasy feeling in her stomach.

"Yes, they were delivered. But not by Lukas. I was expecting Lukas, but instead, that black bitch entered my home with two other employees of the gallery."

Elsa's eyebrow shot up. "And? What does that have to do with anything?"

"Didn't I just say?" He looked at her as if she should understand, but something in his eyes was not quite right.

"No, you didn't."

"I was expecting Lukas. I was expecting the one person I'm familiar with, that I trust, to deliver my items. Instead, he sent that filthy woman into my home. There are many things in this world that I do not tolerate, and Ms. Bishop is one of them."

"The woman that works with Lukas?" Elsa's brain churned on this information. What was this man's problem? "What in the world does that have to do with me?"

"Your boyfriend has offended me. He sent that filthy black woman into my home. And she doesn't like you at all, by the way."

This surprised her. "I don't even know her. What problem could she possibly have with me?"

Ivchencko laughed. "Apparently, you have something she wants, something she wants badly. In fact, her jealousy is so profound, she went out of her way to dig up a little dirt on you. You can thank your friend Christiansen for that."

Elsa's face lost all composure. "She wants Lukas? This is all about Lukas?" Her tired thoughts were jumbled as she considered his words. Ms. Bishop wanted Lukas. She viewed Elsa as a threat, and then did what? Seduced Paul for information on her? Goddammit! She was going to throttle that drunken fool. And now because this cold Russian psycho had personal prejudices toward black people, he'd threatened her all because he was mad at Lukas.

"Look. Whatever your problems are with Lukas, you can take them up with him. I've only just met him. Last night was our first date. After this nonsense, it's also our last. Good day to you." She turned and began walking to the double doors where she came face to face with a young man with dark hair.

"Excuse me." She tried to go around him, but he reached out and grabbed her neck. She felt a sting, and then a warm sensation followed by intense lethargy before she lost all consciousness.

Chapter 10

"We have a hit on our Koslov search." Mahler noticed the ping on her computer and clicked to open the message.

"What is it?" Heinz looked up from a stack of files.

"It's out of Pskov." She read the information on the screen.

"Where is that?"

"Western Russia. There was a Koslov, Boris J., who accrued quite a record for public intoxication, battery, larceny, and beggary. Wife named Emily, and one son, Gregor." She caught his eye as Heinz came to stand behind her chair and read over her shoulder. "This was more than ten years ago, though."

"And where is this Gregor now?" He leaned down, the action bringing his lips not far from her ear.

A shiver ran down Birgitta's spine. She focused on the information. "No record. But Boris has popped up in Ukraine and the Czech Republic since for similar charges. Oh, wait. There's an obituary." She clicked on the link. "Hmm. It's for Emily Koslov. Two years ago. Cause of death is listed as natural causes."

"That's not helpful." Heinz straightened and went back to his files.

She scrolled to the next page. "Well, that is curious."

He looked up again. "What?"

"The obituary says nothing at all about the son. No mention of Gregor Koslov at all."

"Maybe that particular Koslov is dead too."

"No. I've found no obituary for him. He's last mentioned in a census from 2002. Son, Gregor Koslov, age fourteen."

Heinz's interest piqued. He went to stand behind Mahler again to read the screen. "The age sounds about correct. Any family members listed?"

"Not on the reports." She continued scrolling through the police reports.

"What about churches in the area? Any orthodox churches?"

Mahler switched to Google and searched for churches in Pskov, Russia. Two Catholic churches, one Russian Orthodox, and one commune came up in the results, the Order of Rasputin.

"That one." Heinz pointed to the Order listed on the screen, which effectively placed his arm around her. "What is that? A monastery?"

Her skin prickled as she clicked on the link. The page opened to a pastoral scene of congregants working on a farm. The site was very basic with a tab to donate, and an address to write to for more information. No phone number.

"Google that one. See what we come up with." Heinz waited while Mahler worked her magic with the search engine.

"Here we go. It's an offshoot of the Khlysty. They're very much 'back to basics.' Old school orthodoxy. And that's just the Khlysty. Not this third-hand manifestation. No telling what they believe, but the name Order of Rasputin ought to give us some clue, yes?" She read further down the page finding some local articles by bloggers. "Hmm. They believe in self-flagellation for their sins and often enter into ritual orgies. How about that? And I thought religious orders were no fun at all." Her dry humor caused Heinz to smirk. She grinned back. Their eyes locked.

Heinz's phone rang. He answered thinking it might finally be Elsa. "Where have you been? I called over an hour ago?"

"Joseph," a confused voice replied.

Heinz's brow furrowed. "Anno? What is it?"

"I was hoping you'd know where my sister is. She hasn't come home, and I've texted her several times. She's not answering." The young man's voice sounded full of worry.

"Calm down, son. When was the last time you spoke with her?" He straightened and began pacing.

"Around four. I got a text from her saying she'd be home in an hour. She said she was running an errand, but that was almost three hours ago now. I've sent her five texts and called three times, and she isn't answering. Is she still at work?"

Heinz sent Mahler a look. "I don't know but let me check. I'll call you right back, okay? Don't worry."

"Do you think this has anything to do with her new boyfriend? I don't want to interrupt if her errand was him, but she should let me know." Anno tried to be mature about it, but if his sister was just off with the new man, he was going to be really pissed at her for causing him to worry.

"What do you know of him?"

"Not much. Just that he works at the gallery, and it was really early this morning when she came home from their date."

Heinz didn't want to hear that. He rubbed his hand over his face. "Okay. Let me call Captain Keller. I'll find out where she is and then call you back." He ended the call.

"What's going on?" Birgitta looked at Joseph.

"Elsa hasn't come home. Anno said he last communicated with her nearly three hours ago." He picked up his desk phone and dialed the operator. "This is Kommissar Heinz. Get me Captain Keller at the Hauptbahnhof, Tiergarten."

The line rang twice. "Keller. Mit wen spreche ist, bitte?" The gravelly voice answered.

"Keller. Ist es Heinz."

"Joseph." Keller's tone lost its gravelly edge. "What can I do for you?

"I'm looking for Elsa Kreiss. Is she still on duty?" Heinz tapped a pencil on his desk as he spoke.

"Let me check." Keller put the phone down and shouted, "Hey! Is Kreiss still on duty?"

Moments ticked by as both men waited on a response. Finally, Keller came back to the line. "Sorry, Joseph. She clocked out three hours ago. I imagine she's at home. She's not scheduled to come back in until Tuesday. Is there a problem?"

He sighed. "No, none that I'm aware of. Her brother is looking for her, that's all. Thanks, Keller."

"Anytime, Heinz. Say, I'm organizing a poker game next week. I'll give you a call with the day and time, Ja?"

Heinz chuckled. "Sounds good, Keller. I look forward to it." They hung up. He looked at Mahler and shrugged. "She signed out for the day around the same time Anno last heard from her."

"Maybe she went to see her new beau?" Mahler offered, although she knew Elsa to be more responsible than to just go off without letting her brother know exactly where she was and when she'd be home. She'd been like that ever since the incident. Still, she also hadn't dated anyone that she knew of since. A new love could make a woman a little crazy.

"Maybe." The fax machine rang and began printing out papers. Joseph walked over to the machine and picked them up. He stood reading them for some time, his expression growing dark.

"Mahler, we got part of the analysis back from Doctor Menghala."

"Well? What does it say?" She stood up and stretched her arms over her head. The action tightened her shirt across her breasts. Heinz didn't mean to stare, but it was difficult not to notice. He shook his head and scowled before reading the report out loud.

"The fibers from the deceased's wrists and ankles were polyamide filaments from rope, and the chemicals found therein showed to be high concentrations of DDT and HCB above 200 kilograms per unit. Menghala reports that there is only one port nearby that shows this level of contamination in the sediments." He looked at Mahler. "The Port of Hamburg."

She blew out a breath. "Sailor's rope?"

"Yes. So it would seem."

"And Greg Koslov said he is a sailor"

"A sailor who says Yuri Ivchencko is his uncle. An uncle who's major shipping enterprise is based in Hamburg." Heinz looked like he just won a prize.

"And what about Elsa?"

"I think we need to pay a visit to her new boyfriend." He picked up his coat and put it on.

"For Anno?"

"Yes, and also because his gallery just made a delivery there. Someone was inside that house today and can give us some intel. I don't know if there's a link, but we need to find out. And if not, maybe we can use the gallery to our advantage somehow."

"But we don't know his home address." She grabbed her own coat.

"Of course we do." He grabbed a folder off his desk separated from the stack given him by Faust.

"Joseph! Is that his file?" She caught up to him as he walked out of the office.

"It is. Are you going to fuss at me again about spying on her new boyfriend?"

"No. I'm going to read it. Now, hand it over and don't forget to call Anno." She pulled the file out of his hand and walked ahead flipping the pages.

"You're getting to be as bad as me, Mahler." He hit REDIAL on his mobile.

She didn't even look up. "I learned from the best."

Heinz smiled. "We'll need to call Faust next. I'll have him run a check on the Gregor Koslov we found and see if there's any connection to the Khlysty commune. If so, we have a point of origin. As it is, I think we have enough to get a warrant to search Ivchencko's home."

Mahler reached down to open the door, then slid into the passenger's seat of the car. "It's all circumstantial, but it does add up. I'm going to run a criminal check on our friend Ivchencko. I don't care if it's just traffic tickets. I want no excuses when we contact the judge. I have a feeling about this."

Joseph closed her door as he passed and walked around to get in. "So do I."

He thought about the last time he encountered anything to do with Ivchencko Enterprises. His gut was telling him there was far more to this than a few missing girls. And his gut was never wrong.

The loud pounding on Lukas's front door interrupted his arm curls. He set the fifty-pound hand weights down, grabbed a towel, and wiped the sweat off his forehead as he went to answer the insistent knocking. A smile crept across his handsome face as he thought it might be Elsa. Who else could it be?

He flung the door open without looking through the spy hole and his smile died. A tall gentleman with graying hair and a very serious visage stood on the threshold next to a petite dark-haired woman.

"Can I help you?" A badge flashed in front of his face

"Lukas Trommler?"

"Yes."

"I'm Kommissar Heinz, and this is Detective Mahler. Do you mind if we come in?" Heinz cast a look over Lukas's shoulder glancing around the interior of his apartment.

"What's this about, Kommissar?" He didn't move from the doorway.

"Officer Elsa Kreiss."

Lukas was immediately alarmed. "Elsa? Is she okay? What happened?" He stepped back and let the two investigators enter.

"That's what we're here to find out," said Mahler. "Her brother called in saying she'd failed to come home after work. He thought maybe she might be with you."

Lukas put his hands on his hips, perplexed. "That was only a few hours ago. I thought a person had to be missing for over twenty-four hours before the polizei were called in?"

"So, she's missing?" Heinz eyed him sternly.

"No. Not as far as I know. That's not what I said. I'm just surprised that you're looking for her here. Last I heard from her, she said she was going home to sleep."

Mahler walked further inside the living room, scoping out the apartment. "And when was this?"

Lukas walked over to the side table and picked up his mobile. He tapped the screen and then handed it over to Mahler. "Around lunch. I invited her over, but she declined as you can see."

"And this made you angry?" Heinz stood with his hands behind his back and feet apart, interrogating Lukas without shame.

"What? No! I was disappointed, sure, but not angry. Why would I be angry?"

"So, you have no idea where she might be?" Mahler handed back the phone.

"I assumed she was home. It's only been a few hours since she got off work. She probably just went shopping or something banal like that. Why would her brother call the police?"

"He didn't," said Heinz.

Lukas looked even more confused. "But you just said...and you flashed your badge!"

"Anno didn't call the police, he called his family friend," Mahler filled in.

Lukas registered this information, and then his face relaxed. "Oh, I see. This is unofficial." He walked to his chair and then indicated they should take a seat on the couch.

Mahler sat first, then Lukas, and finally Heinz who continued to glare at him. "Tell me what you know about Yuri Ivchencko."

Lukas's eyes grew wide. The question stunned him. "Herr Ivchencko? Why would you ask me about him? What does he have to do with Elsa? This is all very strange." He sat back with his hands on his knees.

"It doesn't have anything to do with Elsa, but everything to do with why you were at his home today." Heinz spoke casually, but his eyes watched Lukas like a hawk, taking in every response.

Trommler's face grew even more perplexed, and his mouth hung open as he digested the statement that sounded more like an accusation, but for what, he couldn't fathom.

"I wasn't at Herr Ivchencko's home today. Why would you say that? I've been home all day."

"Come now, your gallery's delivery truck was parked there early this afternoon." Heinz turned to look at Mahler. "Around two, wasn't it?"

Mahler flipped through her notebook. "Yes, that's accurate."

Lukas went from confused to tense, and he didn't like it. "I'm sure you're right. It would have been my gallery's delivery truck, but I was not the one making a delivery. I don't make deliveries. I set up exhibitions and handle all the public relations for Galerie George Nothelfer. I also, on occasion, am a buyer, but deliveries? No. That would have been Otto and Imani Bishop. She was to ensure delivery and setup today. Now can you please clue me in on what the hell is going on?"

Heinz stared at Lukas a few seconds longer weighing just how much he would reveal. It was obvious Trommler was telling the truth. It was also obvious that the man was vain, cocky, and not good enough for Elsa. But that was another matter.

"We're investigating a missing person. Not Elsa, but another young lady, actually, three young women. A gentleman staying with Ivchencko is a person of interest in this case." Heinz left out that Ivchencko was also on his list. The less information, the better. "However, we don't have enough evidence yet for a warrant. What we really need is to get inside that house and have a look around."

Mahler picked up the conversation. "We were hoping you had access, knew the layout."

"Imani would know after delivering the canvases today," Lukas stated.

Heinz's phone rang. He whipped it out and walked toward the tall, marble fireplace mantle. "Heinz," he answered. He looked at the pictures in the frames. "No. We haven't heard back from her yet. Yes, we've checked with the new boyfriend." He looked over at Lukas. He returned Heinz's stare. "No replies to your texts still?" He waited. "Hold on. We're going to try something." He walked over and stood in front of Trommler. "Have you tried texting Elsa since lunch?"

"No. She made it clear she wasn't going to come over, so I left her alone. She can be very stubborn," Lukas added, his eyes forlorn.

Mahler grinned to herself. Heinz reached down and picked up Lukas's mobile, handing it to him. "Try again."

Lukas took the phone and pulled up Elsa's last text. He hit REPLY and began typing with his thumbs. "What should I say?" He looked up at Heinz.

"Tell her that her little brother is worried sick and calling all over Berlin to find her. And Heinz is pissed."

"Joseph—" Mahler began.

"She has us chasing down her lover to find her, Birgitta. After what happened with Anno, she should know better." He sounded every bit like an angry father.

"I heard about that last night, that her brother had been kidnapped by Christiansen's uncle. What a sick fuck. She even texted Anno when we got back..." He looked at Mahler, who had one eyebrow raised expectantly, and then at Heinz, who looked like he wanted to smack him. Lukas steered the conversation away from all talk of the night before. "Anyway, she made a point of letting her brother know where she was. I can't think why she would not do the same today."

Lukas watched his phone, waiting for a reply. Mahler and Heinz exchanged looks. They, too, were now beginning to worry that this wasn't just Elsa forgetting to check in with Anno. She never forgot to check in with him. She was adamant about it.

"Mahler, call Hummel and ask him to check traffic cameras from Elsa's station to the nearest tube. Let's see if we can track where she went. Have him check which train runs to Köthener Straße at the hour when she clocked out. There should be closed-circuit video we can view."

She began dialing as she stood and walked over to the French doors that opened onto a large terrace.

Heinz sat down on the edge of the couch, his expression serious. "I need you to call this Imani Bishop and get her over here as soon as possible."

"What should I tell her?"

"Whatever it takes to get her here, but don't mention Ivchencko. I don't want to spook her, and since I don't know the nature of her connection to him, it's best to keep that quiet until I can question her."

Lukas blew out a breath. "She has no connection to him. Last night was the first night she ever met him. I usually deal with him. Today would've been the first day she stepped foot in his home, and that's only because I sent her with Otto to make sure the canvases were hung properly. Herr Ivchencko is very particular about things."

"Get Otto over here as well." Heinz's expression never wavered.

"Well, fuck. I may as well invite Bruce, too, because he helped Otto carry the damn paintings inside." He began to dial.

Heinz reached over and patted Lukas on the shoulder.

"Now you're getting it."

He stood and paced, thinking he needed to call Elsa's partner, Hugo Beimer, and get him over here too. He was the last person to see Elsa that day, and he was familiar with the habits of his partner. Plus, they would need help. A persistent voice sounded like it was coming from far away, and he looked around the room, then down, and realized he still had Anno on the line. He lifted the phone slowly to his ear, annoyed with himself for forgetting the boy was still practically in the room with them. He was sure he'd just caused him undue panic, especially since they didn't know anything just yet. "Anno, how much of that did you hear?"

Chapter 11

A persistent pain throbbed in her forehead. It felt like ten jackhammers trying to pound their way out of her skull. Elsa lifted a hand to rub the spot between her eyes, but nothing happened. Her hand couldn't get past a certain point. She tried again but still could do nothing to relieve the pain. She tried opening her eyes, and discovered it was much harder than usual. She managed to get one lid to crack open, but the other remained closed, the lid extremely heavy. She moaned and turned her head to the opposite side. Why couldn't she wake up?

"Shush! They'll hear you." A low voice from far away warned.

"Wha...?" Forming words was difficult. Her tongue felt swollen in her mouth.

"You're not alone. I'll be here when you can awaken fully," the voice whispered.

Elsa tried to open her eyes again, but her efforts were thwarted as darkness carried her under once more.

Sounds occasionally penetrated the fog. A door closing. Footsteps. Low talking. A girl crying. A man pleading, shouting, panting. More crying.

Finally, her lids fluttered open. The room was dark except for an amber light coming from one corner. A lamp, perhaps. Elsa realized she was lying on a flat, cushioned mat. She couldn't quite grasp where she was, the time, or even what day. For a moment, she had no idea where she was supposed to be. It was that strange phenomenon when a person awakens somewhere that is not their own bedroom.

She tried lifting her hand to rub her eyes and found she couldn't. She tried the other hand, and it, too, was immobile. Elsa then tried to sit up but couldn't move much. Her feet and hands were strapped down. Panic set in.

"Hey! What the fuck is this?" She tugged at the straps.

"Shush! Keep quiet or they'll come down here!" A voice whispered just loud enough to be heard.

Elsa twisted her head trying to find the source of the voice. It came from behind her somewhere.

"Who is that? Where are you?"

"I'm back here behind you in this." Metal rattled indicating some kind of gate or cage. "You need to stay quiet or else they'll know you're awake and come down."

"Who is "they"?" Elsa's voice dropped down to a whisper.

"Greg and the other man."

Elsa heard fear as the name passed her lips. "Who are you?"

"I'm Liliya. Liliya Avilova."

"Why are you down here? Are you tied up, too?"

"No. I'm in this cage." The despair in her voice was heartbreaking.

"How did you get here, Liliya?" Elsa asked while feeling around the bed as much as she could with her fingers.

"I was on my way home from school. A boy I knew from my church pulled up and offered me a ride. I didn't know." Her voice choked up as tears began to fall. "I didn't know he would hurt me. He seemed so nice before."

"Hey, now. Don't cry. It's going to be okay. I'm a cop. People will be looking for me." She tried to reassure the girl, and herself.

"You're a cop?" The hope in her voice was high. "But how did you end up down here?"

"Ivchencko. I came here to see him. The bastard was threatening me." The anger in her words sizzled. "I was leaving when I..." She had to think a moment. Her memory was still a bit fuzzy. "I saw a young man with dark hair."

"Greg! His name is Greg." Hatred seeped into Liliya's voice when she said his name. Hatred and fear.

"The sonofabitch pricked me with a needle, and that's the last thing I remember."

"That's what happened to me, but I was in the car. When he went past the exit to my house, I asked where he was going and that's when he reached out. I felt something sharp in my arm and then I passed out."

"When was that?"

She sighed. "I'm not sure. Maybe three or four weeks ago now. I kept thinking papa and mama will be looking for me. They'll find me. But each day, no one came to rescue me. Each day, it was only him. Sometimes, the older man would come down and watch me, but he hasn't touched me. He says I'm Greg's reward for his hard work. I don't know what that means. I just know I want him to stop touching me. I can't take it anymore." She dissolved into tears again.

Elsa's heart broke. What was happening to this girl could have happened to her brother three years ago. Anno was lucky, but this poor young woman was not. She remembered the sounds she heard while she was still drugged and put two and two together. "He was down here earlier, wasn't he?" She asked gently.

Liliya sniffed. "Yes. They both were."

"Both?"

"The older one sat next to you."

"What was he doing?"

"Watching."

"Watching me sleep?"

"No. Watching Greg...rape me."

"What?" The outrage flew past Elsa's lips.

"Shush! Keep it down. Please!"

Elsa craned her head around trying to look at Liliya. She could barely see her through her peripheral vision.

"That dirty, sick fucker! Liliya, I'm going to get us out of this. I don't know how just yet. But please trust me. There are people who will be looking for me. Other cops. Do you believe me?"

There was a pause, and then she could hear the girl pulling herself up to stand. "Yes. But please...what's your name?"

"It's Elsa. Elsa Kreiss."

"I'm glad to meet you."

"And I, you." The words were softly spoken. Both women knew they were in the worst possible predicament. The only consolation was in the fact that they were not alone.

"Elsa, you said the older man was threatening you. Why?"

She sighed. "Before I became a police officer, I worked in an industry that although isn't illegal, wouldn't go over well with my captain. Somehow, Ivchencko found out. Well, because of some nosy, jealous bitch, he discovered my past career. He tried threatening me with that information, but why, I'm not sure. Something completely stupid about his prejudice toward women of color, my boyfriend, and how he doesn't like changes in plans. The man is psycho."

"It's true. I think he's also a germophobe. He is always going on about being clean. He keeps a jar of hand sanitizer over there by you. I think that's why he only watches. He's afraid to get his hands dirty."

Elsa chuckled darkly. "Great. I'm kidnapped by a psychotic clean freak. No wonder it was the other man who did the dirty work." She looked down at herself noticing her jacket, gun, and belt had been removed. It was dim in this room, obviously somewhere in the basement. Her eyes had adjusted by now, so she cast them about, finally finding her items on a chair in the corner not too far from her left foot. Somewhere in her coat pocket was her cell phone. She prayed that Anno had called someone by now, hopefully Heinz. He would know what to do. If her phone was still on, and her kidnappers hadn't discovered it and shut it off, then she could be traced. She just prayed it was still in the pocket, and that it wouldn't ring. Even though it was on vibrate, it would be heard in this quiet room.

"Liliya, how old are you?"

"I'm seventeen."

She sounded younger. The idea that she'd been caged down here for weeks suffering rape at the hands of an animal made her blood boil. What the hell was their deal, anyway, these two men? "What's Greg's connection to Ivchencko? Are they related?"

"No. I thought the old man was family. At least, that's what he led me to believe at first, but now I don't think so."

"Why not?"

"He never calls him anything except Gospodin Ivchencko. It means 'boss'. And the old man is always ordering Greg about. In fact, Greg isn't his name, apparently. Ivchencko calls him Gregor."

Elsa thought about that for a moment trying to piece anything together that she could. "Have there been any other girls?"

There was a pause, and then finally, "Yes. There were two others here when I first arrived. One girl named Anna, and another named Natasha. The old man ordered Greg to 'move them to storage' whatever that means. I don't think he did it right, though."

"What makes you say that?"

"That night, Greg came down here in a foul mood. He was pacing around and saying things like *"I didn't mean to do it."* Then he did the oddest thing. It was quite sickening."

"What?" Elsa waited wondering what could be sicker than raping a young girl.

"He stripped off his clothes and knelt in the middle of the floor. He had one of those whips on the wall over there in his hand, and he started praying out loud. He whipped himself until he bled. And he also..." Her voice trailed off.

"Yes? He also what?" Elsa turned her head to the right and saw, finally, the items hanging on the wall. A whip, a flogger with metal barbs, a metallic rod, and medieval-looking clamps. These didn't alarm her. She knew how to use each item, quite effectively, actually. But it was the trays of knives and large mallets that had her worried. She was trained to inflict pain without causing harm. Ivchencko obviously wished only to inflict pain with maximum harm. The kind a person wouldn't recover from.

"He... he spilled other fluids from..." The shame in her voice clued Elsa in.

"It's okay. You don't have to say it."

"I never knew such things about boys before. My papa wouldn't even let me date yet. If I ever get out of here, I just can't tell him. He can't ever know." The sheer misery in Liliya's tone broke her heart and caused tears to sting Elsa's eyes. She blinked them away and tried to keep a clear head.

"So, this boy is religious, you think?"

"Yes. He makes me pray with him after he... after."

"He sounds very messed up, but maybe we can use that to our advantage. And Liliya, none of this is your fault. You have no shame in this. You understand?" She tried, again, to twist enough to see her.

"But I got in his car."

"No! You did nothing wrong. He had no right. No right to touch you. You didn't ask him to, so he had no right. Tell me you understand."

She sniffed. "I understand." The whispered words carried very little conviction.

Just then the door opened, creaking loudly on rusty metal hinges. Both women went silent and waited to see who was entering the room and walking down the stairs. Each step down had Elsa rattled. Once the bottom step was reached, the soft soles of the shoes made little sound on the concrete floor.

"Finally awake, are you?"

The low tone of Ivchencko's voice sent a feeling of dread through Elsa. She kept quiet, refusing to say anything.

"Good. Comfortable?" He tugged on the strap of her right hand as he came into view.

He had changed the clothes he'd been wearing earlier, and now wore black slacks and a long-sleeved black T-shirt. He still looked cold and evil.

"I've been waiting all day to try out my new toys. Would you like to see them?"

He walked over to the table with all the knives and picked up a wooden box. He carried it over and stood at her side. Slowly, he opened the lid and tilted the contents to show her. Inside, a curved, short-handled knife resembling a small scythe lay next to a glove with razors attached to the ends of each finger. Both looked quite old.

Elsa's eyes grew wide as understanding set in. He was going to torture her. And it wasn't going to be pleasant. She tried for bravado.

"What's the matter, Ivchencko. Can't get it up? Need a little help, do you?" She saw the flash in his eyes before his hand snaked out and smacked her hard across her face. The sound was loud in the small room. The sting on her cheek burned. She heard Liliya suck in breath and whimper.

Using the only knowledge of him she had, Elsa spat, "Did you like touching my skin? I've been around dirty criminals and filthy beggars on the tube. I wonder when was the last time any of them bathed?"

Ivchencko put down the box and went quickly to grab the hand sanitizer where he slathered it all over his hands and halfway up his arms. His anger made his movements jerky.

"Watch your mouth, you filthy slut!" The look he sent her way promised she would be sorry. He reached out and plucked a pair of rubber surgical gloves from a box next to his torture devices. As he pulled them on, he turned to look at her, composed once again. "You'll regret your hasty words, Mistress Elsa. But I am eager to know your opinion of my skills at inflicting pain. I've not yet had a guest with your professional background before. I trust you'll appreciate this more than my past submissives."

His conversational tone, and the fact that he referred to her as a guest put Elsa on edge. The man was truly insane. Still, she tried to maintain her composure. She'd be damned if she'd let him see just how scared she really was.

"Oh, I'm a guest now? If that's the case, then shouldn't the guest get to choose the device?" She hoped to stall for as long as possible while she worked on a plan. Any plan.

"Too soon for these, you think?" He looked at her with one eyebrow raised.

"Well, you have to build up to that slowly. Otherwise, it's like sex without foreplay." She smiled seductively hoping to charm him into trusting her.

He leaned on his hands, mulling over her words. "Well, I'm certainly not a barbarian." He clapped his hands. "This is exciting, Elsa. By all means, please choose a device for me to start with. I assure you, I'm an expert in all." He swept his hand out magnanimously, showcasing the items hanging on the wall.

Elsa knew her time was growing short, and if she didn't come up with something soon, she was going to be tortured by a man who did not know the meaning of the phrase 'safe word'.

"Come, come. Which one!" he prompted her.

She scanned the wall trying to decide which would be the lesser evil. She took a deep breath and pointed with her restrained hand. "That one." He followed her eyes where they lingered on a leather whip.

"It's a bit amateurish, but lady's choice. The whip it is." He walked over and grabbed it off the wall giving it a hard flick that snapped in the air.

Her heart sped up, but it didn't begin to pound out of her chest until he came back, laid the whip over her legs, and plucked the small scythe from the box.

"I thought you were starting with the whip?" she asked, trying not to sound alarmed.

He smiled. "I am. But we must dispense with these first. I hate to waste a single lash." And with that, he began slicing off her shirt, her pants, and then her underclothes. Before long, she lay naked. Ivchencko reached under the side of the table and hit a button. A motorized sound filled the room as the table slowly lifted her into an upright position. With nowhere to put her feet to support her weight, she dangled by her wrists and ankles. It hurt. She clenched her teeth and fought back the tears, anger flooding her. If she got out of this, if she broke loose of her bonds, she was going to kill this man.

Yuri Ivchencko moved to stand a few feet in front of her. He held the whip as he let his gaze travel up and down her body.

"No wonder Lukas wants you. You're quite perfect. Lovely skin. So white and smooth." His expression was much like the one she first witnessed when he was looking upon Paul's art, a sort of sick rapture. "You're a blank canvas, my dear." His words echoed the one's Lukas uttered in passion only the night before. The parallel wasn't lost on her, but now, she knew she would be experiencing terrible pain instead of incredible pleasure. She had no control over this situation that she could see. She needed to think harder.

"Ivchencko, you don't really want to do this." Her eyes pleaded.

He laughed. "Oh, but I do!" He raised his arm and cracked the whip.

"We've got something." Mahler crooked her finger at Heinz who just ended a rather long and awkward conversation with Anno. He tried reassuring the boy that everything was being done to find his sister. Somehow, he had failed to do so, but he did manage to calm him down enough to get off the phone. He promised to send an officer over to sit with him and be liaison for all information as they received it. Then he'd called Hugo Beimer, who was now on his way over. He hadn't seemed at all surprised that Lukas was Heinz's first person of interest in the disappearance of his partner.

"Where?" Heinz looked over her shoulder at the small screen on Mahler's tablet.

"The tube. She never got off at her stop. Closed circuit shows her continuing on and exiting three stations up, then switching to another train to Charlottenburg." Birgitta turned and looked up at Heinz. "Street surveillance from a storefront opposite the exit from the UBahn showed her walking toward Baumgartenstrasse. The time was right about when we left. Joseph, she may have gone to Ivchencko's home. But why? How is she caught up in this?"

The sickly green pallor that was now Heinz's complexion showed how truly worried he was. "Get HQ to run a trace on her mobile. If it's still on, we can triangulate her position. But tell them not to call. If she is in trouble, we don't want anyone to know we're tracking her."

Heinz looked over at Lukas who appeared bewildered and upset. "You said Ivchencko was at the gallery last night. Did he have any contact with Elsa?"

Lukas leaned his forearms on his knees and looked down, nodding his head. "Ja. They met."

"And?" Heinz prompted the man.

"And she may have pissed him off." He looked at Heinz.

"How so?"

"She berated him for liking Christiansen's art. Told him only diseased minds would find it fascinating. Her words did not appear to be well-received."

Heinz nodded, understanding Elsa's swift anger in the face of any reminders of that dark time. He'd had his own run-in with her red-headed temperament back then. "Her tongue can run away with her. Did he say anything to you?"

"No. He just reminded me to make sure his purchases were delivered today."

"And that's when you had Ms. Bishop take over?"

"Yes. She's good at her job. Trustworthy. But I can't think of any reason why Elsa would go to his home, if that's where she went. She didn't like him. I could see it all over her face. She doesn't hide her emotions well." The doorbell buzzed. "I'll get that."

Mahler approached. "We're getting a hit off her cell. She's still in the area. We can accurately narrow it down to within five miles all the way around Ivchencko's house." Her voice dropped low. "Joseph," she placed her hand on his arm. "there's nothing else around that locale where she might be as far as we can tell. Her last text to Anno came from that exact spot. If she's there, and we're right about Koslov, she's in danger. We need a plan."

Hugo Beimer barreled past Lukas the moment he opened the door. Behind him, three people followed, looking at Trommler and the detectives in bewilderment.

"Kommissar, what's the situation? What has happened to my partner?" Beimer's eyes reflected deep concern.

Heinz nodded at Hugo and pulled him aside where he gave a brief, private explanation, and then turned to look the newcomers in the eyes one by one. "No doubt you're wondering why you've been called here." Imani, Otto, and Bruce looked at each other, and then back at Heinz.

"Yes, we are. Just what is going on here?" Imani asked, irritation in her tone. She thought Lukas might have come to his senses when he phoned and asked her over. His words had been aloof, deceptively evasive, but they had sparked hope in her. But now, with all these people gathered in Lukas's living room, she was confused and annoyed.

"Sit down, everyone." Heinz indicated the couch while he stood facing them, Mahler at his side. "I'm Detective Heinz, and this is my partner, Birgitta Mahler. And this is Officer Beimer." He gestured toward Hugo who stood off to the side. "Before you get worried, you're not in any trouble."

"Then why are we here?" The terse question shot out from Imani's lips. Lukas was quick to reply.

"Imani, please. They need our help. Elsa has gone missing, and it's somehow mixed up with their investigation of some missing girls." His tone was gentle, but firm. Still, worry laced his words.

Imani, however, couldn't quite hide the small lift to her lips. "Oh, really? Well, what does that have to do with us?"

The look he threw her told her in no uncertain terms that she'd said the wrong thing. "Detectives, please proceed." He turned his head away and let Heinz have at her.

"Today, you delivered paintings to the home of Yuri Ivchencko. Mahler and I tracked a suspect to that same house. We noted your delivery truck parked outside at the time. Did you happen to see a young man with dark hair, early twenties, while inside?"

As he spoke, Imani's face fell. She could still hear the foul, old Russian asking her questions about Elsa, questions he would not have thought to ask had she not run off at the mouth. Ivchencko was not a good person. She knew this. She saw it in the way he treated her with disdain, and the way he spoke to her. He was a man filled with hate, but was he capable of kidnapping? She thought it best to keep her mouth shut from here on out, and limit what she said to this detective. If Lukas knew what she'd revealed to Ivchencko, he'd never talk to her again. But if she kept quiet, and the man had Elsa, the redheaded bitch might be harmed. Did she really want it to go that far?

Otto spoke. "We only saw Herr Ivchencko, and briefly at that. Imani spoke to him more than we did." Bruce nodded.

Imani seethed, promising to make Otto pay for that revelation later.

Heinz turned to her. "Well? Did he happen to say or do anything that might be considered suspicious?"

"No. He was perfectly pleasant. We simply hung the paintings and then left." She smiled sweetly.

Otto's eyes popped. "But you told us—" He looked at Imani who cut him off quickly.

"Yes, Otto. I know." She turned back to Heinz. "There was one small thing, but it may have been just my perception."

"And what was that?" Mahler asked, facing Imani. She didn't like what she read on the woman's face.

"Well," she turned to Lukas. "He seemed a bit prejudiced. I got the feeling he might have an issue with women of color." She cast her eyes down.

Lukas leaned in, concerned for his co-worker. "What happened?"

"He made it very clear that he was expecting you to make the delivery. He didn't seem pleased to find me on his doorstep."

"Why didn't you tell me immediately? Did he say anything else? He didn't hurt you, did he?"

"No, Lukas. He showed me where he wanted the paintings, and Otto and Bruce did their jobs. Then we left. That's all. And I didn't think it was important enough to remark upon. I'm sorry." She reached out and touched his hand. Lukas pulled back, clearly uncomfortable with the gesture.

Mahler watched this interplay with interest. "Would you be able to draw a map of the house? The parts you've seen?"

"Of course. Any help I can offer, it's yours."

Beimer addressed Lukas. "It would help if you could get paper and a pen."

Lukas tried not to roll his eyes at Hugo as he rose to retrieve the items from his desk. His dislike of the man needed to be put aside. Elsa was more important, and the level of his worry escalated with each passing minute.

He returned, and Imani began making a map of the home of Yuri Ivchencko.

"He has a very strange butler." Bruce, who'd been quiet the entire time, surprised everyone when he spoke.

Heinz walked over to where the younger man sat. "What do you mean? Strange, how?"

"Well, while were in the gallery hall, I saw him taking a tray of food through a doorway on the far end."

"What's strange about that?" Heinz's brow furrowed, irritation emanating from his brown eyes.

Bruce continued, unaffected by the detective's expression. "Herr Ivchencko was in the library with Imani at the time. So, who was he taking food to? Plus, it looked too much for one person."

"Did you happen to notice what kind of food?" Mahler asked.

"Sure. Some bottled waters. Fruit. Bread. Cheese." Bruce shrugged. Mahler looked at Heinz.

"What did this butler look like? Was he young?" Heinz broke in.

"No. He's an older man. Short, and round like a barrel. But not fat. Stocky. He seemed pretty strong, too. He helped me hold up one of the large canvases while Otto hung it."

"Did he have a name?" Mahler was writing down the details in her notebook.

"Ivchencko called him Dutch," Otto offered.

"Bruce, can you indicate on Imani's map where this door is that the butler went through?" Mahler picked up the paper Imani had drawn the map of the house on and brought it over to him.

"Ja, sure. Let's see." He looked at the picture. "It was here." He made an X in the far corner of the long hallway off the entryway.

Heinz stared at it. "Could be a basement. Or it could just be a guest room. Hugo," he turned to Beimer. "Call the city hall in Charlottenburg and ask them to fax the blueprint of Ivchencko's address to Herman Faust. He's LKA." Heinz fished a card out of his wallet and handed it over. "This is his fax number."

Beimer pulled out his mobile and made the call. Heinz grabbed his phone and dialed.

"Faust. It's Heinz. We may have a break in the case. I'm having a blueprint faxed over to you. I need you to check and see if there's a basement off the gallery on the first floor. And Faust, one of my officers has gone missing. We have reason to believe she may be in the hands of your murderer."

"Christ, Joseph, I just gave you this case a few days ago!" Faust swore.

"And already I've discovered a break. Listen," Heinz walked to the French doors that led out to the terrace and stepped outside. Mahler watched him go, knowing he needed to give a report to Faust. Her woman's intuition told her things were bad. They were right about Koslov, and Elsa was in grave danger. Time was not on their side. But then, in their line of work, it never was. She turned to look at the group gathered in the living room. Beimer was working on getting the blueprint. Otto and Bruce were sitting together looking confused as hell, and Lukas was pacing around like a caged animal. Everyone was either working to help, or deeply concerned. But Imani Bishop did not look concerned. In fact, she seemed rather pleased although she tried to hide this whenever Lukas made his way in her direction with his endless pacing. Her expression changed from unfazed to sympathetic as she stared at his shirtless form. It was clear the woman fancied Trommler. What was not clear was whether she'd been telling the truth earlier. Something wasn't right, and Birgitta decided to go push a few buttons.

"So, you work with Lukas?" She sat down next to her.

"Yes." Imani scooted down giving Mahler more room.

"And how is that going?" She leaned back.

"It goes well. He's very easy to work with." She stared at Lukas as he stood watching Heinz through the glass.

"He's very easy on the eyes, isn't he," Birgitta replied, stating the question more as a casual observation.

"Yes, I suppose he is."

"And single, too. I understand he was on a date with our Elsa last night. Did you meet her?"

Imani took a deep breath, then said, "No. I can't say that I did. I only saw her across the room."

"Oh, so Lukas didn't introduce you two. I'm sorry, I didn't realize you were not close like that. You're just co-workers then."

Her spine stiffened, and she flashed a look at Mahler. "We're not just co-workers. We're friends."

"But not the kind of friend he would introduce his girlfriend to, it seems," Birgitta said with innocence.

"She's not his girlfriend! It was only a first date, nothing more." Imani's anger bubbled to the surface, and her attempt to quell it didn't work as well as she intended. "I mean, they only just met. Who knows if they'll even see each other again?" She smiled, but it didn't reach her eyes.

"Well, I'm no expert, but I'd say the way he's pacing through here like a caged lion says he's already hooked."

Imani looked at Lukas who'd resumed his pacing. "Perhaps. Perhaps not. Like you said, you're no expert." She let the insulting words roll off her lips as she gazed at the man in question.

Mahler watched the woman, knowing now, that Bishop truly hated the idea of Lukas dating Elsa. But did it have anything to do with Elsa going missing?

"Hmm. I wonder how Ivchencko met her. Lukas doesn't know him half as well as he knows you, yet he introduced them." She said this as if just speaking out loud to herself.

"The way I understand it, she insulted Herr Ivchencko, so I wouldn't exactly say they were politely introduced. It was probably just Lukas's way to smooth over a situation she caused with her lack of culture."

"Lack of culture? How would you know Elsa lacks culture? You've not met her?"

Imani wouldn't look at her. "I don't need to meet her. I know her type."

Mahler sat forward, stifling her own anger under a calm exterior. "And what type is that?"

The ebony woman finally turned and looked at Birgitta. Her expression was calm, until she noticed her eyes. They flashed dangerously, and Imani knew she'd said too much—again.

"Cops. Schutzpolizei. You know…"

"No, I don't. Tell me." Mahler never lost eye contact. It was a method detectives used to cause suspects to be ill-at-ease. The more nervous they got, the more they babbled. The more they babbled, the harder it became to keep their lies straight.

Imani squirmed a bit in her seat, pissed at the detective. "I don't know, really. It was just something Mr. Christiansen said." She dropped eye contact and looked away, but she could still feel Mahler's eyes on her. They never wavered.

"And what was that? What did Paul say about his friend Elsa?" She stressed the word 'friend'.

"Something about her past career, before she was a cop."

"Paul told you about Elsa's past career. And what career was that?" Birgitta's voice was sharp. Lukas looked up and noticed the two women talking.

"What about Elsa? What are you two talking about," he asked, then sauntered over to stand in front of them.

Mahler finally looked away from Imani and focused on Lukas. "Ms. Bishop was just telling me of her conversation with Paul Christiansen about Elsa."

Lukas looked confused. "When did you talk to Christiansen? He was with me all night."

Imani fidgeted, her eyes looking everywhere but at Lukas or Mahler. "Some time in the evening. I don't remember."

"And what did he say?" Trommler placed his hands on his hips and waited for Imani to explain herself. He knew she couldn't have possibly talked with Paul because Paul had been with him and Elsa most of the night. Prior to that, he was surrounded by adoring fans, and Imani was working with the buyers. Something wasn't right.

"It was just something about what she did before she was Schupo." She looked at her lap, knowing she was cornered.

He addressed Mahler. "Do you know what she's talking about?"

She stood and looked up at him. "Nein. And Ms. Bishop better start explaining why she's lying, why she lied earlier."

"I didn't lie!" Imani shot to her feet.

"Woah!" Lukas found himself between two very angry women. He addressed Mahler. "What do you mean? What did she lie about?"

Biemer got off the phone and joined them. "What the hell is going on here?"

"She's not told us the whole truth, have you Ms. Bishop?" The hard stare was back in place.

Heinz stepped back inside to find his partner giving 'the look' to Imani Bishop with Lukas and Beimer standing around them. All eyes were on the tall, lovely black woman, even Otto's and Bruce's. The woman in question looked like she was about to blow a gasket. He waited, standing by the French doors. He knew better than to get between two pissed off women, especially when one was his partner smack in the middle of an impromptu interrogation.

"I told you everything." She crossed her arms over her chest. "Lukas, tell them!" She pleaded with him with her big brown eyes.

Now he could see what Mahler saw. Imani was hiding something. "What else happened at Ivchencko's? And don't lie to me, Imani. Your job is on the line."

Tears welled in her eyes, but they were not tears of sadness. They were angry tears. "He knows about her, okay?"

"He knows what?" Lukas asked. He took a step toward her.

Imani backed up and blew up. "That she was a whore! Did you know that? Your new girlfriend used to work in a sex club. She spanked men for a living. That's what you think is so great! That's the woman you dated last night. And Ivchencko knows it, too. I don't know if that means anything or nothing. I just know he was interested in Elsa and asked about her."

"Who told you this shit?" Lukas's anger blasted their ears.

"Paul Christiansen. I already told you that." She gave him a look of evil satisfaction.

"When?" Heinz spoke from the back of the room. "When did he share this with you?"

"Yes, Ms. Bishop, when?" Mahler asked.

"Last night," she snapped.

"But you weren't around him at the exhibit. Not at all. You were working the buyers." Lukas's eyes now looked like the very animal he appeared earlier while pacing. Wild. Feral. Dangerous.

"I met him at his hotel, Lukas." She let that sink in, hoping to see some sign that he cared, that it bothered him. She was grasping at straws now knowing her chance with him was blown.

He didn't blink. "After we dropped him off?" His eyebrows rose in question.

She sighed, defeated. "Yes. After you dropped him off."

He looked at Mahler. "He was very drunk last night. He could've said anything. So what?"

It was obvious he didn't believe it. Beimer stood behind him wearing the same expression. He, too, didn't want to believe that Elsa was anything other than who they believed her to be.

"Paul is quite the joker. I imagine if he was drunk, it would just be worse." Heinz approached the group, but his eyes were on Mahler. They said, *"Work with me!"* His words were carefully selected to protect Elsa.

"That's true," she said.

"Still, if you repeated this to a man like Ivchencko, then you may very well have put Elsa in danger."

"I don't understand," said Imani. "What do you mean '*a man like Ivchencko?*' What kind of man is he?"

"Didn't you tell us that earlier? I thought you'd already drawn that conclusion. You said he mistreated you," Heinz pointed out.

"But that may only have been my perception," she replied.

"Perception is instinct, and people should trust it more. Some years ago, a young girl was abducted. The trail went cold at the port in Hamburg. It's the very port where Ivchencko Enterprises docks all their commercial shipping vessels. I've reason to believe he was involved. And now that Elsa has gone missing at a time when Mahler and I are investigating three missing girls who all had contact with a suspect living at his residence, well, it's not just a coincidence. You said he asked about her. A man like that doesn't ask idle questions. Now, from the beginning. Tell us what happened." The coldness in Heinz's eyes sent a shiver up Imani's spine. She started over and told them everything. When she was done, Lukas spoke.

"You're fired. Don't bother to come back to the gallery. I'll have Otto bring you your things. Now please get out of my house." He turned his back.

"Lukas..." She reached out. "I'm sorry." Her hand dropped to her side. Imani turned to grab her purse and leave. Heinz stopped her and handed her his card.

"We'll be in touch." He stated it like a promise, and not the good kind.

When the door shut behind her, Beimer looked at Heinz and Mahler. "It's not true, is it?" He looked hurt.

"What?" Heinz asked.

"Elsa didn't actually work in a sex club, did she?" Beimer sounded like a little boy asking if Santa Claus was real and expecting the worst.

Mahler noticed Lukas's shoulders were stiff, and he stood stock still while waiting for the answer. She patted Beimer on the arm. "No, Hugo, it's not true." She lied through her teeth sounding for all the world as if she were telling the truth.

Heinz's eye caught hers. He mouthed *'thank you'* behind the backs of the other two men.

Lukas's shoulders slumped in relief. He sat down.

"Why would Mr. Christiansen say that?" Beimer asked. He was struggling with his opinion of Paul, a very favorable opinion of the man except for his flirting with Sigrid, saying something so degrading about his partner.

"Paul has a very strange sense of humor, Hugo. Remember, he was abused growing up. You know the story. It was all over the news," Heinz added.

This made sense to Hugo who latched on to the explanation.

"He's getting therapy for it," Mahler shared.

Hugo nodded. "That's good. But I don't want him maligning my partner ever again, and I'll tell him so if he comes back to Berlin."

"But right now, Elsa is in danger as far as we can tell. What are we going to do about it?" Lukas turned, speaking up.

"That's what I came in to tell you before I saw Birgitta boring into Ms. Bishop." He smiled at her, then looked at Lukas and Beimer. "We have a plan. Faust will meet us in Charlottenburg in an hour. Hugo, you ride with us."

Hugo stood tall, puffing out his chest. He was ready to ride in on his white horse and save Elsa. Lukas waited to hear what he was supposed to do.

"And what about me?"

"You'll wait here," said Heinz.

"The hell I will!"

"Trommler, you're a civilian. We can't bring you into this. You'll just get in the way, and I can't focus on finding Elsa if I'm having to look out for you." The two men glared at each other.

"You don't need to look out for me, Kommissar. I can look out for myself. I'm ex-military," Lukas stated as he crossed his arms over his chest.

"What? When? I didn't see that in your background check." Heinz looked perplexed. There was no such information in Trommler's file, only a period of four years where no job was listed. He'd assumed the man was just an unemployed bum.

Lukas's eyes narrowed hearing that Heinz had run a check on him.

"I spent four years as a Marine. Kapitänleutnant Trommler at your service. I was attached to a select group. What we did was classified, and that's why you would not find record of my service in a simple police background check. You'd need higher clearance." The insult was apparent, and Birgitta could see Heinz's eyebrows sink lower indicating he was about to explode.

She stepped between them, whispering under her breath, "Oh, lord." Mahler addressed Trommler, putting an end to their pissing contest. "Can you handle a weapon, Lukas?"

"I can handle all manner of weapons, and even make weapons, if need be, detective. I spent my first two years in Kosovo, and the last two in Afghanistan. My specialty is explosives."

"Why'd you get out?" Heinz asked, still stunned by this turn of events, and still looking for a reason to dislike the man.

"That's my business. Now, can we please go find my girlfriend?"

"No," said Heinz.

Lukas started to protest.

"Not until you put on a damn shirt," Heinz stated angrily. Lukas relented, walking to his bedroom to grab a shirt.

He came back out in jeans, black, long-sleeved shirt, black boots, and strapping an MP7 at his side, and a Glock 17 tucked into a rear pants holster. He slid a large knife up his sleeve into a sheath and then put on a long trench coat to cover the lethal weapons. "Ready."

Beimer gave a grudging thumbs up. Mahler grinned. Heinz blew air out of his nose like an irritated old bull, then said, "Let's go."

Chapter 12

Elsa hung forward in her restraints, covered in welts. They were hot, swollen, and hurt like hell. The angry red lines crisscrossed her torso and thighs. Amazingly, there was no blood spilled, not yet, but Ivchencko was just getting started.

"You see? What did I tell you?" He smiled, proudly standing with arms wide open waiting for praise. "Did I not say I'm an expert?" He stepped forward and traced a welt that ran across her breasts with his gloved finger. "No broken skin, and not a single drop of blood spilled." He admired his handiwork. "Lovely. They match your hair, my dear?" He looked up at her and casually swept the hair aside hanging over her eyes.

Elsa panted; her shallow breaths taken with great care since deeper breathing seemed to stretch her tight, inflamed skin painfully. Despite this, despite her need to scream, and possibly faint, she maintained as much composure as possible. "You did. You did say you were adept."

He smiled. "There, now, was that so hard to admit?"

She looked him in the eye. "You know, of course, I'm going to kill you."

He laughed. "That's the spirit, my dear!" He patted her arm. She flinched and winced in pain.

Elsa could hear Liliya sobbing behind her. Every crack of the whip brought forth an involuntary yelp from the girl who watched from her cage as Ivchencko tortured her.

Yuri wandered over to his wall of tools and picked out the next device, a long metal rod. He smacked the table with it a few times for effect and then came back to stand in front of Elsa.

"My choice now. This has always been a favorite." He eyed the instrument, stroking up and down in a sexual manner. "Women just can't seem to get enough of my rod, Mistress."

"Rather small and thin, isn't it?" She knew this would piss him off, would backfire on her quickly, but damned if she'd let him break her.

"I admire your wit, but it won't save you. Let me know how small and thin you find it afterwards. He eyed her body as if trying to decide where to begin. Fear gripped Elsa's heart causing it to pound in her chest. His lips unfurled at the edges into the most evil smile she'd ever witnessed. Then he stepped back, raised the rod, and swung, connecting with her knee.

Elsa let out a scream as the pain flooded her body. She was sure something just broke, and the tears streaming down her face making new tracks in her already smeared mascara, dripped off her jaw and hit the floor.

Liliya cried out. "Please stop! Please!"

"Shut up over there or I'll call Gregor down. Or is that what you want?" He tossed a contemptuous look at the dirty girl in the cage. How Gregor could touch her was beyond him. She needed to be scrubbed.

"No!" Liliya panicked.

"It's okay, Liliya. Stay quiet, please." Elsa begged the girl not to bring attention to herself despite her own agony.

Ivchenko gave her an admiring look. "You're sensible. I like that about you. And tougher than you look." He began to raise the rod once more when the door slammed open and Gregor stepped in.

"We have a problem." He stood leaning on the railing, looking down at them.

Ivchencko was not pleased with the interruption. "What problem?"

"Dutch informed me there are detectives at the door." He glanced down and away. "And I may have accidentally led them here." His admission sent Ivchencko into a rage.

"You did what?" He threw the rod down and marched over to the staircase where he began to climb.

Gregor bravely turned to face him. "In church this morning, I met a couple." He lowered his voice. Elsa strained to hear. "They were with Liliya's parents. I didn't know they were police. Now they're here asking for you."

"How do you know it's the same two people?"

"I saw them following Dutch into the library. They're the same ones. I thought it strange that they asked so many questions earlier about Liliya, but her friends said the couple were family. I didn't know."

The coldness in Ivchencko's voice could've frozen fire. "You fucking idiot. I'll deal with you later. Go out the back and take the Mercedes. It's time for you to return to port."

Gregor immediately looked at Liliya. "But I can't just leave her."

He smacked Gregor across the face. "Do as I say! I'll take care of your mess."

He sent one last look at the girl, and turned, disappearing through the door. Ivchencko cast a regretful look at Elsa. "I'll be back." Then he left, closing and locking the door behind him.

As soon as the lock clicked, Elsa fought through the pain in her leg and her entire body. "Liliya, can you hear me?"

Through sniffles, the girl answered. "Yes. Are you okay?"

"Don't worry about that right now. Tell me, is that rod close to you? Can you see it?" Elsa struggled to turn her head as far to the right as possible trying to see where it landed. She heard the girl shuffle as she moved around.

"Yes, I see it," she said.

"Can you reach it? Is there any way you can grab it?" She gasped at the excruciating pain radiating up from her knee.

"I don't think so." She heard the strain in her voice. "Hold on. Let me see." More grunts were heard as Liliya tried to extend her arm through the bars of the cage. "Almost."

Elsa heard the metal slide across the concrete floor. "I've got it! Elsa, I got it!" Liliya's words were triumphant. "Now what?" she asked, not knowing what she needed to do next.

"Try to pry open the door to your cage."

"I don't know if it will work. This cage is strong." She sounded doubtful.

"Just try. Get it between the floor and the bottom bar and pull up. You might be able to lift the door off its hinges or at least loosen up the lock."

"Okay." Liliya proceeded to slip the long metal rod under the small space between the gate and the floor and pull upward. "Ugh!" She took a deep breath and tried again. "It's not moving much at all. I'm not strong enough."

"That's okay. A little at a time is okay." Elsa tried to encourage her through terrible pain. Then a lock clicked, and the door at the top of the steps swung open and closed quickly. Footsteps bounded down the stairs at a fast pace. Liliya began to whimper as she hid the rod behind her and stepped backwards up against the wall of her cage.

"I couldn't leave without you. Quickly, now. We have to make haste," Gregor spoke as he unlocked Liliya's cell door.

"No! You can't take her. You've done enough to her," Elsa screamed.

Faster than she thought possible, Gregor came to stand before her where he reached out and slapped her hard across the face. "Quiet, whore," he said in a low voice. "She's mine, and I won't leave her behind with him. Look what he's done to you! I won't have my Liliya treated this way." The look on his face was sheer madness. He spoke of the girl as if they were a couple and not predator and victim.

"And how you treat her is better? You've taken her against her will. You raped her! She's just a girl!"

His expression vacillated between horror and anger. "I love her. And she loves me!"

Behind him, Liliya let loose a primal scream.

"No, I don't! She brought the metal rod down on Gregor's head with every ounce of rage she possessed. Once, twice, and then a third time, the sound of metal connecting with bone filling the space. He fell over, unconscious.

She stood staring at him, eyes wide with shock, panting hard. His head was bleeding from her heavy blows.

Elsa brought her back to reality. "Liliya, good girl! Okay, now unstrap my hands and feet. Quickly!" The girl dropped the rod and brought unsteady hands to the task of releasing the leather straps. With her hands free, Elsa had to lean onto Liliya, who bent down to get the restraints at her ankles. "No, not that one yet." The pain in her voice indicated this was the leg Ivchencko brutally injured. Liliya bent her blonde head to the other leg and let that one down first. With Elsa balancing on that foot and leaning on her, she gently undid the second strap. A loud groan of pain passed her lips as Elsa tried to put that foot down.

"Here, let me." Liliya supported her on the injured side and helped her over to the chair where her clothes lay.

"Scheisse! I don't have anything to put on." She eyed the shirt and pants that lay there in tatters. Tears slid down her cheeks as she sat down gingerly.

Liliya looked at Gregor. "Well, he won't be needing his clothes." She walked over cautiously and kicked him. He didn't move.

"Wait! Get those handcuffs off the wall... just in case he wakes up." Elsa directed as Liliya grabbed two pairs of manacles. She used them to shackle Gregor to the upright table one wrist at a time while she pulled off his shirt. She tossed it over to Elsa who pulled it on. Now secured to the bottom end of the table that met the floor, she pulled off his pants. The look of disgust and fear on the young girl's face showed that it took a great deal of courage for her to complete the task.

"Here." She handed over the pants and then stepped in to help when it became apparent Elsa couldn't do it on her own. At least her shoes were still intact. Getting it onto the foot of the injured leg, however, was a trial, but they finally managed. She used her ripped shirt to wrap around her knee, tying it tight for support.

Elsa rummaged around in her coat pocket and found her phone. There were several missed texts and calls from her brother, Lukas, and Heinz, but at least it was on, and now she knew they were looking for her. It might even be them upstairs, but she didn't know, so she strapped on her holster, and took the safety off her gun. She wasn't sure if she could even walk. It was beyond painful, and she was sure her knee was broken. If Ivchencko came back through that door, she was going to shoot him. For now, she sent a text to Heinz.

Dutch led the two detectives into the library. "Herr Ivchencko will be with you soon." He then exited the room, closing the double doors, the look on his face suspicious.

"Strange man, indeed. He looks more like a Russian mafia thug than a butler. Bruce was right." Mahler watched Heinz check out the room, noting exits as he lifted books off a shelf and then picked up some papers off the desk to read their content.

"We just need to keep him talking for fifteen minutes, unless that warrant comes through sooner. Then Faust will be storming the house."

The door swung wide, and Yuri Ivchencko entered. "Good evening, detectives. What can I do for you?"

Mahler noted the tall man wearing all black had the coldest, gray eyes she'd ever seen. There was a flush on his cheeks she was certain was not natural, but rather, came from some form of exertion. She wondered exactly what they'd interrupted.

Heinz spoke first. "I'm Kommissar Heinz, and this is my partner, Detective Mahler."

Ivchencko's cold, gray eyes narrowed, focusing on Heinz. "Heinz, you say?"

"Yes." In that moment, Heinz knew that Ivchencko knew exactly who he was. The look that passed between them was not lost on Mahler.

The Russian recovered his composure and went to the side bar to pour himself a drink. "So, what is it you need?" He tossed in two ice cubes and swirled the amber liquid around the glass.

"You have a young man living here with you. A Greg Koslov?" Heinz asked.

Ivchencko walked over to his wingback chair and sat down indicating Heinz should do the same. He declined. "I did. He's no longer here, though. Why?"

"Is he your nephew?" Mahler walked to the opposite side of the room where she could better view Ivchencko.

"No. He's an employee." He took a sip of his drink, completely calm.

"What does he do for you exactly?" Heinz asked, walking two steps closer to the roaring fireplace.

"He's a hired hand on one of my ships. What is this about, Kommissar?"

"It's about three missing girls. We need to question him. Where is he now?"

"I'm afraid he's gone back to port. He ships out tonight, back to St. Petersburg."

"What was he doing here so far from port?" Heinz asked.

"That is not your business, Kommissar Heinz. That is my business. Are you planning to charge my employee with a crime?"

Mahler paced the length of the room and was coming back up behind the chair where Ivchencko sat when she noticed a wadded-up piece of paper on the floor. She bent down to retrieve it as Heinz continued his questioning of the Russian. She smoothed the paper out and saw *Elsa* written across the backside. Her eyes widened. She unfolded it further and began reading.

"At this time, Koslov is a person of interest only. It seems he went to church with these girls. Any information he can share with us about the last time he saw them would be helpful."

"Still trying to solve missing girls' cases, eh?" Ivchencko murmured quietly, but Heinz caught it. He looked over at his partner and saw the look on her face. It was pure rage, something only someone who knew her well would recognize. Anyone else would see only a blank expression, but Heinz saw the fire in her eyes. She glanced down at the paper in her hand, then stepped forward.

"Aren't those Paul Christiansen's paintings?" She pointed above the mantle.

Ivchencko, caught off guard, smiled. "Why, yes, they are. I acquired them yesterday. Are you an art appreciator, detective?" He stood, facing the paintings.

"Not really, no. I do know the artist. He was having an exhibit last night. One of our officers attended. Perhaps you met her. Elsa Kreiss? Lovely woman. She's a friend of the artist, as well."

"Can't say that I did." Ivchencko's voice flattened as it lost any passion for the subject at hand.

"Really? Are you sure? Red hair? She was on a date with one of the gallery's employees, Lukas Trommler."

Heinz watched as Mahler tightened the verbal noose, waiting to see exactly what she was getting at. It seemed to have something to do with the paper clutched in her hand. His phone vibrated in his pocket. He pulled it out and glanced at the screen.

Heinz, I'm locked in the basement of Yuri Ivchencko. He lives in Charlottenburg, 1211 Baumgartenstrasse. Get here fast! He has an accomplice who kidnapped a girl. I'm with her now. Bring help, and hurry! Elsa

Heinz's expression darkened. He now knew what Mahler was getting at. She knew Elsa was here. He quickly forwarded the message to Faust. The warrant they were waiting for would be granted now, but how fast was another question. He added Trommler and Beimer to the forward knowing they were outside trying to find their way in from the back of the house.

He looked up and saw that Mahler was practically in Ivchencko's face.

"You don't believe me? I see you've drawn your own conclusions, detective." He set the glass down noting the paper in the petite woman's hand. His eyebrow rose, and a smirk tugged at the corner of his thin lips. "And you'd be right!" He reached out and grabbed her hand, swinging her around and forcing her arm up behind her as he whipped out a handgun from his pocket. He pointed it at her temple and spun them both facing Heinz.

"Don't do it, Kommissar, or I'll put a bullet in her head." Heinz ceased reaching for his gun and put his hands out, still holding the cell phone.

"There's no need for that, Ivchencko. Calm down and listen."

"Listen to what? You came here looking for your officer, didn't you? Well, she was great fun, but I'm generous. You can have her back. However, I'll not be coming with you. You need to back up over to the side." He tilted his head, indicating the direction Heinz should go.

"Yuri," Heinz began, "there's nowhere for you to go. There are officers outside right now. One has a warrant for your arrest. So don't make any foolish moves. Just put the gun down."

"I don't think so, Kommissar." The voice came from behind Joseph. He glanced back and saw Dutch emerging from a hidden door behind the bookshelf with a shotgun drawn and aimed at his head.

"Tie him to a chair," Ivchencko ordered. Dutch prodded Heinz in the back with the barrel of the gun, propelling him toward the desk chair.

Heinz refused to sit down. "You're not going to get away with this. You're outnumbered."

Dutch smacked him on the side of the head with the butt of the shotgun. Heinz fell back, and as he lifted his hand up to his face, the butler clenched a beefy fist and punched him hard, sending Heinz reeling.

"Joseph," Mahler screamed, unable to break out of the hold Ivchencko had on her.

Heinz was quickly tied to the chair with both hands secured to the oak wood arms. Then his feet, despite his kicking and struggling, were tied tightly to the thick oak legs.

Ivchencko forced Mahler's arm higher behind her back. She cursed, spitting out expletives Heinz had never heard pass her lips before. Her face was ashen from the pain in her arm forced into a position near-breaking.

Joseph's own complexion paled dramatically seeing Birgitta in the clutches of this man who he was now one hundred percent certain kidnapped Marlessa Schubert or ordered someone else to do it. He couldn't protect the girl then, and he was unable to help Mahler now. He hoped Beimer, Faust, and Trommler would hurry the hell up and get in here.

"Don't hurt her! You bastard, I'll kill you!" Heinz struggled against the ropes.

Ivchencko laughed. "That's the second time today my life's been threatened. Funny, I'm still here and breathing. Dutch, come here and confine the lovely detective."

Dutch grabbed more rope and bent down to wrap it around Mahler's legs. She kicked him in the face, bloodying his pug nose.

"Now, now, detective. We'll have none of that." He looked at the butler. "Dutch?"

Dutch punched Mahler, knocking her out cold.

Heinz howled with fury. "You fucking dirty bastard! I'll kill you! Mark my words. I'm going to kill you both!"

"Get in line," said Ivchencko. Mahler's hands and feet were tied. Dutch hoisted her over his shoulder. Then he picked up his shotgun, and he and Ivchenko moved to the hidden door behind the bookshelf.

The Russian turned to look at Joseph with a smile on his face. "Always so close, Kommissar. So close, yet not quite close enough to save the girl, eh?" He smirked at the rage in Heinz's eyes. "Well, better luck next time." He turned and disappeared into the hidden corridor. As the door closed behind him, he could hear Heinz yelling impotently at his retreating back and laughed.

"I'm coming for you, Ivchencko. There's no place on Earth you can hide where I won't find you. Count on it!"

Beimer felt his mobile buzz and looked down at the screen as he pulled it out of his pocket. His eyes widened, and he turned the device toward Trommler.

"Fuck! Okay, Beimer. This is what we're going to do." Lukas quickly outlined a plan where they would enter through a back window on the right side of the house. The blueprint indicated it was a powder room so no one would hear the glass shatter.

Hugo pulled his hand inside the sleeve of his jacket and punched through the glass. He used the tip of his gun to break away more of the shards and reached inside to turn the latch. He swung the old window in and turned to Lukas. Bending down, he let Trommler step up onto his back so he could climb through. Once inside, He reached out to help steady Beimer as he scaled up the wall and fell through nearly on top of him.

"You could lose a few pounds, you know." Lukas extended his hand to help him up.

"Bite me," Beimer replied, irritated. They picked up their weapons and moved to the bathroom door, cracking it open to look out into the hallway.

Trommler signaled all was clear, and they slipped out, guns drawn, heading toward the doorway at the end of the long hall that, according to the blueprints, led down to the basement.

They stopped when they heard a door close at the other end of the hallway. Silence again. They quickly came to the door at the back of the hall. Lukas dropped low and reached to open it, keeping his gun aimed in the event someone was inside. Beimer protected his back. They inched their way in, noticing the landing and a staircase beyond. As the door closed behind them, a shot rang out, zinging past Trommler's ear and barely missing him. He turned right and aimed, ready to pull the trigger when he heard her.

"Lukas! Oh, mein Gott! Lukas!" Elsa was shocked as she recognized the face behind the gun aimed at her. She lowered her weapon and tried to stand, but the pain was too great, and she fell back into the chair. Liliya hid next to her.

"Elsa? Scheisse." Lukas ran down the stairs and bounded forward falling onto his knees at her feet. He wrapped her in his arms, and she screamed. He backed off, looking up at her. "What is it? Are you hurt?" He ran his eyes over her body and saw the makeshift field bandage around her knee.

"Yeah. My knee. I think it's broken." Her green eyes welled with tears, but her expression was a weird combination of pain, happiness to see him, and anger.

Hugo ran up behind Trommler. "Kreiss! Damn, I'm glad to see you." He looked around the room at the instruments on the wall, then down to the body unconscious and handcuffed on the floor. Finally, he looked at the girl stuck like glue to Elsa's side.

"And who is this?"

Elsa sniffed and wiped away the tears streaming from her green eyes. "Hugo, this is Liliya Avilova. She was kidnapped and was being held here." She took the girl's hand. "It's okay now, Liliya. These are my friends, Hugo, my partner, and Lukas, my..." she looked at him.

"Her boyfriend," he supplied.

Liliya smiled through her tears. "Hello."

"Heinz will be happy about this," said Hugo. "We need to get you both out of here." He reached out to help the girl up. She stood and immediately went to Beimer's side. He stuck out a foot and kicked the man on the ground. "What's his story? Is he dead?"

Elsa leaned onto Lukas who simply scooped her up into his arms. "Nein. But he's going to wish he was. That's Gregor. He kidnapped Liliya. He also works for Ivchencko. They're trafficking girls, stealing them from families here in Berlin.

"So that's Koslov." Beimer pulled out his phone and texted Heinz. He waited, but there was no answer. He tried Faust who replied right away asking if they'd found Elsa. He let him know they had and dialed so he could speak to the agent. It was faster than texting.

Faust answered. "Talk to me!"

"We have both Elsa and the girl. It's Liliya Avilova."

"What? She's alive?" The relief in Faust's voice could be heard through the speaker. "Okay, get them out through the back door in the east hall just off the main corridor. I have four men waiting there for you. I'm still waiting to hear from Heinz, but he's not responding to texts. Either way, we're coming in. The warrant just came through."

"Ja wohl." Beimer hung up. "Faust is about to storm the castle. We have to get them out."

Lukas looked at Elsa. "Don't worry, I got you. Just keep your weapon at the ready. My hands are full, and we're going to be moving quickly. I'm sorry in advance because it's probably going to hurt you." He gave her a quick kiss on her cheek. He looked at Hugo and Liliya who was now glued to Beimer's side. "Put her behind you and I'll follow. We'll keep them both between us, but you're going to have to take the lead. Can you handle it?"

Beimer snorted and said, "Piece of cake, Trommler."

"Good man. Let's go."

Beimer took point, pulling Liliya along behind him. Lukas brought up the tail as they went up the stairs and back out into the main hall.

Elsa whispered in Lukas's ear. "How did you convince Heinz to let you come along? And where did you get that gun?" She glanced down at the small H&K submachine pistol hanging from a strap over his shoulder.

He winked. "I guess there's a few things I hadn't gotten around to telling you yet."

"Yeah, like, your artsy boyfriend is German Special Ops," Beimer muttered under his breath.

"What? No shit? Well, I can't say I'm unhappy to hear it. My hero," she said, kissing his cheek.

They found the east hall and after making sure the coast was clear, nearly ran down to the end of it, finding the door that led out onto a side terrace.

"What happened to your knee?" Lukas turned carefully so as not to bump her leg going out.

"Ivchencko." She couldn't say any more. She knew questions were coming, and she wasn't sure yet how the hell she was going to answer them.

"He hit her with a rod," Liliya supplied.

"Motherfucker! I'll kill him!" Lukas's face turned dark with rage.

"No. That pleasure will be all mine," said Elsa.

Four men rushed forth and tried to take Elsa, but Lukas wouldn't let her go. "We need an ambulance. Now. Where's Faust?"

"He's entering through the front. Our men are with him," said the officer.

"What about Heinz and Mahler? Did they come out?" Beimer stood waiting. Liliya refused to leave his side.

"Not yet. They still haven't responded to texts."

Beimer looked at Lukas who glanced at Elsa. "Something's wrong. Joseph wouldn't just not answer," she said.

"I agree. He should've been out by now." They made their way to the guard gate where their unit had commandeered the small building, arresting the guard and placing him into the back of a police cruiser. An ambulance was called, and Lukas sat Elsa down on the grass near the road. Liliya immediately joined her, taking Elsa's hand.

Lukas looked at Beimer. "We can go back in where we came out. We'll sweep the rooms. You up for it?"

"We can't let you do that, sir," said the officer.

"You can't stop me, either. My training far outweighs yours in this situation, and I outrank you."

Hugo was impressed. "I'm with you, Trommler."

Lukas knelt by Elsa, taking her hand. She looked at him closely, seeing him through new eyes. Her cocky art dealer turned out to be a kickass soldier boy. "Be careful. Ivchencko is dangerous, and quite mad."

He offered a half smile, and kissed her tenderly, fearing causing her any more pain. Then he stood and began walking back to the house. He turned and looked at the officer. "Well? Are you coming or what? There's a suspect handcuffed in the basement. Get your men in there and get him out. We'll need to question him."

The officer gave him a long look, then signaled his men to follow.

<hr />

Heinz twisted and pulled at the ropes binding him to the chair. "Motherfucker!" He shouted the all-too-American expletive to vent his anger and frustration, and his agonizing fear for Birgitta. Going for broke, he threw himself over sideways and heard a satisfying crack as one of the wooden arms snapped off from the chair. He wiggled his right hand free and was just beginning to untie the left when the library doors burst open. Faust, followed by Trommler, Beimer, and four men in combat police gear stormed inside and stopped when they saw Heinz on the floor.

"Joseph! Scheisse, are you all right?" Faust ran forward, reaching for the ropes. He tried to untie Heinz, but the knots were tight.

"Here. Let me." Lukas pulled a wicked looking hunting knife out of his sleeve and sliced through the bindings.

Heinz rose quickly, frantic. "Did you get them?"

"Yes. We got Elsa and the girl out," Beimer replied.

"No! Not them," he shouted.

Lukas stood and looked around. "Where's Detective Mahler?"

"He has her! Damn it. Did you get them? Didn't you see them leave?"

Faust cursed, then turned to his men. "Radio out to the gate. No one leaves. Tell them to be prepared." He looked at Heinz. "Which way did they go out? We didn't see anyone."

Heinz turned and walked to the bookshelf looking for the trigger to open the trick door. "Here. They went behind this damn thing. Help me find the lever."

The four men rushed forward and began pulling books off the shelves, lifting boards, and yanking and pushing at the thing. When that didn't work, Lukas stepped in and instructed them to pull the whole case off the wall. The five of them leveraged themselves and pulled. On the third try, it separated from the hinges and crashed to the floor.

"Beimer, Trommler, you're taking the lead with me. Let's go." Heinz pulled his gun, and the three of them entered the hidden hallway.

It was dark inside, but they had just enough light to see that it began to slope down and then turned right onto a long ramp. At the bottom, it opened to what appeared to be an underground garage. A long, dark tunnel went out the back side completely opposite the front gate. It was clear this was how Ivchencko managed to leave without being seen by the police.

Heinz threw his hands in the air and then gripped the top of his head turning in circles, cursing, and kicking the ground. "He has Birgitta. We have to get her back!"

"We have Koslov," said Faust, catching up to them.

Heinz turned, looking at him. "Where? I want to question that piece of shit right now." The sheer rage on his face sent Faust back one step. He'd only seen Joseph like this once before, and it nearly destroyed him.

"Take it easy, old friend. We'll find her." Faust pulled out his phone.

"Who're you calling," Heinz asked.

"I'm putting out an all-points to all rails and airports. He's going to try to leave the country." Faust issued the alert, then led the way back topside.

"Tell them to track her mobile. Here's the number." He read it off to Faust who relayed it to dispatch. "We may not have much time with that before they discover it and destroy the phone. Hurry!" Heinz turned to Lukas. "Is Elsa okay?"

"No. I think her knee is broken. The girl said Ivchencko hit her with a rod." Guilt emanated from his face. He felt responsible. Heinz could see it.

"You didn't know, Lukas. How could you have?"

The younger man looked at him, self-recrimination in his hazel eyes. "I'm trained to know people, know who's dangerous and who isn't. I failed, and it nearly cost Elsa her life."

Heinz couldn't argue with that. He felt the same. He took a deep breath. "Then don't fail again." He planned to take his own advice. His partner's life depended on it.

The medical tech was gently probing Elsa's knee when they arrived back at the guard gate. Heinz went to her side and gave her an awkward half hug. He grilled the EMT. "Well, what's the diagnosis?"

The tech, a young man with reddish-blond hair looked up. "I'm not a physician, sir, but I think she has a fractured patella." The knee in question was now swollen, and a dark shade of purple.

"What the hell does that mean?" Heinz had lost his patience and had none to spare.

"It's my kneecap, Joseph," Elsa said, as she leaned back, finally feeling the effects of the pain killer they injected into her hip.

Heinz watched as she fell backwards onto the gurney and closed her eyes. "Elsa!" He reached out and grabbed the tech by his shirt collar. "Do something! She's crashing." Desperation laced his words.

"Sir, she's okay. It's just the sedative mixed in with the pain killer. She's fine, really."

Heinz relaxed, then realized he was still gripping the man's shirt. He let go. The tech unbuttoned Elsa's shirt halfway to apply the EKG strips to monitor her on the way to the hospital. Huge red and purple welts greeted their eyes. Hundreds of them covering her torso. Heinz sucked in a breath, shocked by the sheer number of wounds.

"What is that? What's happened to her?" He looked like he was about to grab and shake the tech again when Liliya spoke up from the other gurney where she waited to be attended.

"Ivchencko. He whipped her. He hurt her badly." Her voice was so small, as if she were afraid to speak.

Heinz looked at the girl, and back at Elsa, then over at Lukas who was walking toward them. He tried to say something, anything to stop the younger man from seeing the evidence of his girlfriend's torture, but he wasn't quick enough.

"What the...?" Lukas stopped in his tracks. He slapped a hand over his mouth and stood staring. He'd seen men whipped before. Grown men who'd cried out because the pain was so great. They were reduced to blubbering balls of agony as they curled up on their cell floors unable to take it. Elsa had been whipped, yet she hadn't succumbed to the intense pain. She still maintained herself trying to protect the girl. No wonder she'd cried out when he touched her.

The tech gently looked beneath her shirt, doing his best to preserve her dignity, but what he saw made him step back and retch.

Lukas turned away, quickly wiping tears from his eyes. When he turned back, the tech had recovered and was covering Elsa with a sheet tucking it around her body. The sooner they got her to the hospital, the better. Lukas turned to Liliya.

"And what about you? What haven't you told us? Did he whip you too?" He kept his voice gentle.

Liliya's blue eyes welled with tears. "No. He never touched me."

Heinz saw the haunted look on her face. "And what about Koslov?" He knew. He felt like complete shit for even having to ask, but Faust and his crew would be asking the same questions soon.

Liliya looked away. She couldn't say it. Heinz reached over and took her hand. "It's okay now. You're safe. You're safe." His crusty heart broke for this young girl, for Elsa, and it was in agony for Birgitta who was now in Ivchencko's clutches.

He turned to Lukas. "I have to get her back, Trommler. I can't let him do to her what he's done to so many."

"You won't be alone. I'm coming with you." He reached out, and Heinz, acknowledging the help for what it was, shook his hand. The pact was made, and now they needed a plan... fast.

Chapter 13

The helicopter landed on the deck of the Vledelets, Ivchencko's first commercial ship in his empire. The name translated to *Dominus* - Latin for 'master' or 'owner'. His ego embraced both, and so being the first in the line, was aptly named. Deckhands ran up ready to assist their corporate overlord.

"Take her below deck to my suite. Make sure she's secured." Ivchencko gave the order to Dutch who directed two of the hands to carry Birgitta Mahler out of the helicopter. She was awake now, had been halfway through the two-hour flight. Dutch taped her mouth at his boss's command. He was in no mood to spend the last hour of the flight listening to a woman's hysterics. Little did he know, Birgitta Mahler was not the hysterical type. She was the calm, cool, and collected type who observed her surroundings and made mental notes. One of those notes was that, as far as she was aware, neither of these two had dispensed with her cell phone. If she was right, as she had been unconscious for a while, then the police had a way of tracking her. She didn't want to ruin that by bringing attention to herself, so she remained quiet.

Another point she observed was that the deckhands didn't seem to find it unusual that their boss had shown up with a bound and gagged woman. Now why was that? She rode the shoulder of a large man with a shaved head. She noticed his hands when he grabbed and hoisted her over. He had a five-pointed star tattooed on each. One point meant a year in prison. Two five-pointed stars added up to ten years. This man had been in prison, a Russian prison. *So, Ivchencko employed criminals.* She might've given the man the benefit of the doubt, he'd done his time, and was earning a living in an honest trade. But here she was being hauled like a sack of grain below deck, and the man hadn't questioned who she was or why. That certainly ruled out any honesty on his part.

Her ride was uncomfortable, and it was all she could do to keep her breath as each bounce down the steep metal stairs sent his shoulder into her abdomen. She concentrated on her surroundings looking for anything to identify the ship and counting how many decks down they went. If she managed to get loose, she'd need to have some kind of working knowledge of the layout, at least, how to get back topside. Still, she'd need help. She thought of Joseph, and prayed he was okay. The last thing she remembered was seeing him tied to a chair and struck by the barrel-shaped butler. It was clear now that Dutch wasn't a mere servant. She'd bet her chips he also spent time incarcerated. It was becoming evident that there may be a tie-in to Russian mafia, and most definitely, sex trafficking. Just where did Yuri Ivchencko fit into it?

Three flights down they came to a short, narrow corridor that led to a stateroom on the left. Inside, the man who was her mule, tossed her onto the large Captain's bed. He stood over her expecting a fight. When she simply sat up and looked at him, he grunted and backed up a step, looking over at Dutch and the other man. Birgitta finally got a good look at the second deckhand. He was shorter, wiry, and rather swarthy looking. His age appeared to be around forty, and his dark hair was liberally streaked with gray. He had crowns tattooed on his fingers. Further up his arm, bared by the rolled-up sleeves, was a skull.

The smaller man was higher in rank, and the tattoos indicated he was a murderer. This wasn't looking good.

Dutch pulled up a heavy chair. "Set her here, Ivan." The larger man looked at Birgitta and crooked his finger at her.

"Come!" He said in a guttural accent.

Mahler sat there wondering just how he expected her to move with her hands tied behind her. She could've, but she chose not to comply. Instead, she gave him her best '*fuck you*' eyes.

Ivan laughed, and reached out grabbing her ankles yanking her until she was on the edge of the bed. Then he lifted her up like a rag doll with one arm and tossed her unceremoniously into the chair.

Dutch handed a length of rope to the shorter man. "Tie her feet, Vitaly, but be careful. She kicks like a fucking mule." The butler rubbed his nose, and Vitaly, noting the swelling and bloodstains, raised an eyebrow and grinned.

Dutch began untying the rope that bound her hands. Momentarily free, Mahler punched Dutch dead-on in the nose, making the man howl, and kicked Vitaly in the groin before he could secure her legs. She jumped up and was immediately stopped by Ivan who picked her up and tossed her over his shoulder again and began spanking her hard on her bottom. It hurt. She pummeled his back and clawed like a cat.

Dutch recovered, yanking her back into the chair where he smacked her hard across the face. "You bitch!"

Ivan laughed as Vitaly slowly rose back to his knees still covering his groin protectively. The look he gave the larger man silenced him quickly.

"Trust me when I say you'll pay for that, and what you did to Vitaly, many times over...very soon." Dutch tied her hands, and Vitaly made short work of her legs before she could strike again.

When they finished the task of securing her, they left, locking the door behind them. Mahler sat there, her face still stinging from the slap. She opened her mouth and worked her jaw, making sure all her teeth were still intact. Then she unclenched her hand and began the task of repositioning the switchblade forward that she'd swiped while the big Russian spanked her. Silently, she thanked him for carrying the damn thing in his back pocket. She hoped it would be enough to get her free and save her life.

———————◆○◆———————

Yuri Ivchencko walked onto the bridge, and the men immediately stood at attention. Captain Andrei Oberin saluted, not dropping his hand until Ivchencko acknowledged the gesture. "Captain, is all in readiness?"

"Aye, Gospodin Ivchencko. The ship has already been inspected and cleared to leave port prior to your arrival as directed. If you are ready to give the order, we're set to cast off for St. Petersburg."

"Koslov is on his way. He will be at least two hours behind us, but we will wait for him." Yuri stared out the window at the now dark, massive port in Hamburg. Containers and cargo were being loaded and unloaded from other commercial vessels all around, even at this late hour. His own ship had been cleared by port authority to depart when ready. No one would know he was on board not having been here when inspected. Even if they noted the helicopter among all the activity, no one would give it a second thought since it was too small for any significant contraband, which was all they worried about.

Captain Oberin objected. "Sir, we should be on our way. If the authority decides to double check after your arrival, we could have a problem."

Ivchencko turned cold, gray eyes on him. "Who is in charge here?"

Oberin was immediately contrite. "You are, Gospodin Ivchencko. Of course."

"Gregor has been loyal. He's also key to our collaboration with the Order, and we need them. So, for now, he has value. We wait, captain."

"Vasha volya, moi ruki." *Your will, my hands,* he muttered.

Dutch entered, approaching his boss and rubbing his face as he walked. He stopped, waiting to be acknowledged.

"Well? Did you secure our guest?" Ivchencko turned and looked down at his henchman, noting the fresh redness around his already broken nose. He answered his own question before Dutch could reply. "I see she got you again. You're getting slow, old friend," he chuckled.

"She's got one hell of a kick." Dutch sniffed, then grimaced.

Ivchencko raised a dark eyebrow. "That's almost a compliment coming from you."

"Maybe I just have a soft spot for small, feisty brunettes."

"Ha! If you have a soft spot, I've yet to see it. But if she impresses you, even a little, then I'm happy to make a gift of her to you, old friend...after she outlives her usefulness to me."

Dutch smiled, but it wasn't a smile any woman would welcome. "Might be a bit of fun." He offered a slight bow of his head in thanks. "I do admire her spirit. Breaking it will be exhilarating."

"Call Koslov and find out where he is. Get an ETA. As soon as he arrives, we pull anchor."

"On it, boss." Dutch pulled out his mobile and dialed. After five rings, the voicemail came on. "Fuck sakes." The irritation in his voice was obvious as he waited for the beep. "Gregor, it's Dutch. Call me back ASAP." He hit END and waited.

"Let me know when he does. I'll be downstairs checking on the cargo." Ivchencko left the bridge, a purposeful gleam in his eyes.

"His phone is ringing." Trommler stated the obvious as Heinz stared at the gadget in his hand. It took them an hour to track the last record-ed ping off Mahler's phone, which turned out to be within a mile of a heliport. From there, it was easy to gather the intel that Ivchencko kept a flight service on call, and a warrant was issued for them to hand over the flight plan. The helicopter was headed to Hamburg, and now, so were they.

Lukas called in a favor with his old unit, and two of the men joined him, Heinz, and Beimer on a military flight via the Bell UH 1D transport helicopter. StabsKapitanLeutnant Kristof Jager piloted the craft, and Korvettankapitan Dieter Kelner rode shotgun. Lukas, Heinz, and Beimer sat in the back. Faust stayed behind, calling in to his LKA contact in Hamburg to notify them of the situation and gain their assistance.

Heinz hit the button for voicemail and struggled to listen over the noise from the engine. He looked at Trommler. "It was the butler. He wants Koslov to call him back."

"Well, we can't do that without giving ourselves away now can we?" Lukas raised an eyebrow. "Here." He grabbed the phone from Heinz and began typing on the keypad.

"What are you doing?" Heinz asked, peering over Beimer who sat between them.

"I'm sending a text. I just wrote *unable to call. Text me.*"

"Smart thinking," said Beimer.

Heinz harrumphed, and they waited. The phone buzzed.

The boss wants your ETA.

Lukas tapped Jager on the shoulder and spoke into his headset. "How far out are we?"

"About an hour and a half."

Trommler looked at Heinz. "If Koslov was to have left at about the same time, he'd still be at least an hour behind us depending on traffic. So, he'd still be two to two and half hours out on the road. It's nearly 2100 hours now so that would make his estimated time of arrival approximately 2300 to 2330 hours."

"That sounds right. And we'll be there a good hour before, which gives us time to strategize with the local police." Heinz's mind was going a mile a minute. Every second would count to get Birgitta back safely.

Lukas texted back and hit SEND. A minute later, the phone buzzed again. *Don't be late!*

"We better not be. Please, God, not this time," Heinz muttered the silent prayer, his heart breaking.

———◄O►———

Elsa lay in her hospital bed with her knee bandaged in a tight splint. The patella was only fractured, amazing considering the force of the strike against it. She was ordered to stay off it for six weeks. As for the whip welts all over her body, they were treated with a topical steroid cream for the inflammation, and oral painkillers to manage the pain. The doctor stated she was lucky Ivchencko did not actually break the skin lest she be worse off and possibly fighting infections from the wounds. Feeling a bit groggy, she slowly woke from a short nap searching out her water glass. She sipped a little trying to refresh herself. Faust walked in as she was mentally going over all that had happened in so short a time.

"Officer Kreiss, how are you feeling?"

Elsa liked Faust. She'd met him once before, back when Heinz first made the push to get her into the academy. He'd cajoled the man into writing a letter of recommendation afterwards saying *"You're a fine judge of character, Herman. Tell me you don't see what a fantastic cadet she'll make?"* Heinz played off his friend's ego, and it worked. Faust had written a glowing recommendation, and between the two of them, got her admitted the following month to begin training.

"Drugged." She smiled.

Faust chuckled. "Well, considering what you endured, I'd think that's a good thing."

"I'm not complaining." She struggled to sit up.

Faust immediately rushed forward, hand up. "No need to stress yourself. Just relax." She eased back down. "I came by to let you know that Liliya Avilova has been reunited with her parents."

"That's wonderful!"

Faust eyed her, then glanced away. "I'm happy for her, too. It's rare to recover a girl alive once she's been abducted. But I'm not sure how wonderful her life will be after all of this. What that man did to her..."

"I know. But I think Liliya is strong. She proved herself in that basement. I wouldn't have gotten free without her."

"Funny, she said the exact same thing about you." He turned and paced. "I'll be questioning Koslov soon...upstairs," he added, glancing over his head. "We know he had the third girl, Natasha Kirolova, by Liliya's testimony, but she doesn't know what happened to the girl after he took her out of the basement. My gut tells me she's dead, but I've been wrong before."

"She said something about Ivchencko telling him to deliver the cargo. Do you think maybe she could be on one of his ships in Hamburg?" Elsa thought about Heinz and Lukas. Heinz was more distraught than she'd ever seen him. He blamed himself for Mahler being taken, and she feared he might get himself killed in the attempt to rescue her. Finding out about Lukas's military service was a surprise, but a good one in this case. The fact that he readily volunteered to lead a rescue mission, that he was capable of such a thing, was still stunning to her. Even more startling was the bond that had developed between him and Hugo. Those two couldn't stand each other, and now they were behaving like brothers in arms. The three of them collaborating with Lukas's old unit was like something out of an action movie. But Elsa couldn't focus on that. They had to get Birgitta back. Losing her was not an option. And she wanted them to capture Ivchencko—she hadn't forgotten her promise to kill him. When she'd first issued that promise, she wasn't sure if she would be able to keep it, never having killed anyone before. But after learning he'd kidnapped Mahler, and was, by her best guess based on bits of information, involved in the routine abduction and trafficking of young girls, knew she could, and would not regret it. Especially after the torture he'd put her through.

"It's entirely possible. The more we dig, the more we find, and the more evidence mounts against him." He stuck his hands in his pockets, his face serious. "So, if you're finished with laying around like a pampered princess for now, I thought you'd like to join me in interrogating this piece of shit."

The invitation surprised her. Elsa knew she was being granted a privilege. She looked down at her hospital gown and bandaged leg. "I'd be happy to, sir, but ..." She glanced up.

"Yes. Clothing would be a good idea. So, I brought you something to wear, and a little help." A female officer walked in carrying a bag. "Kreiss, this is Officer Imler. She'll be assisting you. I'll go round up a wheelchair while you dress." Faust walked out leaving Elsa alone with Imler.

"It's Hannah, by the way," she said.

"Nice to meet you, Hannah. I'm Elsa."

Hannah Imler pulled out a pair of dark sweatpants and matching police sweatshirt. "It was the best I could find at this hour. Sorry."

"No, no. That's fine." She noted that Imler did add a sports bra, socks, and slippers.

"They're mine. Hope you don't mind." She smiled and helped Elsa change.

"I'm grateful, really. Good thing we're close in size."

The pants took a bit of work, but she was finally dressed by the time Faust returned with a wheelchair, and a concerned nurse.

"She really shouldn't be getting out of bed, Herr Direktor." The nurse, who rushed in behind him, was top-heavy with a bosom that threatened to burst the buttons on her white uniform. The forbidding expression on her rugged face emphasized the hard angles of her cheekbones and jaw. She looked like a professional body builder on steroids stuffed into a dress. And the boobs had to be fake by Elsa's calculation because she possessed zero body fat. Women without body fat didn't boast big boobs. The nurse stood her ground facing Faust over the wheelchair. Officer Imler and Elsa watched the battle of wills waiting to see who would come out on top.

"Now, nurse..." he looked at her name tag, "Eichmann. My officer is more than capable of a short ride, for fresh air, of course. Plus, her brother doesn't need to see her looking as she did. He's young and it might traumatize him. You know who she is, yes?" He raised an eyebrow and glanced at Elsa.

Nurse Eichmann looked down her nose at Faust. "Of course I do. She is my patient," she huffed.

"Nein. You do not. Think back nearly three years and place her name. This is Elsa Kreiss. Her brother is Johann Martin Kreiss. Anno." He waited for the name to sink in, and saw understanding slowly dawn on her swarthy features.

She looked at Elsa. "Entschuldigung! I did not realize." She turned back to Faust. "Still, she should not be out of bed. She needs her rest." She placed her hands on her hips and stood, feet apart, daring the Direktor to defy her.

"She needs to reassure her brother so he can go home and come back tomorrow. She also needs to be with me to question a piece of shit upstairs in the psych ward no later than now. We do not have time to debate with you Nurse Eichmann because the life of a kidnapped girl and one abducted female detective hang in the balance, so unless you want to be the reason we do not get the information we need to rescue these women before they are sold into the sex trade or outright killed, never to be found again, I suggest you stand down and move aside!" Faust's voice rose steadily as he spoke and ended on a sharp note. The vein in his temple throbbed, indicating he'd lost his patience.

The nurse stepped aside.

Hannah lifted the foot pedals on the wheelchair and turned to help Elsa stand. The two struggled with coordinating this on her one good leg. Nurse Eichmann pushed Imler aside, stepping in to scoop Elsa up as if she weighed nothing and sat her gently on the seat. She fixed the pedals raising the left one to extend out and allow her injured leg to remain supported. "I'll be here when you come back with some nice painkillers for you, officer." Her voice was gentle, yet a bit manly. It was all Elsa could do not to laugh at the spectacle they all made.

"Thank you, Nurse Eichmann. I appreciate all your help."

"Adelein, please." The nurse stepped back, pinning Faust with a dubious stare. "Do not keep her too long. She is injured."

Faust nodded and pulled Elsa's chair away from the bed, backing out of the room carefully. He wasn't worried too much about accidentally hurting Kreiss by banging the chair against a wall or door so much as what the manly nurse might do to him if he did. Officer Imler followed them as they made their way down to a lounge where Anno sat half asleep in a chair.

His eyes were closed, and his head lolled over onto his hand. Blond lashes lay like fans on his cheeks. Elsa's heart constricted in her chest.

MICHELE E. GWYNN

She knew that he must have been worried sick. Faust wheeled her closer and she reached out to shake his knee.

"Hey, sleepy boy," she said, her voice gentle.

Anno sat up, alarmed, then saw his sister and grinned. "Elsa! You're okay!" He leaned over to hug her, and she swallowed a gasp at the pain not wanting to frighten him any more than he'd already been.

"Yes. I'm okay. You're squeezing too tight, though. I can't breathe." She eased him back and then saw tears in his blue eyes.

"I was so worried! When you didn't come home or answer your phone, I didn't know what else to do so I called Joseph. Elsa, what in the hell happened? No one will tell me anything except you were injured in the line of duty." His voice, so deep now, rose an octave, and she could see the young boy he'd been, still was deep inside beneath the surface of the young man he was now. So like their father the older he grew.

"I wish I could tell you more, Anno, but I can't. It's just my knee, really. I have to stay off it for six weeks, but then I'll be all right. But you did the right thing. Calling Joseph got me the help I needed." Her own voice contained the beginnings of a sob and she swallowed. No need to get weepy over the fact she'd nearly been killed. Definitely no need to ever let Anno know how close she'd come.

He sat back and looked at her. "I don't like it! I don't like that you got hurt."

"I don't like it, either. It was quite painful. But I'm okay now. Listen, I want you to go home and get some sleep. That's what I'm going to do. Come back tomorrow and bring some of my clothes. I'm in good hands here as you can see." She gestured to Faust and Imler.

Anno gave Faust a quick look, and then glanced at Officer Imler. His inspection of her took a bit longer, but the worry in his eyes dimmed, to be replaced by a smidge of flirtation. He returned his attention to Elsa.

"Okay. For now, I won't give you a hard time." He sighed. "What do you want me to bring?"

Elsa rattled off a short list of clothing items. "They might discharge me tomorrow so be prepared. Drive my car. The keys are on my dresser."

He stood and leaned over, giving her another hug, but not quite as tight as before, then looked at Imler. "Take care of my sister, please." Imler nodded and smiled. Anno began to leave, then turned back around and said, "By the way, Jan called. He was looking for Joseph, said his mother hadn't come home, and he's worried. She's not answering her phone. Was she with you? Is something going on?" The tired look on his face said he already knew the answer but was not looking forward to hearing it.

Faust responded before Elsa could. "She's on an assignment. It's undercover so she can't answer. Let him know if you can. It was last minute so there was no way she could give him a heads up." He reached into his pocket and pulled out his card, handing it over to the young man. "Give him my number. If he has any questions, he can call me anytime."

"Thank you, Herr Direktor. I will." Anno waved at Elsa and walked out.

"Thank you for that. I don't like to lie to him." Elsa chewed her lip, her anxiety ignited all over again at the reminder of Mahler's abduction.

"I figured. Certainly, after what you two went through." He wheeled her back out into the hall. "Now, let's get upstairs and rattle Koslov's cage. He only just woke up before you. Young Liliya may have given him a concussion. Good girl." The glee in his words was not lost on Elsa and Imler.

"Why is he on psych?" Elsa wondered out loud.

"It's the only ward in this hospital with the capability to lockdown and secure a patient. I have two officers guarding his door as well."

Officer Imler hit the UP button on the lift, and they waited for the elevator to arrive. Elsa reflected inwardly, knowing that eventually Faust would question her as to why she'd gone to Ivchencko's in the first place. She didn't like lying. Not at all. But Heinz told her many times over not to reveal her past career. Keeping it out of the press three years ago was hard enough, and only happened with Joseph's help. His credibility is what carried her. That, and the fact that he'd redacted that information out of the first police report where he'd interviewed Elsa after she initially called Anno in as missing. Letting that cat out of the bag now would not only sink her, but would drag Heinz down, too, for supporting her new career all this time. She couldn't do that to him. He'd gone above and beyond for her and Anno. She could do no less for him. So, when that time came for those pointed questions, she would have to do the one thing she hated most in the world—lie. She just didn't know exactly what that lie would be yet.

Chapter 14

Gregor looked around the room. The walls were a sick shade of green. The radiator by the window blew out heat that didn't quite make it to where he lay strapped down onto the hospital bed. He was cold, and his head hurt. The doctor informed him he'd had to sew up the deep gash with ten stitches. He also warned him that he might begin to experience blurred vision, nausea, possible vomiting, and headache—all signs of a concussion. He'd been kept awake for an hour while the doctor tended to his head wound. He couldn't believe Liliya had done this to him. The last thing he remembered was her voice screaming that she didn't love him. After all they'd shared. He thought he'd earned her trust, her love. Out of all the women he'd encountered since leaving Pskov, Liliya was the one who filled the hole left in his twisted heart by Irina Bromovich's death. He tried telling Liliya about Irina, about how he felt when he first laid eyes on her, first touched her skin, and then the horror when she died. He didn't tell her the girl died at his own hands. He was afraid of scaring her. He knew he could never do such a thing to Liliya. He'd gained control over himself—almost. He slipped up with Anna. He knew that, but Anna wouldn't let him touch her, and he wanted very badly to touch her soft skin. Still wanted to touch her skin. It worked out because he saw Liliya at church, and knew she was the one.

The odor of strong bleach and chemical cleaners filled the air, offending his nose. Gregor stared at the fluorescent light overhead trying to figure out how to get out of this room. He needed to get out, to get back to port like Gospodin Ivchencko told him. He revered the man who'd given him a job when he was living on the docks in Riga, Latvia. After leaving the home of his cousin, Ivan, Gregor made his way across the border into Latvia where he traveled, mostly by foot, through the country until he reached the port city. Months went by with no job. He'd resorted to stealing once his meager funds had run out. He was considering finding the nearest Orthodox order and begging to be allowed to join when the Vledelets anchored.

He watched from under a platform as a tall man with silver hair, followed by a shorter, barrel-shaped man, and three sailors disembarked stepping off the gangplank onto the dock, and straight into a waiting luxury car. Hungry, filthy, and bone-tired, he curled up into a ball and slept. It was dark when he was awakened by the sound of a vehicle pulling up. He opened his eyes and saw that it was the same car from earlier followed by a dark van that parked behind it. One of the three sailors got out of the driver's side and stood, waiting. The tall man and the barrel-shaped man got out of the car. They looked around, saw no one, and then the tall man nodded. The sailor who drove the van walked around to the back and knocked twice on the door before opening it.

Gregor could see that the other two sailors were inside. They stepped out and began pulling at something. Several somethings. All wiggling. As they were pulled out and into the dim light provided by the half-moon, he saw they were girls. Three of them, all bound and gagged. They were trying to get away, but with hands and feet tied, and gags shoved into their mouths, they didn't stand a chance. One had long, blonde hair, and she stood defiantly facing the men. *Irina?* His mind, deprived for nearly three days of food, water, and sleep played tricks on him. He stumbled forth seeing only the girl.

The girl's eyes widened in hope at seeing someone else on the dock. She began making noises that sounded like pleas for help. The first sailor smacked her, and she fell over. The other two turned and sighted Gregor. The tall man and the shorter one also turned to see who had come up on them. The shorter one drew a gun and aimed while two of the sailors pulled switchblades out of their pockets while coming at him. All Gregor saw was his Irina go down. He shouted "No!", then stumbled and fell, reaching out, desperately trying to touch her. The two sailors were upon him. The first one grabbed him by his shirt and hauled him up. Now delirious, Gregor could only utter one word, one name. The only person in the world who cared what happened to him. "Ivan," he whispered.

The man stopped. The other sailor asked, "How does he know you? Who is he?"

The first man replied in a deep, guttural voice. "I do not know this filthy rat." He seemed convinced of that, yet...

"Well, he certainly seems to know you!" the shorter one said, pointing out the obvious.

The tall man approached. "What's the holdup? Who is this creature?" He said the last with a disgusted sneer, observing Gregor's dirty and disheveled state.

"Ivan says he doesn't know, but the boy clearly called his name. He looks like he's delirious. Probably starving by the look of him."

"Well, we can't leave him here. He's seen us." He looked at Dutch. "You know what to do." Then he walked to the gangplank, ascending to the ship.

Dutch stepped forward, pulled back a fist, and knocked Gregor unconscious. The world went black. Then it changed. It changed so completely that he couldn't believe his luck, and he'd be forever grateful to Gospodin Ivchencko for as long as he lived, even if he did have a Godless, evil streak.

The lock clicked and the door opened. A female officer walked in followed by a wheelchair being pushed by an older man. He let his gaze travel to the woman in the wheelchair. It was the redheaded whore from the basement, the woman who turned his Liliya against him. A sneer curled his lip, and hate filled his eyes.

Seeing Koslov again so soon was unsettling for Elsa. She could only imagine how much worse it would be when she came face to face with Ivchencko in the future. Still, a part of her felt only steely resolve and the need to squeeze every last drop of information out of him so they could get Birgitta back safely. She saw the hatred in his eyes and remembered the other thing she saw in his eyes down in that basement—lunacy. She couldn't afford to forget that this young man was unbalanced. He thought Liliya was his girlfriend, truly thought they were a couple despite the glaring fact that he'd kidnapped her and forced himself on her.

His lip curled into a sneer. "You!"

Instinctively, she tread carefully with her words. "Yes. Me."

Faust parked her chair at the foot of the bed keeping Elsa out of reach although he knew Koslov was strapped down by his wrists and ankles as well as handcuffed to the bedrail. He eyed the suspect taking note of the scars on his chest knowing they continued onto his back crisscrossing in raised, red and white welts of permanently damaged skin. The attending physician who examined the head wound was shocked, and said he'd never seen anything like it. He concluded by their placement that they were self-inflicted.

When Faust asked who the hell would do such a thing to them-selves, the doctor responded, "The only cases I've read involved reli-gious rituals of self-flagellation." As strange as he found that answer, it fit in with the information slowly coming together about Gregor Koslov. He found the three missing women via a church community. He was still waiting to fill in the blanks from the information Heinz and Mahler dug up about a Gregor Koslov out of Pskov, Russia. The records ended with an old census. It was entirely possible the boy had been raised by, *or sold to*, a religious order. He would have been too young at the time to voluntarily enter one. Faust was not a fan of religion. He considered it poison to the mind and a crutch used by those looking for reasons to justify their own personal agendas of hate, bigotry, and hypocrisy. People didn't need religion to know right from wrong. All they needed was empathy. Without that, they lived in pure selfishness.

"Where is my Liliya? What have you done with her?" He jerked against his restraints, spittle flying from his lips.

Officer Imler stepped forward, but Faust put up a restraining hand. "It's okay." He looked at her. "You can wait outside." She began to object, but then followed the order from her superior.

Once the door closed, Elsa asked, "Why'd you send her out?"

Faust pulled up the only chair from the corner and sat next to Elsa. He leaned forward, placing his forearms on his knees. "Because some of what gets said from here on out needs to not leave this room."

"Like what," she asked, curious now.

"Like how you ended up at Ivchenko's in the first place." His steady gaze seemed to say he already knew, *but that couldn't be possible...could it?*

Elsa returned his gaze, giving nothing away. She decided to go with as close to the truth as possible without going into details. She hated lying. "He invited me."

"I understand you'd only just met the night before. Why did he invite you?" Faust patiently gauged her responses.

Gregor watched the exchange, both angry that they were ignoring him and not answering his questions and fascinated as it seemed the redhead might be in trouble herself.

This question was not so easy to answer. "He was interested in me." It was as close to honesty as she could get without saying why Ivchenko showed interest.

Faust changed tactics. "And were you interested in him? I thought you and Trommler were dating?"

Elsa's eyes widened. "God, no! To being interested in Ivchencko, not to dating Lukas."

"Still, you responded to his invitation." It was a statement and not a question, yet she felt compelled to answer.

"He really didn't give me much choice," she muttered, shaking her head, and looking at the wall. When she turned back, Faust was watching her intently. Then he nodded, seemingly satisfied with her answer.

He turned to Koslov then. "You're in quite a bit of hot water, young man. Kidnapping a minor, forced imprisonment, assault and battery, and rape. That's a five-year sentence for the kidnapping, five for the assault, and fifteen for each time you raped Liliya Avilova." Faust exaggerated the last a bit. It could be suggested by the prosecution, but rarely was returned by the judge. Even so, instilling fear into a suspect for information was not beyond him, especially a rapist piece of shit who might also be a murdering piece of shit. He was still waiting for DNA results to come back from Doctor Menghala to see if Koslov's matched what was found under Anna Popovich's fingernails and in the semen collected from her body. By Liliya's own testimony so far, he felt ninety-nine-point-nine percent sure it would. "You're looking at spending the rest of your life in prison."

Gregor stayed quiet. It was clear he was thinking about what Faust just said, weighing his options. This act alone showed he wasn't completely crazy. Twisted, but not beyond the fringe.

Finally, he spoke. "What do you want?"

Faust wanted it all. He wanted the man who took all three Berlin girls, and he was sure he already had him right here. But he also wanted what now appeared to be a larger menace—Yuri Ivchencko. The Russian was the head of one of the largest business enterprises in Eastern Europe, was respected throughout the world of art, and even philanthropy from what he'd gleaned off the internet. Taking someone like Ivchencko down would be no easy feat. He had more than the protection of his public image. If he was, indeed, involved in the trafficking of young women, he also had the protection of whatever underground organization he was working with. By all indications, that may very well be the Bratva, also known as the Russian mafia. If that turned out to be the case, it was bigger than Koslov, bigger than Faust. A task force would have to be formed to handle it. Their lives would be in danger if handled wrong. Hell, their lives would be in danger no matter what, but justice was a demanding bitch, and Faust was in love with her. He'd give her anything she asked.

He smiled. "My dear boy, I want your full confession."

"I've nothing to confess to you!" He glared defiantly at Faust.

"Oh, I didn't make myself clear. My apologies. It is not me you will be confessing to."

Koslov looked at him with confusion. "Then who? A priest?" He began to laugh.

Faust stood, then casually walked to the corner where a black duffel bag sat. He unzipped it and pulled out a wicked-looking cat-o-nine tails, not the cute kind couples use in foreplay, but one made of strong leather tied with strips of suede knotted with spiked metal balls. It was heavy and at least three feet long. "Nein, mein Freund. You will be confessing to Mistress Elsa!"

Elsa's eyes popped wide and her mouth fell open. Faust looked at her and smiled. "Your particular skill set is needed, officer." He placed a warm hand on her shoulder and gave a small squeeze. "Mahler's life depends on it."

"How did you know?" She was still in shock.

He leaned down and whispered in her ear. "I've always known. Who do you think advised Heinz to redact that information from your old police report before you entered the academy?"

"Well, scheisse," she said.

"Indeed. By the by. I appreciate your honesty earlier. You could have lied, but you stuck to the truth." He patted her shoulder and straightened his spine.

Elsa gave a wry chuckle. "Minus the sensational bits."

"Exactly. Good job. Now, I feel a strong need to grab myself a cup of coffee. I think it might take me at least an hour to drink it. I believe Officer Imler might like one, too. I'll leave the other officer outside the door there, just in case you have a need. He's very discreet."

"You're going to just let me whip him into submission?"

Faust stopped at the door, giving her a look of astonished innocence. "Me? Why, I know nothing, Officer Kreiss." He opened the door, stepped out, then poked his head back in. "And don't be gentle. He has a mile of scar tissue to get through before you even manage to inflict the least amount of pain." He winked and left. The lock clicked, and Elsa was alone with the rapist of Liliya Avilova, the man who may be the murderer of other young women, and definitely knew where they could find Birgitta and how to stop Ivchencko. All she had to do was dust off her old self and once again be the best of the best, a dominatrix skilled like no other in the art of inflicting pain without damage. Only this time, she could drop that last part.

She backed her chair up and maneuvered to the side of the bed. "So, you like to rape girls." She eyed his scars remembering what Liliya had told her about him beating himself with a similar whip in front of her, and then getting off on it. She knew people found pleasure in pain, but she didn't think that was why he did it, nor its intended consequence.

Gregor eyed her with distaste. "I didn't rape her. Not once did I hit her."

"Really? You're understanding and knowledge of English and German seems quite fluent. And, of course, your native tongue shouldn't be lost on you. So how is it you failed to understand the word *no*?"

His eyes narrowed to slits.

"Hmm. What about nein? Stop? Aufhören?" Elsa lowered her voice and gave Gregor a pitying look. "You raped her. She didn't consent. She is only a teenage girl. Do you know what that makes you?" She waited.

"I'm sure you're going to tell me, whore." His nostrils flared as the hate in his eyes increased.

"But of course I am." Elsa did not acknowledge his insult, but instead, backed her chair up and stood on her good leg, balancing. "I'm going to tell you over and over again until you get it through your thick skull that what you did was unforgiveable, illegal, a sin. And then you're going to tell me what I want to know about Yuri Ivchencko." She hobbled to a better position, one that allowed her to lean onto a metal cabinet that sat against the wall by the bed. She lightly flung the straps of the whip over his stomach to test the distance. Perfect. From here, she was up high enough to wield the whip while resting her body weight on the top of the furniture. Gregor's eyes widened a little as she slowly dragged the leather strips over him.

"I'm not afraid of you." His bravado was sincere. Elsa could hear it in his voice.

"Do you know why Ivchencko had me down in his basement?"

Her question seemed off-topic, confusing him. "I don't question Gospodin Ivchencko."

Elsa smiled slowly, cat-like. "I see. So, you don't even know." She swung the leather strips back and forth playfully.

Suspicion clouded his expression. "Know what?"

"Before I became Schutzpolizei, I had a rather unusual career. I was known as Mistress Elsa. Men, rich men, poor men, and all the men in between, paid very well for my services."

He laughed. "A whore, like I said. So, what are you planning to do? Fuck me into confession? You're not my type!" He spat at her and missed.

Elsa ignored this, looking him straight in the eye. "No, Gregor Koslov. I never had sex with any of those men. They didn't pay me to fuck them. They paid me to whip them. Brutally. And often. I was the best. Still am."

He paled just a little, but still didn't quite believe her. "You're a police officer. You can't harm me." He turned his head away.

"In this room, right now, I'm simply Mistress Elsa, and you will address me as such, and only when I say." She hauled back the whip and let it fly.

Outside, the seasoned officer standing guard at the door flinched as he heard a loud crack followed by a high-pitched scream. He resisted the urge to glance through the small window. His orders were clear. Keep the medical staff out, and only enter if the officer inside requests it. He looked down the long hall at Faust drinking coffee and chatting with the on-duty physician. They both looked his way, having heard... something, but when he showed no alarm, turned and resumed their chat.

The Bell landed three blocks away from the port in Hamburg. It was met by a Spezialeinsatzkommando (SEK) team sent by no small miracle of coordination, courtesy of the LKA. The commander, who was wearing a mask as all those in the unit did to protect their identities, walked forward and introduced himself to Heinz who stepped out of the helicopter first. "Kommissar Heinz? I'm in charge here. You can call me Commander Hammer." He reached out.

Heinz clasped his outstretched hand and shook it. "As in 'drop the...?"

"Precisely. This is my second in command, Howitzer." A man built just like his name stepped forward offering his hand to Heinz.

Lukas and Beimer came up behind them along with Jager and Kelner now fully decked out for combat and carrying H&K MP5 submachine guns.

"Hammer, these are my men, Officer Hugo Beimer, Lukas Trommler, StabsKapitanLeutnant Kristof Jager, and Korvettankapitan Dieter Kelner.

The men all nodded, sizing each other up for strengths and weaknesses. Satisfied, Hammer continued. "We have word that the Marines are patrolling beyond the port, and in position to help should we need it." Kelner nodded. Hammer returned to addressing Heinz. "I have fifty of Hamburg's finest at your command. I understand we have very little time. Shall we?" He indicated they should follow, and all walked to a makeshift command post where a map was already laid out. A red X marked the exact location of the Vledelets.

"What do we know right now?" Heinz asked, leaning over to view the map.

"The ship was cleared to leave port but hasn't yet. We have the harbor master's cooperation." He glanced over at a man sitting on the back of the truck looking like he was about to piss his pants as two masked SEK agents trained their rifles on him.

Heinz grunted. "Good. So, what's the plan? What's the best way to get onto this vessel without raising the alarm?"

Howitzer spoke. "We have ten aquatics on stand-by. They'll board seaside here and here." He pointed out the two best areas of entry in the stern. "No one will be watching the stern. Once aboard, they'll take out and secure the deck, signal all is clear, and we'll board from the gangplank. They still have it out. From there, we put a unit of ten men at each of these stations. One unit gains the bridge, two hold topside, and three take the lower decks. Until we know exactly what we're dealing with, that's the best plan."

"And what about us?" Heinz asked, noting there was no mention of where they fit in.

Commander Hammer looked up. "You're all with me. We're search and rescue. You up for it, Kommissar?"

"And then some." Finally, a plan. Heinz was chafing to get started. The longer they waited, the more anxious he became for Birgitta.

"Then you're going to need protection." He turned and gestured to one of the men who came forward carrying body armor, a helmet, and weapons.

Heinz dressed in the Kevlar vest and got a crash course in both the electronics of the helmet that offered drop-down night vision and communication with the rest of the unit through wireless tech, and the MP5, a weapon he'd not fired since his early years of police training. He still preferred his police issue Sig, but in what could well turn into a battle, this was good, too. He checked the sight, getting as comfortable as he could in the few minutes he was given. Howitzer made sure Trommler and Beimer were similarly decked out. Heinz noticed both looked like boys at Christmas with new toys.

"We have less than forty-five minutes before Ivchencko gets suspicious. He's expecting his man, Koslov, to arrive before they cast off. Now might be a good time to inform your aquatic unit," said Heinz.

Hammer clicked on his speaker and was instantly connected to all fifty men. "The countdown has begun, gentlemen. It's T-minus forty-five minutes."

Elsa's arm was tiring, but she'd never admit it. Faust was right. Twenty lashes in, and Koslov was barely responding to the pain beyond a few howls. Well, he did have an unfortunate erection, but that wasn't anything she hadn't seen happen before. His chest was bloodied, and even though she kept her face expressionless, inside she was unsure about going further. The only thing that kept her moving was the fact that time was not on their side. In order to rescue Birgitta, they needed information. Heinz, Lukas, and Hugo were already in Hamburg. The situation was fluid, and the tide could turn in their favor, or it could drown them in an instant. She couldn't let that happen.

"I see you rather enjoy this. And it's a freebie too. Lucky you."

Gregor's eyes followed the whip as it swung loose in her hand. Sweat beaded his forehead, and his cheeks were flushed. Instead of looking fearful, he now appeared ecstatic. She knew it wasn't working. He was actually enjoying himself even if he wouldn't cop to it. Pain was nothing to him judging by his scars. She would need to switch tactics, but what?

"Fucking whore." His words lacked the loathing they were laced with when he called her that earlier.

"Boring. You've said that before." She feigned a yawn. "Truly, Gregor, I don't believe that you feel so strongly. I mean, there's a little indicator right here that says you like me just fine." She pointed the whip at the bulge in his underwear. He flinched.

"No!" He tried scooting his hips away.

Elsa's eyebrow rose. This was the first fearful reaction she'd seen out of him. She thought about what she'd just done—pointed the whip at his family jewels. So far, she'd whipped his chest since it was the only available exposed skin. His legs were covered by a blanket, which rode low enough to show the top of his underpants. The erection was evident underneath, peeking out a bit at the top.

"No? Did you just tell me no without saying my name?" She straightened her spine, still using the cabinet as support.

"Go to hell!"

"A warm place. Yes, it is awfully cold outside." She looked at his flushed face. "But you look very hot. In fact, you may need to cool off a little. Let me help you." She leaned over, supporting herself with one hand on the bed, and used the other to yank his covers down. Then she made eye contact as she slowly reached up toward the band of his underwear.

"No! Do not touch me, whore!" He began wiggling around. It got him nowhere, so he bucked, but Elsa grasped the material and easily slid the underwear down low enough to reveal his naked member. She stood back up and leaned once again on the cabinet. He panted as he shot her a hate-filled look.

"I think you'd like me touching you, Gregor." She flicked the straps lightly over his thighs, caressing. He groaned. She went on, chatting as if they weren't in the middle of a bizarre situation. "I had a client once, a Herr Schultz. He had a particular fetish. Like you, he enjoyed pain. It made him hard too." She maneuvered her wrist to slide the leather straps up and over him. The contact made his eyes roll back.

"Stop. Touching. Me. There." He panted out the words. "You're not her. You're not good enough."

Elsa chuckled. "Oh, I assure you. I am good enough. Anyhow, as I was saying. His fetish wasn't just to have me whip his chest or back, but also his buttocks, his thighs...and his cock!"

Gregor's eyes flew wide. "No! You can't!" He bucked again, finally reacting as she'd intended.

Had I known this earlier, I could've saved myself time and an aching arm.

She smiled wickedly, fully into her old role again. "Tell me what I want to know, and I'll cease. Your confession is your safe word."

"I won't! You whore! You fucking bitch!" He spit, cursed, and bucked.

"You will." Elsa raised her hand and brought the whip down onto his protruding penis—bloodied leather straps, spiked metal balls, and all—with force.

Koslov screamed, this time with fear and pain rather than sick ecstasy.

"Fuck you!" he yelled.

She recoiled and struck again, harder this time. His face turned red, and he opened his mouth to cry out, but no sound emerged. He was tensed up, and out of breath. Finally, he sucked in air like a drowning man and began to cry.

"Stop! Please!"

"Tell me what I want to know, and I'll cease." She raised her hand to strike a third time when he caught her eye.

"No, Mistress Elsa, no! Please, no. I'll tell you what you want, but please stop!" He blubbered like a baby. She guessed that having spiked metal bits strike his testicles and sensitized penis finally got through to him.

"What will he do with Birgitta? Where is he going? We know he's on his ship. How many men are consigned there?"

"Too many questions." Tears fell down his cheeks, and snot ran freely from a nose he could not wipe with his wrists cuffed to the bed rails.

"What will he do with Birgitta?"

"He'll hurt her, then sell her."

Elsa took a deep breath. Hearing him say it out loud made it all the more real. "Where is he going?"

"St. Petersburg."

"How many men on the ship? I need an exact number."

"I don't have an exact number."

She raised the whip, and he cringed, whining again. "Around six-ty-five men."

She thought about that a moment. "Sailors?"

"Sailors, criminals, mercenaries." He tried turning his head into the pillow, the pain still racking him. "I think I'm going to be sick."

"Go ahead," she said, watching him dry heave. Nothing came up. "What happened to the other girls, Gregor?"

"They're in hold." He coughed.

"Hold? What does that mean? Where?"

His breathing evened out. "Containment. They're onboard."

"He's transporting girls now? You're sure? Don't lie to me!" She shook the whip at him, getting angry at the very thought of more girls like Liliya imprisoned in a container, ripped away from their families, abused and terrified. "How many?"

He saw the swift change from calm torturer to menacing bitch with a whip, a whip she could once again wield to strike his tender genitals.

"I don't know exactly. I procured two, but only one made it. There are others around Germany who were to bring in specific types. I don't know how many."

Her eyes narrowed to slits. "You filthy motherfucker!" She raised the whip again and brought it down. He was mid-scream when Faust came back in.

The door shut, and the Direktor leaned on it, effectively covering the window he was sure someone might be trying to look through. He sipped his coffee. His second since he left earlier. "Well? Any progress or are you just having fun?"

Elsa lowered the whip, the look on her face broadcasting her outrage. "Ivchencko is transporting an unknown number of girls on his ship right now. There are approximately sixty-five men on board including Ivchencko, and if we don't stop him from leaving, all those young women, and Birgitta, too, will be sold into sex slavery in St. Petersburg."

Faust gave an opera clap. "Excellent. Now, can you get him to tell us who he's selling to? Who is his connection?"

Elsa turned back to Gregor. "Well? You heard him. Who's the connection?"

Through a haze of tears and mucous, Gregor sniffled, and replied, "I can't. They'll kill me."

"I'll kill you if you don't. And that man over there won't lift a finger to help you." She pointed at Faust.

Faust stepped closer. "But I will help you, Elsa. Here." He offered her his Sig, which she took after throwing the Direktor an odd look.

"I think a bullet is too kind, but if they're going to kill you anyway, I may as well have the pleasure." She released the safety and aimed the gun at Koslov's head. "Who is the contact?"

"You're crazy! A crazy bitch!"

She lunged forward and shoved the weapon between his penis and testicles. He shrank back as far as the mattress allowed, sniveling, panicking.

"Contact?" she demanded, digging the tip further into the sensitive skin of his perineum.

Faust caught Koslov's eye and smiled, giving a thumbs up. "Solid move. A bullet to the taint. She's very good, isn't she?"

Gregor knew after an hour with Elsa that she probably would shoot him in the dick. He also knew he was now dead either way, he

just needed to choose how he would die. He took two deep breaths.
"Bratva. Vladimir Brezhnev."

Faust dropped his coffee.

"Fuck!" The hot liquid splattered at his feet.

Chapter 15

It'd been almost two hours now, and finally, Birgitta felt the rope give way as she managed to cut through it. It was agonizingly slow work. She could only use her fingers to guide the blade, no real strength applied. A time or two she'd nicked her own skin at the wrist as she worked the knife beneath the rope. Sweat poured down her face from sheer concentration, but she was rewarded when her left hand popped free. Now she made much shorter work of her right hand, and then her ankles, sawing like a lunatic, sure that Ivchencko or one of his henchmen would walk through the door at any moment.

She stood and shook her limbs as she moved around the room seeking anything she could use besides the switchblade. She opened and closed drawers in a desk bolted down to the floor. Inside, she found personal files and a ledger. Flipping through, she saw detailed numbers and dates of deliveries. *25 Blonde, 13 Brunette, 7 Redhead.* On the right, these numbers were further broken down by gender. At the top, dates. She set the ledger down and opened the first folder. Inside, a Polaroid was paperclipped to the top showing a dark-haired girl who looked no older than thirteen. She was crying, her eyes terrified. A handwritten page was underneath. *Hessen, speaks German and English. Virgin. Value – High.*

Birgitta was disgusted. She wanted to vomit. She looked around for something to hold these items, wanting to secure the evidence of

Ivchencko's evil. She located a seaman's bag in a lower drawer of the built-in dresser on the wall and shoved the book and folders inside, tightening the drawstring. The bag had a mail-carriers strap that she placed over her head and let rest against her body. Another desk drawer revealed a Russian P-96 9 mm pistol. A box of clips sat next to it. She checked to make sure it was loaded, stuffed clips in her jacket pocket, and took the safety off. She realized she no longer had her cell phone while loading herself down. They'd found it. It would be a miracle if Heinz and Faust had managed to track her this far out of Berlin. She was on her own at this moment, and prayed she'd be able to get off the ship before it left port. She just needed to make it to the port authority office. From there, she could call in help.

A key slid into the lock, and she tensed. Moving silently behind the door, she waited, gun drawn.

Dutch walked in and immediately noticed the empty chair. "What the fuck?" He turned, but it was too late. The butt of the gun came down on the back of his head. He stumbled and dropped to his knees but didn't go completely down as intended. He roared and charged her. Mahler aimed, exhaled, and fired.

Blood spattered, and bits of bone and brain sprayed in an arc as the bullet blew out the back of the butler's head. His large body dropped, the last expression on his face, shock.

She stood unmoving, stunned. In all her years as a detective, she'd only fired her gun in the line of duty twice, and those shots were in warning. No injury resulted. This was her first kill. *Shake it off, Birgitta. Get it together.* She swallowed down the urge to heave.

She stepped over the dead Dutch and out into the corridor closing the door behind her. She made her way back in the direction from which she came, slinking close to the wall, gun at the ready knowing she might need to blast her way off the ship. Fear gripped her, but she pushed it down. She thought about her son who was probably frantic with worry for her by now. Jan was mostly grown, but he still needed her. She wanted to live long enough to see him fall in love, get married, have children, to see his children have children. And she thought about Joseph. Five years partnered together, and the fool still didn't realize what a good man he was, how much she cared. *Heinz, you're awfully blind for a detective!* She sniffed as tears stung her eyes. She hastily wiped them away. No time for sentiment. Taking a deep breath, Birgitta peeked around the next corner. Finding the way clear, she moved on.

The men were all in place. Heinz, Commander Hammer, Lukas, Beimer, and the rest now waited for the aquatic unit to complete gaining the stern and securing the deck. His mobile vibrated in his pocket. Everyone looked at him as he fumbled to pull it out.

"Heinz," he answered. His harsh whisper indicated his stress level.

"Joseph, it's me." Faust's voice greeted him.

"I'm a little busy right now, Herman. What is it?"

"Information. And you're not going to like it. Where are you now?"

"We're about to board ship."

"Hold off!" Faust's reply surprised him.

"What? We can't. It's already begun. A unit is in the process of taking the stern as we speak."

"Scheisse! Well, then you'd better inform everyone quickly. You're facing at least sixty-five of the hardest, most brutal men you've come up against."

Heinz paused. "Who are they, Herman?" By the anxiety in Faust's voice, he knew he wasn't going to like the answer.

"Bratva. And not just any branch of them."

"Who do they work for?" Dread flooded his system.

"The Butcher."

Heinz gasped. Flashes of every media headline plastered across newspapers, televisions, and internet sites hit him. Vladimir Brezhnev had never been nailed down on a single charge, yet he'd slain his enemies and those who crossed him with impunity. His nickname stuck after a 1989 massacre of Yakuza who tried to invade his territory. Even after the initial attack in which he and his men slaughtered the rival Japanese mafia up-and-comer, Yohido Iyushi, and his gang, the Yakuza sent more men after Brezhnev. They didn't appreciate the insult. Honor codes among criminals are written in blood. Still, Brezhnev and his men defeated them too. Brutally. From that day on, he'd been tagged by media as *The Butcher*. The name stuck.

He sucked in a breath. "What else?"

"He's transporting girls on that ship. If you board that ship, you're facing men who spent time in the worst penal colonies in Russia, men who bow to no authority. They're straight-out killers."

"Then that's all the more reason we must do this. We can't let them get away with these girls. I can't let them take Birgitta. Look, I have an SEK team of fifty men plus myself, Trommler, Beimer, and two combat Marines. We have a strategy, and we have the element of surprise. They're not expecting us."

"It may not be enough, Joseph." Faust paused. A woman's voice could be heard in the background. "Hold on. Elsa wants to talk to you."

"Joseph, there's something you can use. Ivchencko is a germo-phobe."

"Yes, so?" He didn't see how Ivchencko being a clean freak would make any difference.

"No, you don't understand. He's germophobic on a crazy level. It's why he won't shake hands with people. He will shy away from dirt, and germs you can't see make him crazy. Use it. If you find yourself in a pinch with him, use it." Her words were insistent.

"How do you know this? Did Koslov confess?"

"Let's just say I had my own experience with his insane fear. And yes, Koslov confessed. Joseph?"

"What?"

There was silence on the line, adding to the tension they all felt. And then, "Be careful, and bring Birgitta home." There was a hint of emotion in her words, the fear of a child talking to a parent.

Heinz bit his lip. "I will. Now put Faust back on."

"She's quite something, this one," Herman stated simply.

"Yes, she is. Listen, Herman, I need you to do something for me."

"Anything. What do you need?"

Heinz looked at Lukas and Beimer. Both were watching him. "If we don't make it...If I don't make it back—"

"Stop talking nonsense, Jo—"

"Herman! You promised."

"I'm sorry. Please continue."

"In the event I don't make it out of this, take care of Elsa and Anno. They need someone."

"I will. Now, stop being maudlin, and go be the hero, for Christ's sake." Faust hung up.

Heinz stuffed his phone back in his pocket and looked at the men. He licked his teeth, and started to say, "There's new information."

Hammer held up a hand. "We know." He reached out and flipped the button on Heinz's mic. "You forgot to turn this off. Everyone knows. And I can safely say that Bratva or no, we're taking this ship, and we're rescuing these girls. There isn't a single man here who isn't onboard with this plan. And Heinz? We're going to kick their ass!"

Elsa's stomach was tied in knots. She feared for Joseph, and for Birgitta, and all those girls. Her arm hurt. She really was out of practice with the whip. Her leg hurt too. The painkillers from earlier were wearing off. She felt physically and mentally exhausted, and her emotions were running high. Officer Imler backed her wheelchair out of Koslov's room. He was still cursing her, but the heat had gone out of his words.

"I hope you rot in hell, you evil devil woman!"

"You first." Elsa flipped him the bird.

"Oh, he will. No worries. Gregor is going to love prison. And by the looks of him," Faust made a wry face, "prison is going to love him." Koslov lay in his bed, penis still out for all the world to see. Faust sighed. "Well, even I can't leave you like that." He walked over and threw the blanket up, tucking it around Gregor's shoulders. He leaned down, smiling. "The LKA thanks you for your cooperation. I'll be sure to let the jail guards know just how much you've helped us. I'm sure they'll want to tell all your cellmates, hold you up as a good example, a model prisoner."

Koslov's eyes grew wide. He'd never been in prison, but heard the men on the Vledelets tell tales, and the one thing prisoners do not tolerate is a man perceived to be in the pocket of law enforcement. He was as good as dead. The idea terrified him.

Faust whistled a happy tune as he walked out. But the tune didn't quite hide the fierce worry running around inside his head. He knew that the odds of Heinz and the SEK coming out on top in this operation were lower than fifty percent. He didn't like those odds at all. Before he'd turned Elsa loose on the rapist, they all thought they would be dealing with run of the mill criminals. After she extracted the information, he knew they were the worst kind. The Bratva weren't just brutal, they were a network with paid informants in places one would never expect. Sometimes, those informants were inside police organizations. He didn't want to put Joseph and Elsa in danger, but it seemed this whole case file of three missing girls was bigger than any of them could imagine. It was only the tip of the iceberg.

He caught up with them at the elevator. "Hell of a job you did, Kreiss. I won't forget it."

"Thank you, sir." Her energy level plummeted further, and she could barely hold her eyes open, yet her mind wouldn't shut down. "You'll keep me posted, won't you?"

The ride down two floors was short. "Will do. I understand how much it means to you." He gave her a pat on the shoulder. They were no more than three steps out of the lift and down the hall when Nurse Eichmann came up on them.

"It's about time!" She looked at her patient. "What have you done to her? She looks like she's going to pass out!" Her eyes narrowed on Faust and her thin lips pursed.

If it weren't for Elsa's immediate need for medication and bed, Faust thought the muscular nurse might just whoop his old ass for keeping her patient up. He swallowed a nervous chuckle. There wasn't much in this world that frightened him. The list was short, actually. His mother-in-law, the Bratva, and spiders—the hairy ones. He'd been known to shoot at them with his Sig. Now, he could add Nurse Eichmann to that list.

"Come, come, Officer. I have your pain meds all ready for you." She commandeered the wheelchair from Imler and tossed a look over her shoulder at Faust. He shuddered.

He stood there, hands in pockets, rocking back and forth on his heels. Officer Imler smothered a chuckle.

"So, are we staying or going?"

Faust ran a hand through his graying blond hair. "I'm staying. You're going. You're relieved for the night."

She started to object, seeing how tired he looked, but wisely chose to do what her boss instructed. "Goodnight, sir." She left him standing in the hall.

He turned and headed down the corridor to the waiting area near Elsa's room. There were chairs in there, and a couch, if he recalled correctly. He could grab another coffee from the vending machine and go have a lie-down while he waited to hear back from Heinz. At least he'd be close by and could let Elsa know what was going on once he knew. In the meantime, all he could do was wait.

Chapter 16

Two hours passed, and still Koslov had not returned. Ivchencko checked his watch again, then his phone. *Where the hell is Dutch?* He put the flogger down and removed his surgical gloves. The sound of crying was annoying him now. It was coming from all around from cages filled with more than forty girls. The one he had manacled to the rack against the wall slumped forward. The brown-haired young woman had passed out on him. *It's no fun if they're unconscious.* The girl was covered in welts and open lashes. She would need to heal before they arrived in St. Petersburg. Ivchencko picked up an antibiotic spray and proceeded to 'water' the girl's wounds like a houseplant. The anticoagulant in the spray would stop the bleeding, and the wounds would not get infected. She'd have some scarring, but who cared?

He used a clean cloth to wipe the sweat off his brow, put his jacket back on, and left the cargo hold. He needed to go check on what was delaying Gregor. He needed the boy. When they arrived back in Mother Russia, the girls would have to be hidden temporarily before they could be sold at auction. When he initially found Gregor on the docks of Riga, he planned to kill him. He'd even brought him down to the cargo bay intending to have a little fun first, but when he'd had Ivan strip him down and seen the scars covering his back, he stopped. Instead of whipping him, he was fascinated, and made Koslov tell him the story of all those scars. He couldn't believe it when he discovered they were mostly self-inflicted. He was even more intrigued by the tale of the Order of Rasputin. Gregor admitted his crime of killing a young girl, but that didn't matter as much as to how and why the young girl was there to begin with. Koslov said he'd often witnessed young women being brought in and tortured in the same manner as Irina. They didn't stay long, just long enough to be broken—made meek and compliant. A car would always come for them in a few weeks, and that car would leave behind supplies for the Order.

It was clear that the Order worked with an organization that trafficked young women. As long as they weren't particular about who paid them, Ivchencko saw this as a golden opportunity. His contact complained often of how difficult it was to break these girls. They had to become addicted to drugs, which became expensive, and then they didn't last long, overdosing faster than he cared. Profit and loss. The bottom line was always the priority. The longer these girls lived, the better for business. If they stayed clean, they sold for a higher price. So, if the Order could break them down for only the cost of food and supplies, that was a win-win for everyone. But he needed Gregor to find the place, and he needed that 'in'. He promised to protect him from the wrath of the Holy Father Matteus and Mother. All he had to do was lead them there and make the introductions. But for that to happen, he needed to be on this ship.

He made his way up to the third deck. He needed to change his shirt, and that meant a quick stop at his state room. If he heard nothing by the time he changed and arrived on the bridge, then they would have to leave without him. That thought put Ivchencko in a foul mood. He reached the corridor and made his way down to his room. He pulled his key out and slid it into the lock. It didn't click. He paused, then pulled the handle and pushed it open. A bloody body greeted his eyes. He stepped inside, seeing no detective tied to the chair or the bed. He bent down without thought reaching to turn the head of the corpse. It was Dutch. *Fuck!* He stepped back. Ivchencko absorbed the fact that he had blood on his hands, and panicking, ran over to the sink to quickly scrub them clean. He had to do it three times before he was satisfied. Then he pulled off his jacket and shirt and washed his upper body as if it, too, somehow became contaminated. He dried off with a towel and grabbed a clean shirt from the wardrobe. Buttoning it up, he picked out a clean jacket. Once all was in order, he went straight to his desk to get his pistol. It was gone. Rage filled him. He picked up his phone. The line connected straight to the bridge. It rang, and rang, and rang. No one answered. He slammed the phone back into the cradle. After a moment of thought, Ivchencko bent down to pull a box out from the bottom shelf of the built-in shelving. Inside was a collection of knives. He pulled out two lethal-looking daggers and palmed them. The look in his eyes promised murder for one petite, brunette detective. He left the room, purposefully pulling on a fresh pair of surgical gloves.

Heinz followed Hammer up the gangplank. It was dark now, and they kept low. The aquatic team took out the guards on deck by hand—knives over gunfire, then signaled to the rest of the team. They were the last to ascend. Lukas took his left flank, and Beimer took the right while Hammer led the way. Howitzer, Jager, and Kelner brought up the rear. Unit two stormed the bridge taking out communication with the rest of the ship. Units three, four, and five began making their way down to the first three lower decks. So far, so good.

The team three leader gave the thumbs up indicating the way was clear down to the first lower deck. Hammer waved them onward, and they took to the stairs. In his ear, Heinz could hear unit two's leader

say, "We got the wheel. Bear on the loose. Possibly third deck. Out."
The *bear*, of course, was Ivchencko. And he was most likely on third
deck. Check. They moved quickly, making their way room by room,
looking for Mahler. The kidnapped girls were most likely in the hold.
It was possible she was with them, but Heinz didn't want to leave any
stone unturned, and they still had a way to go.

Birgitta moved at a painstaking pace. The scent of food filled her
nostrils. She was close to the galley. As she got closer, she could hear
voices and utensils clanking. It sounded like it was dinnertime, and
most of the crew would be inside the chow hall. She backed up, not
wanting to run into any of them. Looking around, she searched for
another route. The corridor branched off right and left. The sounds
and scents of the galley seemed to be coming from the left, so she went
right hoping to find another staircase up to the next level. She tried
reading the directions on the wall, but they were in Russian. No good
to her. Someone whistled a tune, the sound coming closer. She glanced
left, then right. There were three doors. She tried the first. Locked. The
whistler was getting closer. The second door was also locked. Sweat
trickled down her spine between her shoulder blades. The third door
opened, and she gave a quick look before stepping inside and closing it
before the whistler rounded the corner and passed by. It was a supply
closet. She sucked in a deep breath and let it out slowly. Too close for
comfort. She counted to ten, then peeked out the door. The coast was
clear, and she moved fast, taking the corner.

She lucked out when she discovered a back staircase at the end of
the next hall. It was narrow, and darker than the one she was carried
down earlier. Not used as much, but most definitely used if one could

guess by the empty pack of cigarettes wadded up and tossed on the steps. The acrid hint of smoke still lingered. Someone had been here smoking recently. Possibly the whistler, but she couldn't be sure. She climbed the steps, gun at the ready. When she reached the landing, she sent up a silent prayer, then pulled the handle. It squeaked, and she cringed. Slowly, she pulled the heavy metal door open peering through the crack for any movement. Seeing none, she stepped through.

A voice stopped her in her tracks. "Freeze!"

"Put the gun down and turn around with your hands up."

Mahler's heart raced. She thought a mile a minute about how to get out of this. If she put the gun down, she still had the switchblade. She leaned forward and set the gun on the ground using her free hand to reach into her jacket.

"Stop!" The voice startled her. She turned.

"Joseph?" A mountain of hope filled that one word. Her eyes locked on his.

"Birgitta!" Heinz pushed Hammer out of the way, rushing forth to pull her into his arms. He held her tight, whispering words of gratitude into her hair. "Thank God! I thought I'd lost you!"

She pulled back, tears in her eyes, about to respond when he kissed her. Hard. It was brief, powerful, and they were both surprised. When they pulled apart, Lukas cleared his throat.

"Maybe we should save that for later."

Beimer chuckled, muttering, "Elsa nailed it. Can't wait to tell her."

Mahler looked embarrassed, and Heinz's face showed irritation over being observed, and perhaps losing control in front of others. He looked down at his partner whom he still held. "You're okay? He didn't hurt you?"

"Well, he did punch me, but nothing beyond that. Listen, I found documents that implicate him in the trafficking of hundreds of girls."

Joseph fumed. *The bastard hit her!* Murder lit his eyes.

"We know. There are an unknown number onboard now." The anger written all over his face summed up all their feelings.

"How do you know," she asked, still not ready to let him go.

"Koslov confessed. Faust said he turned Elsa loose on him. Can't wait to hear the entirety of that story. But the gist of it is that he's been working for the Bratva, specifically, The Butcher."

"No kidding?" Mahler's eyes grew large.

"No kidding." Heinz reached up and tucked a strand of her loose, curly hair behind her ear. "So where are these documents? We'll need them if we're going to have a chance in hell of indicting Ivchencko."

Birgitta felt her cheeks warm under his regard, and she smiled. "I have them with me." She indicated the seaman's bag over her shoulder.

Heinz smiled. "You're an amazing woman."

Trommler sighed loudly, eyes rolling. Beimer grinned. But Hammer brought them all back to reality. "If you two are finished, there's a dangerous criminal onboard that we need to catch."

Heinz and Mahler looked a bit sheepish but pulled apart. "When I find his 'butler', I'm going to blast several holes in him for punching you," he said.

"You're a little late, Joseph. I already did." Her voice was hollow with suppressed emotion, but her eyes glinted with resolve.

"You took him out?" Hammer asked. She nodded. The commander pressed the button on his mic. "Hammer here. One more down." He added Dutch to the men the aquatic team had already disabled, keeping count so that they could coordinate their attack. Six men on the bridge were also neutralized, so that brought the number of men left on the loose to fifty. The odds were even by number, but heavily in their favor by element of surprise, training, and weaponry.

Hammer once again took lead, and Heinz pushed Mahler behind him. As they moved, he removed his Kevlar vest, insisting she put it on.

"But what about you? You're unprotected," she argued.

"I have these three." He pointed at Hammer, Trommler, and Beimer. "Just do it. I can't stay focused if I'm worrying about your safety," he insisted as she reluctantly took the vest and put it on. It was a little large on her small frame, but Heinz seemed satisfied that she had her vital organs behind a bullet-proof shield.

"Since when did you ever worry about such before," she asked.

He looked her in the eye, cupping her cheeks after cinching the belts on the Kevlar. "Since now. I'd like us to make it out of this alive, woman, so no arguing. We have a lot to talk about later." He kissed her forehead, and then turned, taking her hand to keep her close behind him.

Mahler tried not to grin. It wasn't easy, especially since she realized they were still in the thick of things. But she let her heart be happy for that one moment before switching back into police detective mode.

Heinz tapped Hammer on the shoulder. "I need to get her top-side."

Hammer nodded. "Go back the way we came. The way is clear." He informed the team. "Two coming up. Over and out."

They turned to go, but Mahler stopped. "There's a galley one deck down. Most of the men are in there right now. This door," she indicated the one she'd just come from, "is a back staircase. If you go out to the right, and take the first immediate right, you'll be on track straight ahead to the chow hall. Ivchencko's stateroom is also on that level, south from the three-way split in the corridor, and to the left. Third door down on the left. It's the room with a dead body in it. He wasn't there when I left. I haven't seen him since I arrived."

Hammer relayed that information and thanked her. "Now, take her to the command post. We got this."

⸻◆⸻

Heinz and Mahler stepped off the gangplank and made their way across the dock back to the makeshift post. It was eerily quiet since the remaining SEK had set up a perimeter to keep others out. There were no trucks driving past or cranes lifting large containers on and off the ships. Fog had rolled in during the past hour making it difficult to see more than three feet in front of themselves. The loud reverberation of gunshots sliced through the silence reaching their ears. They both stopped and turned, looking back.

"Do you hear anything?" Mahler asked, looking at his helmet and the com link.

"Nein. We're out of range for the wireless." She heard the frustration in his voice.

"They may need us." Anxiety flecked her words.

"They're highly trained men, Birgitta. Fifty of them, plus Beimer, Trommler, and the two marines."

As they spoke, a figure began to emerge from the fog, but it was too dark, and too hazy to identify him. A shot rang out, and Heinz grunted.

Mahler yelped. "Joseph!"

He slumped against her side, then fell to the ground.

"Back away or you're next." The fog cleared, and Yuri Ivchencko stood pointing a police-issue semi-automatic rifle at her.

"He needs help." She looked at Heinz lying prone on the cold, hard ground, fighting the urge compelling her to go to him. "You can't do this!"

He sneered. "Oh, but I can. You've both cost me quite a bit with your meddling." Two more men stepped out of the fog behind him. One large and tall with a shaved head, and the other, shorter, wiry, and mean-looking. Ivan and Vitaly. Ivan locked eyes on her, an evil grin on his terrifying face.

Mahler kept her body slightly turned, the P-96 still in her hand down at her side.

"I say again, detective, move away! You're only making things worse for yourself."

"I won't." She stood protectively over Heinz.

Ivchencko snorted, anger emanating from his cold eyes. "Ivan, please show the detective that her bravery is merely misplaced stupidity."

Ivan fisted his hands, not even bothering to raise the gun he carried thinking her unarmed. Mahler dropped low quickly, raising her gun, and fired off two rounds into his chest. There was a moment of surprise on his face as he fell forward, dead. Without missing a beat, she sighted right, aiming for Ivchencko before he could shoot, but Vitaly grabbed his boss, pulling him quickly to his left. Her bullet barely missed him. Vitaly aimed and fired, hitting her shoulder. The impact sent her reeling even as the vest saved her.

More shots fired, but this time, they came from behind Ivchencko and Vitaly. Both turned, seeing the agents rushing to Mahler's aid. Cursing, Ivchencko tossed one last, regretful look at Birgitta before fleeing with Vitaly. The fog swallowed them both just as Trommler, Jager, and Kelner arrived.

"Are you all right?" Lukas dropped down at her side.

"I'm okay. It's Joseph. He's been shot. Get help!"

Jager pulled out his walkie. "I need medical transport immediately at my location for an officer down. Gunshot wound." He inspected Heinz, looking for the entry point of the bullet. "Chest, upper right."

He rattled of coordinates, then thrust his two-way at Lukas. "Kelner and I are going after Ivchencko. We'll radio in as soon as we can." They took off in the direction Vitaly and Ivchencko had gone. Within seconds, they could no longer be seen.

Lukas leaned forward over Heinz and pressed down on the wound. Blood continued to leak through his fingers.

"Hold on, Heinz. Help is coming."

Mahler sat up, trying to catch her breath. "Don't you die on me, Joseph Heinz!" She crawled forward and sat on her knees at his side, holding his hand while tears ran down her cheeks.

"Miss me, would you?" Heinz's voice was weak, and his eyes rolled around in their sockets, a direct result of the blood loss and pain. He tried to focus.

"You fool! Of course I would. Now save your strength. Please." She leaned down and kissed his cheek.

"Careful. I might begin to think you love me." Then Heinz passed out.

"Joseph! Joseph!" she screamed.

The wail of a siren signaled the arrival of the ambulance. As they lifted Heinz onto a gurney, more shots rang out in the direction of the ship. The sound of men's voices shouting filled the air. The smell of smoke from gunfire reached them as Mahler jumped into the back to ride with Heinz. Her usually calm, stoic face now reflected anguish and heartbreak.

"I'm going back in." Lukas stood outside the ambulance watching as the medical tech ran an IV. "I'll catch up with you." He closed the back doors and gave the side of the vehicle a tap. The siren wailed as they drove off, heading for the hospital.

He turned and ran back to the Vledelets. Beimer stood on the dock. When he saw Lukas, he met him halfway. "We've secured the ship. Most of the men are locked up in the chow hall now and under guard.

Hammer called in the backup." The sound of large trucks pulling onto the dock met their ears.

"What about the girls," Lukas asked.

"One of the teams is down in the cargo hold now. Just waiting for word. What about Ivchencko?"

"Jager and Kelner are on his heels."

"We should call Heinz and let him know."

Beimer didn't know.

"Ivchencko shot him."

"What? Is he..."

"No. He's not dead, Hugo." Lukas patted him on the back. That's when Beimer saw the blood on his hands.

"Mein Got!" His eyes bulged. "And Mahler? Please tell me she's okay?"

"She's on her way to the hospital with Heinz. She's not seriously injured, but I wouldn't say she's okay.

They stood there, two men who'd seen more in the last twenty-four hours than anyone should ever have to witness. Finally, Lukas said, "You handled yourself very well. Damn good job, Beimer." He extended his hand.

Hugo accepted the gesture, shaking Lukas's hand.

"Thanks. You're not at all what I first thought." He gave Lukas a sideways glance. "You're a good man, Trommler. And you have my blessing to date my partner."

Lukas smirked, then muttered, "As if I needed it." They both grinned.

Truckloads of police officers arrived with prison transport buses ordered to handle the number of men being arrested. It took them two hours to load the prisoners. Once the ship was cleared, the team began the painstaking task of bringing up forty young women from the cargo hold. Another group of trucks arrived along with several emergency medical vehicles to check them out. Most of the girls were taken to a nearby Catholic charity clinic while some were in dire need of a hospital. News crews began showing up and filming the exodus. Police had to tape off the area and push the gathering crowd back. When it was all said and done, everyone was exhausted. But the satisfaction of scoring one for the good guys maintained them throughout.

Lukas and Beimer caught a ride in one of the ambulances to the hospital intending to check on Heinz and Mahler. Jager and Kelner still hadn't checked back in, and Lukas was worried. Still, he trusted in their abilities, and knew they would catch, or at least corner, their quarry. There were still units at the dock, and he made sure to let them know the two marines were out there on Ivchencko's trail. Hammer informed the LKA, and a net was being cast around the city to catch the Russian. For now, they'd done all they could do.

Chapter 17

Elsa awoke to find Faust sprawled out in the chair next to her bed. His head lolled off to one side, and his mouth hung open on a snore. His gray-blond hair stuck out in spikes as if he'd run his hand through it a few times. She checked the clock on the wall. Five-sixteen in the morning. She was exhausted even though she'd slept most of the night. The medication the nurse administered worked well, but it seemed to leave her groggy. She shifted and tried scooting up a bit in bed. The action dislodged something that slid down her pillow onto the sheet. She reached for it, finding a card. She lifted her hand to read it. Printed on it were the initials IE in gold leaf. A logo. Elsa froze.

"Faust, wake up!"

Faust snorted and opened his eyes.

"Wha.."

"Wake up! He's here!" Elsa looked around her room but saw no one.

"Who's here? What are you going on about?" Faust sat up, and he, too, looked around the room.

"Ivchencko!" Fear and anger vibrated in her voice.

"What? Where? Why do you say this?" He rubbed his eyes and looked at her thinking she might be having a nightmare. There was no way Ivchencko could be here.

"This was on my pillow." She handed him the card.

Faust stared at it. He got up quickly and went to the door.

"Stay here." He looked up and down both sides of the hall and then walked to the nurse's station. Nurse Eichmann came out of another room, and seeing Faust, stopped.

"Yes, Herr Direktor, what do you need?" She set the file down that she carried and walked around behind the desk.

"Has anyone been up here asking for Officer Kreiss?" His expression was dead-serious.

"No one asked, but a hospital chaplain stopped by earlier. I told him he'd have to wait until later as she was sleeping."

Alarm bells went off in Faust's head. "What did he look like?"

Eichmann shrugged. "Like a chaplain."

Faust lost his temper. "Damn it, woman! What. Did. He. Look. Like?"

The nurse pulled back, clearly surprised by the vehemence in his tone. "He was tall, gray hair, pale eyes, I think. Slender. Rather quiet."

"Was he alone?"

"Yes. Why?"

"Why do you say he was a chaplain? Did he say so?"

"His I.D. read 'Chaplain'. It was hanging around his neck. And he said he was here to see the young officer brought in yesterday."

"Did you actually look at the I.D.?"

She became flustered. "Well, no. What is the problem?"

"What did he do when you told him he would have to come back? Did he leave?"

"I assume so. I had a patient call. He wasn't here when I got back. What is going on, Herr Direktor?"

"What is going on is the man who tried to kill her left his card on Kreiss's pillow!" He stormed away from the desk and pulled out his mobile. Behind him, nurse Eichmann turned pale, her mouth hanging wide, and she had to sit down before her knees gave out.

He called his officer on the fourth floor, needing to check on the status of Koslov. There was no answer.

"Fuck!" He turned back to the mannish nurse. "Nurse Eichmann, I need you to stand guard outside of Elsa's room until I get back. Do not leave her no matter what, do you understand?"

Eichmann stood, nodding her head. "Good. Is there anyone else working with you tonight?"

"Ja. Nurse Klugman. He's changing out an I.V. in three-twelve."

"Good. Tell Klugman to call hospital security ASAP. I'll have men here within the half hour." He handed her his card. "If that man comes back onto this floor or anyone else asking for Kreiss, you call my cell immediately. Got it?"

"I've got it. And Herr Direktor? I apologize for being so short with you. I wouldn't want anything to happen to Officer Kreiss, and I will protect her." Her eyes were sincere, and her posture alert and ready to fight if necessary.

Faust gave her a brief salute and headed to the lift. He called the station as the door opened. By the time he reached the next floor, he'd ordered a team to sweep the hospital, floor by floor, looking for Ivchencko, and had them issue an all-points bulletin within the city, and beyond. He checked his phone for messages, specifically looking to see if Heinz had called, to see if he'd missed it because he'd fallen asleep. He'd only been awake long enough to walk from the waiting room—where his back cramped from the short couch no normal sized man could stretch out on—to the men's room, and then to Elsa's room where he kept vigil at her bedside... and fell back to sleep. No calls missed. That was odd. He should have heard something by now. He dialed his old friend's number.

The phone rang and then went straight to voicemail as he walked to the psych unit. At their desk, he again asked if anyone tried to get in to see the patient. Again, he heard that a hospital *chaplain* had stopped by. They let him through.

"You did what? What the hell is wrong with you people?" he demanded as he stormed off to Koslov's room. He could see his officer sitting in a chair outside the door.

"Tell me you didn't let the so-called chaplain in?" Faust was on fire. The closer he got, the angrier he became. His officer didn't respond. He didn't even twitch. Faust slowed.

As he reached him, he could see a trickle of blood coming from the officer's mouth. His eyes were wide open, and his body leaned onto the wall giving the illusion from a distance that he was simply reclined. He stepped close and could see a puncture wound just under the right ear. He heard several footsteps come up behind him. Officer Imler and another cop stood looking at their fallen brother.

"Son of a bitch!" Faust took a deep breath and opened the door. Inside, Gregor Koslov hung suspended by his neck from a makeshift rope of tied sheets. The rope had been looped around the visible metal water pipes overhead. His tongue was cut out and pinned to his chest with a knife. His hands, still cuffed to the bed rails, had been yanked tight extending the arms almost to the point of ripping them from the shoulder joints. He turned to Imler. "Stay here and see to this. I have to get back downstairs to Kreiss."

He practically ran to the lift. Inside the elevator, his phone rang. "Faust," he answered, his tone sharp.

"Herr Direktor, it's Hugo Beimer."

"Beimer, where's Heinz?" The floor bell dinged, and the door slid open.

"He's here in Hamburg in surgery."

"What! What happened?" Faust walked out, seeing who he assumed to be nurse Klugman sitting at the desk. He looked down the hall and saw Eichmann standing guard. She nodded at him.

"Heinz was shot by Ivchencko. He got away, him and one of his men. A thug called Vitaly. The two marines, Jager and Kelner, just arrived back an hour ago. They went after them but lost them."

"How serious is it?"

"Not quite sure yet, but the doctor said he didn't think it was life-threatening. That's all we know right now."

"Did you find Mahler?"

"Yes. We got her. She's okay. We also got the ship, and rescued forty young girls that were aboard, caged like animals." Beimer's voice shook.

Faust closed his eyes and sent a prayer heavenward, thankful for that. "You did a fine job, officer. Listen, are your marines there? I need to speak to the one in charge."

"Ja, sure. Hold on." Faust could hear Beimer exchanging words with someone, another male voice.

"Kelner here."

"This is Herman Faust. I'm the local Direktor of the LKA in Berlin."

"Herr Direktor, Heinz spoke highly of you when we met yesterday. What can I do for you, sir?"

"Ivchencko is here in Berlin."

Kelner sucked in a breath. "Say again?"

"He's here. He came into the hospital where we have his man, Koslov, and took him out. He also left our officer Kreiss his calling card."

"Scheisse!" Kelner pulled away from the phone and quickly shared this with Jager, Trommler, Beimer, and Mahler. He came back on the line. "How long ago?"

"No more than an hour."

"He must've left straight for Berlin then. Jager, Trommler, and I are on our way. We should be there in about two and a half hours. Which hospital?"

Faust gave him the name and address. "Good. Now, let me speak with detective Mahler, please. I'll see you soon." Kelner handed over the phone.

"Herman?"

"Mahler. It's good to hear your voice." He sighed, weary to his bones. "I want you to please call me as soon as he's out of surgery."

"I will, I will." She hiccupped and swallowed down the beginnings of a sob.

"He's going to be okay, Birgitta. Joseph is the toughest man I know, and too damn stubborn by half to let one bullet do him in."

"I know. I'm just...just worried."

"Do you need anything? Can I send someone?"

"No. I spoke with Jan earlier, and he wanted to drive up, but I told him to wait. If we can get Joseph stable, we can transport him back to Berlin by medevac."

"Good. Sehr gut."

"You take care of Elsa. If anything happens to her, it would kill Joseph. She's like a daughter to him, you know."

"Yes, I know. She's quite special, that one." He noticed three more of his men stepping out of the lift. They acknowledged him, and then spread out to check the floor. "Don't forget to call me."

"I won't." Mahler hung up, and Faust waited by the desk as his men went room to room.

An hour went by. No Ivchencko. He'd come and gone like a ghost. Their witness was dead, and his killer at large. Faust didn't know what to make of the card. Was it simply to instill fear or was it a direct threat? Either way, he knew that he would have to assign officers to guard Elsa and her brother until Ivchenko was caught. And even then, with his connections, would she ever be safe? How the hell had three missing girls' cases spiraled so far out of control? He turned and headed down to Elsa's room. He needed to let her know what transpired. She was sitting up in her bed gripping her Sig Sauer. She smiled when she saw him and put the gun down.

"Well, I have good news, and I have bad news. Which would you like first?" He leaned on the door. Nurse Eichmann stood behind him, afraid of what he was going to say next.

Elsa bit her lip. "Save the good news until last. Let's have the bad news." She squared her shoulders.

"Ivchencko was, indeed, here. Seems that pretending to be a hospital chaplain makes people forget to do their jobs." He glanced sideways at the nurse who looked down, shame faced. "He killed Koslov, and my officer."

"What! Faust, I'm so sorry!"

"I also don't know if he intended to simply scare you or if his stopping in here and leaving his card was a warning, so we're going to have to put guards on you and your brother until we catch him."

Suddenly alarmed, Elsa's eyes grew wide. "Anno! Oh, scheisse! She grabbed her phone and began dialing home."

"I've sent two officers over already. They should be arriving shortly."

Anno answered, grumbling. Elsa launched into speech. "Anno, are you okay?" The panic in her voice cut through the room. Faust could hear only one side of the conversation. "Good. Listen. There are two officers about to knock on the door. Do not open it until they identify themselves. Use the spyhole for once. They're LKA so no other officers are legitimate. Yes. No. I can't answer that. But don't speak to anyone, I don't care who they say they are." She stopped and looked at Faust. "Should he still come up to the hospital to pick me up?"

"No. Tell him to stay put. I'll escort you home myself."

She relayed the message. "Okay. Love you, too. Yeah, I don't know why this shit keeps happening either. Bye."

She looked at Faust. "Okay, now, please, give me some good news."

"Heinz has been shot—"

"What! How is that good news?" She nearly came off the bed.

"...but he's going to be okay. I think. At least that's what Mahler said. It wasn't life-threatening."

"They found Birgitta?" Her voice rose, caught between being relieved, and anxious.

"Yes. Didn't I say that already?" Faust looked confused.

"No, you did not! Next time, lead with that, thank you." She threw her pillow at him.

"I'm sorry. Yes, they rescued Birgitta, and forty girls who were taken from their homes. We also have the ship. It was Ivchencko and one of his men who got away."

Elsa leaned back, sighing. "Okay, then. Yes, that's very good news. But Joseph. Joseph was shot." A tear slid down her cheek. "When will we know more?"

"When Mahler calls. She promised to do so when he gets out of surgery. They plan to transport him back here once he's stable." He walked over, carrying her pillow, and sat down.

"And what are we going to do about Ivchencko?"

He ran his fingers through his hair, spiking it again. "I've cast the net. We're putting guards on you. That's all we can do right now."

Elsa thought about it. "He's going to be desperate; don't you think?" She looked at him.

"What do you mean?"

"Well, he was supposed to be delivering those girls to St. Petersburg. That's what Koslov said."

"Yes. To the Butcher." Faust steepled his fingers, thinking.

"Now he's lost both the shipment and the ship. And who knows what else he was carrying." She raised an eyebrow, looking at the wall. Her mind was racing. "And by your reaction, I'd say this is a man he wouldn't want to cross, Ja?"

"No. This would not be the man to piss off. He's not called *'The Butcher'* for naught. What are you getting at, Kreiss?"

"I'm thinking that much like my previous career, discretion is the key. The Bratva doesn't like their business known."

Faust started to see where she was going with her thoughts. "So, if we shine a light on Ivchencko's involvement, the bust with the ship, we send him into a panic."

She locked eyes with him. "Exactly. He'll have nowhere to run. He'll be a wanted man not only by German state police, but also by the Bratva. I wonder which he fears more?"

Faust contemplated the danger of a cornered rat. "But it could put many innocent lives in danger." He was thinking of her, Heinz, Mahler, and his own officers.

"Not if we frame it right in the media. It all began from the cases of the missing girls. Feed that to the media. Mention Ivchencko's involvement, but nothing beyond. Don't let on we know the connection to Brezhnev and the Bratva. To avoid being found out, they'll come after their own just like Ivchencko did to Koslov. He'll be desperate, and I'm sure he would consider the LKA the lesser evil. We need to feed a message he'll understand through news stations that he can turn himself in, cut a deal."

Faust smiled. "Kreiss, if this works, we're going to sit down and discuss the next steps in your career."

Chapter 18

"The doctor signed your discharge papers, and I'll have your paper-work ready shortly. You'll need to follow up with him in two weeks." Nurse Eichmann, feeling responsible for putting her patient in danger, stayed on after shift change to follow through with her care. She cast a look at Faust, then dropped her eyes, walking out of the room.

"I feel reasonably sure I don't need to walk on eggshells around her anymore. What do you think?" He sighed and stretched his arms and legs out from where he sat on the chair.

"Perhaps for now. Not sure about any future run-ins." Elsa ran a comb through her hair, then twisted it on top of her head securing it with a rubber band.

"I'll do my best to avoid any. God, I'm tired." And he did look tired. There were dark circles beneath his eyes. More so, worry marred his brow, and it looked as if the weight of the world rested on his burly shoulders.

"Well, you're no spring chicken, Herr Direktor."

He lifted his head. "Maybe it's time you just call me Herman. At least, outside of work. I'd say we've earned being on a first-name basis by now, wouldn't you?" He lifted one bushy eyebrow and smiled.

Elsa chuckled. "Yes, Herman, I think we have."

A knock on the door was followed by Lukas walking in, trailed by Jager and Kelner. He went straight to her bedside leaning down and wrapping his arms around her. "Are you okay?" he whispered into her hair.

Elsa melted into the embrace. The heat from his body radiated into hers. His familiar scent filled her lungs as she breathed in, and she immediately felt safe and secure.

"Yes. I'm okay."

He sat down on the bed next to her, holding her close. "We need to get you out of here. When do you go home?"

"As soon as the nurse brings back my paperwork. She's working on it now."

He kissed her cheek, aware of the others in the room. He nodded at Faust. "Direktor, this is StabsKapitanLeutnant Kristof Jager, and Korvettankapitan Dieter Kelner. Gentleman, Herr Direktor Faust."

Faust stood and shook hands with both men. "Take a walk with me." He indicated the hall. "We'll leave these two love birds alone for a bit." He grinned as he walked out.

"I heard that, Herman," Elsa said. He answered with a backwards wave.

The room was suddenly quiet, and she was fully aware of the man next to her. Elsa looked at Lukas. He was still wearing the clothing she saw him in yesterday when he'd rescued her. He still had a weapon holstered at his back. His hair was mussed, and he had five-o-clock shadow growing along his usually clean-cut jaw. He smelled of gunpowder and man. It was sexy as hell.

He smiled at her extensive regard. "What are you staring at, Officer Kreiss?"

"A very sexy man, Herr Trommler."

"Hmm. I could say the same."

"I'm a sexy man too?" she asked, feigning innocence.

He laughed. "The sexiest!" He gazed at her face, devoid of makeup, and her hair piled loosely atop her head. She wasn't wearing a fancy dress, but rather, police academy sweats. He'd have to ask about that later. Still, he'd never seen a more beautiful woman.

The world ceased to exist when he looked at her like that. Elsa forgot to breathe, and he took advantage, capturing her lips in a scintillating kiss. He took his time, going slow, being gentle and not wanting to hurt her or her tender skin. He kept his hands on her face, caressing her cheeks and neck. When his tongue swept inside, he tasted her, kissing her as if it were the first time, and he was thorough. She felt warm all over, all gooey inside. It was wonderful.

He pulled back and trailed hot kisses to her ear. "When you're better, we'll continue this. But for now, we should probably stop."

Elsa pouted playfully. "No, I don't want to." She smiled, resting her head on his.

"Insatiable woman." He lifted her hand and kissed her palm. "I can't chase bad guys down with a hard-on. Have a little mercy on me, sweetheart."

Elsa opened her eyes and glanced down. Sure enough, his zipper strained. "Just this one time. And only because the situation is dire." She stretched her neck, peering back at him.

"Elsa the merciful. I bow to you, your highness." He dropped another kiss on her forehead.

"How was Joseph when you left?"

Lukas sighed. "Still in surgery. He's going to be okay. The bullet hit on the upper right side of his chest."

"How did that happen?" She snuggled into his side.

"Visibility was low. The fog had rolled in. Ivchencko was able to get off the ship by a different route than the one we used to get onboard. Mahler said he shot Heinz before they even knew it was him. She took out one of his men. Actually, she took out two. She killed the butler as well."

"Dutch?"

"Ja. I don't think she's ever killed before. She seems to be handling it all right though, but once Heinz is out of the woods, she might experience some problems dealing with that with nothing else to distract her."

Elsa chewed her thumbnail. It was something she did when she was lost in thought.

"Oh, and before Beimer can tell you, you were right."

"About what?"

"Heinz and Mahler. He's just dying to tell you, but I'm beating him to it."

"What happened?" Her eyes lit up.

"Oh, you know, they kissed, that's all." He waited to see her reaction.

"What! He kissed her?" She grinned. "I knew it! Finally!"

"Yep. I'd say he's got it bad for her, too. He did seem a little surprised by it, but she didn't."

"Well, she's been in love with him for some time now." Elsa resumed snuggling Lukas. "So, Heinz is in love."

"Looks like."

The nurse walked in and stopped short, staring at Lukas.

"Oh! Forgive me." She looked at Elsa. "I have your paperwork. You can go home now. Just remember to take it easy and stay off your leg for the next six weeks." Another nurse came in carrying a pair of crutches, handing them off to Eichmann. "And you'll use these. Come, stand up so I can make sure they're adjusted to your height."

Lukas got up and helped Elsa to her feet. She balanced on her good leg and leaned on his arm while the nurse made adjustments. In minutes, she was using them, taking a few steps to get the hang of it.

"There's a prescription for pain meds. Make sure to get it filled and follow the directions on the bottle. Oh, and the doctor's office number is on the paper. Call to make your follow up appointment."

"So, I can go now?" Elsa was ready to leave this place.

"Yes, but let me get a wheelchair. Hospital policy." Nurse Eichmann went out into the hall and came back with a chair.

Lukas helped her get settled as Faust came back in.

"We're ready?" he asked.

"Yes, Herman. Very ready." Elsa held her bag that contained her weapon, shoes, and cellphone. She placed it in her lap and held her crutches.

"I'll go get the car and meet you downstairs." He left, leaving Jager and Kelner behind with her and Lukas. The nurse pushed her out, taking her all the way down to the first floor, and out the front door.

Lukas rode with Faust and Elsa. Jager and Kelner left in their own vehicle heading off back to base. On the ride home, Faust filled them in on the plan. By the time they reached Köthener Straße, everyone was up to date. Faust parked as close to her building's front entrance as possible.

"By the way, Mahler called. Heinz is out of surgery and doing well. They got the bullet out without any complications. Apparently, he's sitting up in bed and demanding bratwurst. We've arranged for a medevac to bring him back in the morning."

Elsa stood on her crutches and looked at Faust. "Again, Herman, lead with that! You could have said so the whole ride home."

He chuckled and reached in to grab her bag. She looked at the distance from the car to the building entrance. It never looked so long before. Lukas put a hand up.

"Wait." He handed one of the crutches to Faust, reached down and lifted her in his arms, and let the man take the other crutch. Then he proceeded to carry his woman all the way inside, up the elevator to the fourth floor, and down the hall to her flat where her brother waited, guarded by two LKA officers standing outside the door.

She beamed at him as he sat her down on her couch. "When I'm one hundred percent again, you're going to be rewarded big time, mister," she whispered in his ear.

"I'll hold you to that."

Anno sat next to her and threw his arm around his sister. They held each other close, her brother fighting back the tears that threatened to fall.

He finally sat back and looked at her. "For fuck's sake, Elsa, please tell me what's going on!"

And she did, or as much of it as she was at liberty to say. Faust stayed long enough to corroborate the information, and warn Anno to stay in the house, and not go out without police escort until they caught Ivchencko. Introductions were made, and her brother and boyfriend became fast friends, playing Xbox while Elsa rested. Faust left after filling her prescription at the pharmacy, promising to return the next day.

"As soon as Heinz is back, we're all going to get into one room, and put this plan into action. Pray it works or we're fucked."

━━━━━━━◄O►━━━━━━━

That evening, Taggesschau News reported the rescue of forty kidnapped women from sex-traffickers discovered operating out of Hamburg. The reporter stated that the SEK, in cooperation with the LKA, and working off a tip, captured the ship containing the women who were locked in cages, bound for parts unknown.

"And now, the LKA is working with the owner of that ship, Yuri Ivchencko of Ivchencko Enterprises, to ferret out those responsible. At this time, it is believed that the men captured on the ship acted independently and are connected with a larger operation outside of Germany."

In a small flat on the outskirts of Berlin, Yuri Ivchencko sat sipping bad coffee at an old kitchen table that had seen better days. He watched the small television screen while Vitaly dragged the body of the man who lived there into the bathroom where he lifted, pushed, and kicked him into the tub. The man didn't protest. He was dead, after all. His swollen tongue protruded from his mouth, and his face was blue—a direct result of being choked to death.

"We won't be able to stay here longer than a day. He's going to get ripe," Vitaly said as he walked back out into the kitchen.

"Yes. But we have bigger problems now." He sat the chipped China cup down and pointed at the TV.

"Brezhnev will understand—" he began.

"No! He will not. Nor would I if it were me in his place. If we stay here, our days are numbered." He went quiet, thinking. "We need to get to Switzerland. From there, I can transfer funds to an account I keep on Île de Ré."

"Where the hell is that?"

"It's an island off the west coast of France." He turned his cold, gray eyes on his henchman. "You'll like it there, Vitaly. Lots of sunshine. Lots of tourists, and most of them are women."

"I like it already." He smiled showing a few gaps where teeth were missing. "So, when do we leave?"

"As soon as I take care of Trommler and the redheaded bitch. They've brought me nothing but problems."

"I don't think that's a good idea. This fiasco is on the news. It won't take any time at all for it to reach Brezhnev's ear."

"I don't care!" Ivchencko stood looking down at Vitaly. "In case you hadn't noticed, it was Trommler who came after us along with the police. He lied, misrepresenting himself. He also sent that filthy animal into my house." He began to pace. "He brought that Schupo into all of this, too. All of which led to this moment, and I don't forgive such betrayals. No. We will tie up loose ends, then leave. I need you to stake out Trommler's home. Follow him and find Elsa. He'll be sticking close to her now."

Vitaly kept a straight face, but inside, he cringed. His boss was a strange one, couldn't see the flaws in his own theories. He took things personally that weren't personal at all, and he would lead them into danger by pursuing this small revenge. Vitaly was a criminal through and through, his heart black, but even he would've let this one go. However, he was loyal to Ivchencko. The man took him in straight out of prison, and gave him a job on his ship, the first and most beloved of his fleet. He was paid well, protected, and got to do the things he loved, like steal, fight, and murder; all with impunity. Up until this moment, his life had been uncomplicated. He would not bitch or whine. It was not his way. No, he would do as he was told. That's what a soldier did. He followed orders. If Ivchencko wanted Trommler and the redhead dead, then so be it. He would handle it, and then they would flee to Switzerland, and then south to France.

"Consider it done, boss." He grabbed a coat from the closet, and pulled on a tweed cap.

"When you find them, come back. I want to do this one myself."

Vitaly paused, then nodded, but once he was outside, he shook his head. Considering his boss's phobia for getting his hands dirty, this threw a monkey wrench into him quickly and quietly killing those two. He feared that the Butcher would find them before Ivchencko had time to carry out his revenge. If time got short, would the LKA protect them if they copped a deal? He didn't want to go back to prison, but if that had to happen, a German prison was surely better than a Russian gulag. But would his boss go for that? Probably not. He'd never been incarcerated to date, and his privileged lifestyle was proof enough he couldn't deal with being confined. He might find that he was well and truly on his own. He could go to Brezhnev himself. The Butcher valued loyalty above all else. That was another possibility, throw his lot in with the brotherhood, and hand over Ivchencko. Vitaly had a lot to think about and very little time. He pulled his collar up to ward off the cold as he walked to the nearest tube station. He would have to make a decision by the time he returned.

Standing in a shower on one leg was not easy. Elsa tried leaning against the tile, but it was slippery. All she wanted to do was shampoo her hair, bathe, and then put on clean pajamas.

"Are you okay?" Lukas called through the door. He'd offered to help, but she insisted she could do it herself.

Elsa hated to admit she wasn't faring well. She blew out a breath and cursed as the shampoo bottle slipped through her fingers landing on the floor. "Scheisse!"

Lukas, hearing the crash and her expletive, immediately came into the bathroom.

"What happened?" He waited, not wanting to invade her privacy by pulling back the curtain.

"Nothing. I just dropped the shampoo." She tried balancing while bending over to grab it. His hand slipped under the curtain and found the bottle, holding it up for her while he stayed on the outside. She smiled, taking it.

"Okay now?" he asked.

"Maybe not quite so okay." She needed help. Her knee hurt, and her skin still felt tight.

Lukas crossed his arms over his chest and leaned on the wall, a grin tugging at the corners of his lips. "Is that your way of asking for my assistance?"

She poked her head out from behind the curtain and looked at him. "It might be." She looked down, suddenly self-conscious. "But I don't want you to see me like this. My skin..."

He reached out and touched her face. "Is beautiful. You're beautiful. Nothing is going to make me think otherwise."

Elsa chewed her lower lip. "Do you think you could shampoo my hair?" Her voice was soft, unsure. It was so completely opposite the confident, tough woman he knew her to be, and it endeared her to him more than he could say.

In answer, he began tugging his shirt over his head. Then he unbuckled and pulled off his pants and underwear. Kicking them to the corner, he stepped into the shower behind her and took the shampoo bottle from her hand. While she steadied herself with her hands on the wall, he lathered her hair, gently massaging her scalp with strong fingers.

"That feels nice." She leaned her head back, letting him rinse the soap thoroughly before he worked the conditioner through her silky strands.

Lukas smiled. He loved the feel of her soft, red hair slipping through his hands. He was enjoying himself until he glanced down and caught sight of the angry, red welts on her sides and front. The doctor told her they would heal, but she might be scarred for life. Eventually, they would be thin, white lines, barely visible, but she would have a constant reminder of being tied up and tortured. As for his own feelings on the subject, he knew that if he got the chance to be in a room with Ivchencko, he'd kill him.

"How about the rest of you?" He left her hair piled on top of her head to soak.

She glanced over her shoulder. "Gently." Her eyes contained hesitancy, fear of the pain from being touched, and also a hint of seduction.

Lukas knew he would do everything in his power not to hurt her. He grabbed the soap and used his hands to first clean all uninjured areas of her skin. He started with her feet, giving them a gentle rub, even between each toe. She giggled. Then he worked up her shapely calves, caressing her good knee, and barely skimming the injured one. The front of her thighs had welts, so he avoided that part and moved to her backside, which was untouched by the whip. He allowed himself the pleasure of running his soapy hands freely over the back of her thighs, her lovely ass, and up her back to her shoulders. She purred.

That sound resonated all throughout his body causing no end of havoc. His erection rose, prodding her. He tried to maintain a little distance. After all, she was barely able to stand, and they had company out in the living room by way of her brother and two officers. Elsa arched her back bringing her rounded bottom up against his throbbing hardness.

"Elsa, don't. I don't want to hurt you," he whispered in her ear.

"Then we'll be careful." She turned her head and kissed him. He kissed her back awkwardly as there was nowhere he could put his hands without causing her pain. Standing behind her, he could only touch her arms. But there was one other spot in front, down low that was unblemished by the whip. She placed his hand there, and when his fingers slid between her thighs, she melted.

Slowly, carefully, he worked her, rubbing softly. She pressed her back against his chest seeking closer contact.

"Lukas, please."

He wouldn't tease her tonight. She'd been through too much. He moved to enter her, holding her up under one arm, and by his own hand pleasuring her from the front. She was hot and slick as he slid in inch by inch. They were surrounded by steam and the scents of soap and her conditioner. It was like a scene out of one of his fantasies. Any sound would echo in the small bathroom, and it was an exercise in discipline to be inside her and not be able to verbalize the sheer ecstasy of it. Elsa leaned slightly forward onto her hands, supporting her weight as she pushed back and down onto him. His thrusts increased and his fingers kept time on her sensitive nub. She was close, so close. Her stomach muscles tightened, then everything exploded. The spasms felt so damn good. Only a moment after she orgasmed, Lukas tensed and came inside her.

Elsa straightened, feeling him slip out. She turned, and the look in his eyes before he kissed her senseless took her breath away.

He pulled back and held her chin. "You are the most beautiful, incredible woman I've ever known."

She didn't know what to say, so she simply kissed him, putting all her feelings into it.

Smiling like fools, he rinsed her hair, and ran the soap back over a few parts again, including his own body. He helped her out of the shower, wrapped her in a towel, lifted her up, and carried her to the chair in her room. He dried himself off and quickly dressed. By the time he walked back into her room, she was wearing an old Oktoberfest T-shirt and a pair of shorts. He grabbed a comb off the dresser and settled in next to her, combing her hair.

"Lukas Trommler, you are a very good boyfriend."

"I am, aren't I? Who knew?"

Anno called out from the living room. "Hey! What's taking so long? Is Elsa all right? Does she need anything?"

Lukas laughed. "She just needed a little help."

"I'm fine, Anno," she yelled. To Lukas, she asked, "What's he doing out there, anyway?"

"He's playing World of Warcraft with one of the officers."

"Some guards." She shook her head.

"They're all right. You need to put the steroid cream on those welts. Want me to do it?"

She looked down at herself. "No, I can do it."

He handed her the tube. "It's about time for your pain medication, too. I'll get that while you do this." He got up.

Elsa eyed him. "Not sure I need any. I think you already took care of my pain, Doctor Trommler." She grinned.

"Anytime you need an injection, madam, I'm here." He winked, and walked out to the kitchen, chuckling.

Chapter 19

Heinz arrived back in Berlin by lunch. With his shoulder bandaged and his arm in a sling, he was released home after a nurse checked his wound. Mahler stayed by his side, making sure he got home safely. She left him long enough to go home and pack a few things. Heinz didn't get a chance to object. She'd appointed herself his personal nurse. Who was he to argue?

Faust showed up before she returned, ringing the doorbell. Heinz struggled to rise off the couch and answer.

"Good. You're alive."

"Is that your way of saying you were worried about me?" He backed away from the door and walked cautiously to the sofa.

Faust closed the door and followed. "No. This is." He sat down and looked at his friend. "I'm sorry, Joseph. I didn't mean to drag you back into all this and put you in danger."

Heinz sighed. "Well, now I'm one up on you as you've never been shot before."

Faust grunted. "Not sure that's a race I'm willing to pursue. How'd it feel, by the way?"

Heinz's eyebrows shot up. "How do you think? It hurt like hell!"

"Yes, well." He looked around. "Where's Mahler?"

His irritation faded and a small smile appeared on Heinz's otherwise grumpy countenance. "She went home to grab some things. She's insisting on staying here while I recover."

A look of mock surprise lit Faust's blue eyes. "Is that so? Hmm, it seems at least one good thing came out of this then. And it's about time, too."

"What do you mean?"

"Joseph, it's been obvious for a while."

"What's obvious?"

"That you two—"

Mahler walked in.

"Herman, are you bugging my patient already?" She dropped a large bag on the floor next to her purse.

"Forgive me, detective, but time is not our friend right now. I've invited Kreiss and Trommler over as well as Jager and Kelner."

"I know. I saw them pulling up as I walked in." She came around and sat down next to Heinz. The look Faust threw at Joseph read, "*See?*" He returned his attention to Mahler. "Beimer should be arriving shortly." He checked his watch. "We have much to go over. A lot happened overnight, and Elsa came up with a good plan."

This surprised Heinz. "My Elsa? Really?"

Mahler elbowed him. "Why are you so shocked? She's a sharp young woman."

"Yes, she is. I guess I can take a little credit for that," said Heinz. "She's had the benefit of my wisdom for the past three years." He leaned away before Birgitta could swipe him.

'Oh, Joseph. Honestly!" She got up as the doorbell chimed.

Elsa and Lukas came in. Elsa stopped and hugged Birgitta. "I'm so happy to see you!" The two women fought back tears.

Behind them, Jager, Kelner, and Hugo waited, uncomfortable with all the female emotion. Finally, everyone got through the door, shook hands or hugged, grateful to be together again.

Once they were all settled, and Mahler passed around bottled water and cokes, Faust spoke.

"Last night, Ivchencko snuck into the hospital and killed Koslov. I'm sure he could've easily done the same to our Elsa, but he left his card instead."

"What! Why am I only hearing this now?" Heinz sat forward, alarmed.

"Because, Joseph, you were in surgery, and then recovery. And then we had to wait for you to arrive back home. Believe me, this is the earliest I could inform you." Faust stated the facts.

He took a deep breath to calm himself. "Proceed, Herr Direktor." Sarcasm dripped from his words. Mahler reached out and took his hand.

"As I was saying, Ivchencko could have done far more damage, but he chose not to, at least for now. We're not sure if he meant to intimidate or threaten. And so far, we've heard nothing of him trying to get out of Berlin or the country. I would bet my last euro he's still here. As Elsa said, he's going to be desperate. He lost the shipment of girls. He lost the ship, and the cargo, which, by the way, contained nearly two thousand kilos of raw heroin." Whistles sounded around the living room. "The Butcher is not going to just let that slide. So, we're manipulating Ivchencko into coming in, and making it impossible for him to go anywhere without being discovered. And that plan began yesterday evening with a very carefully worded exclusive news report to the Taggesschau." Faust went on to explain the rest, taking questions from the marines and providing as much information as he could.

An hour later, he said, "And it has to work. If not, we'll all be on the Butcher's shit list."

———◄O►———

After everyone left, Birgitta picked up her bag and went to sit on the floor by Heinz. He was lying on the couch now that they were alone. Dark circles stood out under his brown eyes. He looked tired.

"Can I get you anything?" she asked.

"No. I just want to lay here and enjoy a few moments of peace and quiet with you." He reached his hand out, and she took it.

"We didn't tell Herman about the files and ledger." Her soft voice trailed off.

He stared at the ceiling. "No, we didn't." He turned to look at her. "I'm not sure I like this plan. It could go wrong so easily. If it does, we're all in danger. But those files and that ledger, they're leverage. Let's just keep it to ourselves for now." He tugged her hand, pulling her closer.

She came up on her knees at his side, smiling. "You need something?" Her question, benign.

"Yes. I need something." He snaked his hand behind her neck and pulled her down for a slow, sexy kiss.

Birgitta's heart pounded. For nearly five years, she'd dreamed of this moment, and now it was here, and she was nervous, like a schoolgirl all over again.

He pulled back, staring at her face. "Birgitta..."

She loved hearing his deep voice say her name. "Yes, Joseph?"

"Let your hair down."

Of all the things he could've said, she didn't expect that. She smiled, reaching up and pulling out the pins. Her hair tumbled down around her shoulders in glossy black curls. The scent of her shampoo surrounded him, and he breathed it in.

"You're so beautiful." He kissed her again until neither of them could breathe properly. "So, detective...would you go out on a date with this old man?" His easy smile, so rare, warmed her.

She dropped a quick kiss on his lips. "I'll think about it." She pulled away.

"Where are you going? Come back here. I need my nurse." He started to sit up and come after her.

She dropped down by the bag and pulled out the files and ledger. "We should really go through these. There may be vital information we could use."

"Now?" He looked at the files, disgusted by the idea.

"Yes, Joseph, now. Like Faust said, time isn't our friend."

"All right, all right. But only if you promise to keep your hair like that." He reached out to twirl a lock around his finger.

She grinned as she opened the first file and handed it to him. "If it makes you happy."

"It does. You do." They began to inspect the material, perfectly in sync with each other.

Lukas stopped by his place on the way home to pick up a few things. He knew he'd be staying with Elsa until this situation was resolved. "Wait here. I'll be quick." He left her in the car with the engine running as he ran upstairs to grab some clothes and personal items.

She was listening to music when a knock on the window made her jump. She looked up and fought a scream. The short, wiry man stood waiting. She could see the tattoos on his hands. *Vitaly?* She glanced around for her purse. Spotting it, she made a grab for it fumbling to open the flap and pull out her gun when he busted the window and gripped her wrist.

"I wouldn't do that if I were you, officer. Now sit still and listen!" His fetid breath blasted her as her heart pounded.

"Get your hands off me!" She tried to break his hold.

"Damn it, woman! Stay still!" He grabbed her other wrist and leaned in close. "I'm not here to hurt you. If you want Ivchencko, then shut up and hear me out."

Elsa stilled. "Say your peace," she spat, her expression clearly furious.

"Yuri is on the outskirts of town at 115 Weide Strasse. He won't be there after tonight, so if you and your cop friends want him, act fast."

"Why are you telling me this? He's your boss, Ja?"

"I'm not willing to die over his petty vengeance. He wants you badly. And your boyfriend, too."

"What? Is he still pissed at Lukas? For what?"

"He's an odd duck. Not right in the head. This is your chance. I won't be there, and don't come looking for me. I have nothing against you, but if you come for me, I'll have no other recourse than to kill you. Verstehen?"

Elsa nodded, and he let her go, walking away before she could get her Sig out. She was covered in glass when Lukas came back down to the garage.

"What the fuck happened?" He came around to her side, pulling her out, and slapping glass shards off her clothing.

"We have to call Faust right now. That was Vitaly. He told me where we can find Ivchencko."

"What? Why would he do that?"

"I think he's disillusioned with his boss. Says he's not willing to die, all because he wants revenge on you and me."

"Why the hell is he pissed at me?"

"You sent Imani Bishop into his home. Apparently, he has a real problem with black people."

"But that's absurd!"

"I know, but Vitaly said Ivchencko isn't right in the head." She made air quotes around that last phrase.

He looked at her busted out Peugeot. "Well, we'll take my car." He seemed happier about that and unlocked his Mercedes. Once he helped her in, and slid her crutches into the backseat, she dialed Faust.

He answered on the third ring.

"Herman? Elsa. Change of plan. I know where Ivchencko is hiding." She relayed the story and then sat through his speech about her not being careful enough. When he'd exhausted his ire, he ordered them both to go straight back to her place where he would meet them. He had calls to make to the tactical team first.

The ride back was quiet. Elsa's mind was racing. If they let this play out, Ivchencko would be arrested. This might sound good at the outset, but with his wealth and connections, he would escape justice. He'd tortured her, tortured countless numbers of other young women, and sold them into bondage. He also shot Joseph nearly taking yet another person from her that she cared about. Vitaly said he was also intent on killing Lukas, not to mention herself. This man couldn't be allowed to run free and hurt anyone else. What if he came after Anno? The idea of any of them being harmed made her heart break and her blood boil. No. Arrest was too good for him.

"What are you thinking about over there?" Lukas cast a sideways glance at her. She was chewing her thumbnail again. A sure sign her mind was at work.

"Nothing. I'm just worried is all."

He took her hand. "Don't. I'm here. And I'm not going to leave your side again. I'm so sorry that I did." He looked at the road, mentally beating himself up for leaving her in the car, thinking she would be safe. It was thoughtless and amateur. He knew better.

She squeezed his fingers gently. "It's okay. I'm okay."

Lukas sighed. "It's not. But it will be, I promise."

When they arrived home, Elsa excused herself, going to the restroom. She needed a moment alone, even away from Lukas. He paced the living room, trying to field the questions flying out of Anno's mouth. He was relieved when Faust finally arrived. While they waited for Jager and Kelner, he explained the new plan. Elsa was to remain behind with her brother and the two guards. Heinz was out because of his injury. Mahler insisted on being a part of it against Joseph's wishes, but with the SEK set to storm the flat in two hours, she would be stationed behind the lines while they did the dirty work. Hugo wanted desperately to go along, but Faust circumvented that request by going through his captain who assigned him to guard Heinz. The marines were liaisons to the unit on call in the event Ivchencko got away. They could travel over international lines with the surrounding countries and pursue. With all possible scenarios covered, Faust gave the go ahead. Everyone had their part to play.

<hr />

Heinz fumed a little. He didn't like Birgitta going on this bust, but she wouldn't listen to him. He sat in the living room with Hugo who damn near pouted about not being included.

"Believe me, Beimer, if I could bring her back, I'd send you in her place."

"I'm not complaining, Kommissar. It's an honor to be looking out for you."

"I'm surprised you said that with a straight face." Heinz ran a hand through his hair. Hugo blushed, knowing he hadn't sounded sincere when he said it, although he very much respected Heinz.

With nothing else to do, Heinz put down the stack of files and picked up the ledger. He began going over the names on the first page. The book was thick, and the dates indicated it contained more than ten years of entries. This would take a while.

Epilogue

Elsa was smiling like a fool as she patrolled the Tiergarten with Beimer. It was a beautiful spring day, cool outside, but not cold. Bright green leaves dotted tree branches, and tulips and irises bloomed. It was almost Easter, and in two weeks, she would begin the next level of training thanks to Direktor Herman Faust. She'd been put on the fast track to the LKA. It would take many years of hard work and classes, but her career was set. Hugo also made an impression during the Ivchencko affair that got him noticed by the SEK. He would begin his own training next month. Even better, he'd proposed to Sigrid, and they were planning a fall wedding.

Her relationship with Lukas deepened. She'd made the colossal step to moving in with him and leaving the flat to Anno. He was now nineteen, and still in college. Grown. She continued to pay the rent, but the deal meant he had to keep his grades up and stay on course for graduation. It also meant he had to work part time to afford his own things. Growing up always came at a cost, but she was proud of her brother.

She was proud, also, of Lukas who gave him that part-time job making deliveries for the gallery. After her knee healed, she'd rewarded him many times over. Theirs was a very passionate relationship. Thankfully, her scars healed down to barely visible white lines. The less severe lashes disappeared completely, which was great. But it was the news she received that morning that had her feeling on top of the world.

Birgitta called her early. She'd barely arrived at work to clock in when her phone rang. "What's wrong," was Elsa's first response due to the hour.

"What? Is that how you answer your phone?" She laughed.

"Well, it's early. Okay, then, hallo! And what can I do for you today, Detective Mahler?" Elsa popped some coins into the vending machine, seeking coffee.

"Well, dearest girl, you can agree to be my maid of honor." She let that hang.

Elsa stopped. Then she jumped up and down, squealing. Beimer thought she was having an epileptic fit.

"Are you serious? He proposed?" She couldn't stop smiling, and she kept hitting Hugo on the arm.

"What are you going on about? Stop that!" He pulled away.

"Heinz proposed to Mahler! They're getting married!"

Hugo grinned. "Well, it's about time, don't you think? They're old, after all."

Birgitta yelled through the phone. "I heard that, Hugo!"

He laughed, then leaned over the speaker and said, "Congratulations, Birgitta."

Elsa immediately agreed. "Of course I'll be your maid of honor. We have so much to plan! I can't wait. I'll come by after shift, okay?"

"Yes, that's perfect. Bring Anno. Joseph would like us all to go have a family celebration dinner."

"Okay. See you then." She ended the call.

Her day had been glorious since. She and Hugo discussed their relationships, his upcoming wedding, and now Heinz and Mahler's wedding. The morning flew by. As they made another circuit around the park, a dark sedan pulled up, keeping pace with them. Hugo finally noticed, and he put a hand on Elsa's arm. She turned to look, seeing the car. It stopped.

The door opened, and a tall man with a dark, short beard stepped out. He adjusted the lapels on his tailored suit. His clothes said *money*, but the hardness around his eyes, and the tattoos visible on his fingers said *criminal*. He approached.

"Officer Elsa Kreiss?"

She noted the Russian accent in his deep voice. "Yes." She was on red alert. Beimer stood just in front of her, hand ready at his holster. It didn't seem to faze the man at all. He didn't even look Beimer's way.

He reached into his jacket. Hugo unlatched the strap and gripped the handle. The man pulled out a white envelope.

"This is for you." He extended his hand, and Hugo took the envelope, passing it back to her without taking his eyes off the Russian.

The man turned and got back into the car. It drove off, disappearing in traffic. Hugo exhaled, and relaxed a little, still rattled. Elsa looked down and saw her name written in a flourish on the outside. She ripped it open, and found a letter addressed to her.

Dearest Officer Kreiss, your assistance was appreciated. If you ever need a favor, find me. I am at your disposal. V. Brezhnev, a.k.a., The Butcher.

"Well? What does it say?" Hugo asked, trying to see as she folded it quickly and stuffed it into her pocket.

"It's nothing, Hugo. Nothing." She resumed walking.

"It's not 'nothing'. Come on, Kreiss. After all we've been through?" He followed at her heels.

"That's exactly why it's 'nothing'. It's better left buried. Trust me. We're all going to be okay."

He wasn't satisfied with her answer, but he also knew she was stubborn as a mule, and unless she wanted to tell him, he would not hear it otherwise.

Elsa knew he was mad, so sought to get them back to the easy mood before the Russian showed up. "Don't pout, Hugo. Your face will freeze like that." She elbowed his side in a good-natured fashion. "Tell me, where will you and Sigrid go on your honeymoon?"

The mention of his beloved's name never failed to make him smile. He let her have her secret, then launched into a list of places the happy couple had discussed visiting. For now, all was right in their world.

Sneak Peek

Prologue

Leningrad, USSR

July 8, 1969

The ice cream melted down his small hand, dripping onto his best shoes. The leather was scuffed, and the brown laces were becoming tattered on the ends, but they were still considered new despite the wear. It was summertime in Leningrad, and the day was hot and humid. The breeze coming in off the Baltic did little to cool the stifling heat, and the clouds gathering overhead were a clear indication that rain was imminent. It would ruin the party if they didn't let him open all the pretty packages soon.

"Vladi, come! It's time to open your presents." The little towheaded boy turned away from staring at the clouds and ran back to his mother's arms. She stood by a table set on the front lawn of the tenement building where they shared a flat with his uncle Pavo's family. Kommunalkas, or communal apartments, were common in the distressed neighborhoods throughout this major port city of the USSR. The Soviets called it good economic policy. All low-income families had a free apartment, but the people knew what it was really all about, keeping the poor corralled, so that the aristocratic and privileged military families that ran the government and the major businesses could snatch up prime real estate for luxury condominiums. The market for property was booming in the northern region while the urban ghettos were ripe with poverty, crime, and suffering. But at the tender age of six, young Vladimir Alexei Brezhnev knew only that he had a table full of brightly wrapped presents to open. His friends were herded in from their playtime to come and watch him. He was about to rip the paper off the first one when his father noticed the ice cream on his shoe.

He grabbed the boy's arm.

"What's this," his finger pointing down.

Vladimir looked, noticing for the first time the mess on his foot. He shrugged. "I don't know, papa."

"You don't know!" His father's anger, always lurking beneath the surface, exploded. "This is how you care for the nice things I buy you with the money I work so hard for?" He shook the boy.

"Kirill, please!" His mother, Olga, pleaded as she ran over and bent down, quickly wiping the sticky sweet cream from the shoe. "There, see? It's all fine. No harm." She remained on her knees trying to gently pry her husband's fingers from Vladimir's arm.

"Of course there is harm, woman!" He shook her off, his expression fierce. "The boy must learn to respect me, and to respect the things we provide for him. You cannot baby him anymore. He's six years old. Unless he is retarded, he understands that he is to take care of his belongings." Kirill turned his attention back to his son. "Are you retarded, Vladimir?"

The boy looked around at his cousins, his uncle who stood with his eyes averted, his aunt Ava who gathered her youngest to her side, and his friends from the apartment building, some of whom were laughing at his predicament. He looked back toward his father, keeping his eyes lowered and staring at the whiskers on his scarred chin. "No, sir."

"You like your shoes?" The tone in his papa's voice was deceptively soft.

"Yes, papa. I like my shoes very much." Vladimir's lip began to quiver. He knew his father's outbursts never ended well.

"You want to keep your shoes?"

"Yes, papa."

"Kirill, please, it's his birthday—" Olga began.

"Shut up!" He looked back at the boy. "I think you need to learn a lesson, a man's lesson. You wish to be a man, yes, Vladimir?"

Tears ran down the boy's cheeks now. He sniffled. "Yes, papa."

"Good. This is good. I'm going to teach you to respect me, and to respect what you own. You know how I am going to do this?" His son shook his head in the negative. "You are six now. Six is an age where you must start becoming a man. No more clinging to your mother's apron. So, Vladimir," his father put his arm around his small shoulders and turned him toward the crowd of children watching. "You're going to give away all of your presents to these children."

Vladimir gasped. "But papa—"

"No *'but papa,'* Vladimir! You will stand here and pass these gifts out to your friends, and you will thank them for coming to your party. When you are finished, you will go to your room and clean it. I expect it to be spotless when I come up and inspect." The look in his dark, brown eyes said, *'or else'*.

Vladi wiped the tears blinding his blue eyes. Sobs wracked his small body as one by one, he handed out all seven of his gifts to the children who lived in the building. His uncle would not let any of his own children step forward. The look of shame in his eyes, and the tears escaping from his aunt and mother became too much to bear. Finally, the last package left his hands.

"Tha-thank you for coming to my pa-party," he hiccupped. With that, he ran inside and up the four flights of stairs to the small flat with three rooms. No one else was inside, and little Vladimir Alexei Brezhnev slammed the door of the tiny space he shared with his older brother, Nikolay, and cousin, Oleg. He threw himself down on the cot and cried.

———————◆◇◆———————

St. Petersburg, Russia (Modern day Leningrad)
  July 8, 2015

"Happy birthday, my son." The tiny gray-haired woman placed a small pineapple cake on the table in front of the well-dressed gentleman sporting a short salt and pepper beard. With shaky hands, she lit the single red candle that stood up from the fruit ring in the center.

"Mama, you don't have to..." Vladimir began.

"Shush. I am but an old woman, but I can still bake a cake for my baby boy." She set the lighter down and cupped his face, smiling as she peered at him through rheumy blue eyes. "Fifty-one today, and still my baby." She kissed his cheek.

Vladimir smiled as he patted her hands. Olga Brezhnev was seventy-six now, and her back hunched with osteoporosis. "Bal'shoye spaseeba, mama."

Inside the small but well-appointed flat decorated with the best furniture money could buy, his mother lived with his Aunt Ava. His Uncle Pavo passed the year before, and his own father met the wrong end of a butcher knife more than thirty-five years earlier.

"Ya tibya l'ublyu, Vladi." Olga pinched his bearded cheeks.

"I love you, too, mama."

"Now, make a wish, quick, before the wax drips onto the cake." She stood behind his chair with her hands on his shoulders.

Vladimir closed his eyes and pretended to make a wish to please his mother. He didn't believe in wishes, not since his sixth birthday. That was the day everything changed. No longer could his mother protect him from his father's wrath although she never stopped trying. The drinking Kirill indulged in sporadically became a daily occupation as lack of work drove his father to the streets. It was there he started peddling drugs for a local boss. Kirill was at first disgusted with this turn in his life, then began to embrace it. He worked hard, selling the poisonous product to the poor who could little afford such a habit. He helped contribute to the vicious cycle of poverty and suffering in the ghettos with no empathy whatsoever. If someone overdosed, it was an opportunity to sell to the deceased's friends so they could numb themselves to their grief.

Kirill trained his oldest son, Nicolay, in the art of the deal when he turned thirteen. At first, he succeeded in passing the cocaine to his friends in the neighborhood. He was proud of his oldest son until Nicolay, becoming too cocky and trying to impress a young lady, took his first hit of the drug. Before long, he was hooked and getting high on the inventory he was expected to sell. When he couldn't pay for the powder he'd blown through, Kirill had to step in and pay the boss out of his own pocket. Angry at the loss of money, his father showed his anger by beating Nicolay within an inch of his life. The beating was so severe, it broke Nicolay's leg costing Kirill even more in medical treatment. Nicolay eased the pain with more drugs, and when he couldn't afford more, he began stealing from papa's stash. Two weeks before his fifteenth birthday, Nicolay was found dead, a needle hanging from his arm.

Vladimir was devastated. As a boy, he had looked up to his big brother. He also knew that despite his coke habit, Nico had never once injected the stuff into his veins. He snorted or tasted, but he was acutely afraid of needles, a fear he never admitted to anyone except Vladimir. No one ever questioned his death, but Kirill's demeanor grew more violent and erratic. He would come home late, and if dinner wasn't waiting on the table or not to his liking, he would beat

Olga with his belt, and often with his fists. He didn't seem to care if Vladimir or his cousins saw him do it, and his Uncle Pavo was too afraid of his brother-in-law to stop him. Life went on like that for a time.

Kirill tried again bringing a son into the business. When Vladimir turned fourteen, he started running the street sales to the other kids. He kept his head down and did what he was told not wanting to anger his father. He also learned from Nicolay to never, ever use drugs. Some of the older kids made fun of him, taunting him about being a "big pussy" too afraid to take a hit, but Vladimir knew that he would always have the last laugh. He would never overdose, and his pockets would always be filled with cash. Meanwhile, they would remain poor and eventually die young or worse, die slowly, aging horribly while addicted to the white pony.

"Blow it out already!" Olga shook him out of his reverie.

He leaned over and blew out the flame. His Aunt Ava shuffled into the kitchen, leaning on her cane. "We're having cake?" She was half blind at seventy-nine, but her appetite had yet to wane.

"Da, Ava. It's Vladi's birthday. You remember. I told you just this morning, you loony old bat," Olga chuckled. "Come, sit. It's time to eat." She turned to her son. "And what did you wish for?"

Vladimir accepted the slice of cake on the porcelain plate with a grin. "You know I cannot say or else the wish won't come true."

"Silly boy." She cut another slice and placed it in front of Ava.

"So, what's the occasion? Is it my birthday?" Ava picked up her fork, smiling through her few remaining teeth. "I do so love cake."

Olga looked at Vladimir who shook his head. His aunt was several marbles shy of a full bag anymore. Soon, he would have to hire a nurse to come in and help take care of them. There was nothing he wouldn't do, no expense he would spare for his mother. She was dearer to him than anyone in the world. The three of them sat eating cake and sipping strong coffee for the next hour. Finally, Vladimir pushed his chair back and stood.

"I have to go now, mama."

"So soon? But what about dinner later?" She got up slowly and shuffled around the table.

"I can't. I have a business meeting, but I'll come tomorrow and take you both to lunch, yes?" He leaned down and kissed her forehead. Then, he did the same for his aunt. "I'll call tonight to check on you both."

"Such a good boy. I always knew he would grow up to be so good." Ava muttered through her second piece of cake.

Vladimir headed out the front door to the lift. On the way down, he pulled out his cell phone, hitting number two on his speed dial. It was answered immediately.

"Have the car ready." He exited the elevator and walked through the marble hallway. The concierge held the door open and waited as he walked through.

"Have a good evening, Mr. Brezhnev." The man kept his eyes ahead as he stood at attention. In his uniform for the condominium complex, he resembled a soldier.

"Thank you."

A black limousine waited. A large dark-haired man bulging with muscles covered in an expensive dark suit jumped out and opened the back door. Once Vladimir was inside, the man closed the door and climbed back into the front passenger seat. The driver, who wore an equally expensive suit, but was shorter, huskier, and bald, looked in the rearview mirror. "Where to, boss?"

"The warehouse. We have business to tie up," he said.

The man in the passenger seat smirked. The driver nodded and put the car in gear steering into and merging with the traffic.

A thud sounded, then two more knocks. Vladimir looked up from checking his messages. "Is that what I think it is?"

The man in the passenger seat sighed. "Yes, I'm sorry."

"Well, take care of it! I don't want to listen to that all the way to the warehouse." Vladimir ordered, anger seeping into his words.

The driver pulled over past the bridge onto a dirt road. There, hidden from passing cars by an old, rusted shack, the man in the passenger seat got out and walked to the back of the limo. He popped open the trunk. The *thwack* of a fist meeting bone filled the air, and then there was only silence. The muscular man closed the trunk and came around, sliding back into the front seat. Vladimir leaned forward.

"Make sure that doesn't happen again, Petrovich." He sat back slowly, focusing once again on his cellular.

"Yes, sir." Petrovich let out an inward sigh of relief. He looked down at his knuckles. They were already swelling. Next to him, the driver smothered a laugh. Once again, the car weaved into traffic heading toward the docks and warehouse number 214.

Read more here: *The Redemption of Joseph Heinz*, Book 3 in the Checkpoint, Berlin Detective Series. Visit micheleegwynnauthor.com and download now!

Also By Michele E. Gwynn

Visit my website for these books plus updates on upcoming releases!
micheleegwynnauthor.com.

Checkpoint Novels

Exposed: The Education of Sarah Brown (novel)
The Evolution of Elsa Kreiss (novel)
The Redemption of Joseph Heinz (novel)
The Making of Herman Faust (prequel novella)

Green Beret Series

Rescuing Emma (18+)
Loving Leisl
Freeing Fatima
Saving Christmas
Loving Freddie
Saving Major Morgan (A Green Beret Series prequel novella)

The Soldiers of PATCH-COM

Secondhand Soldier (18+)
Second Chance Soldier

Second Breath Soldier
Silent Night Soldier
C'est la Vie Soldier

The Harvest Trilogy
Harvest
Hybrids
Census
Section 5 (A Harvest Trilogy Spinoff)

Stand Alones
Darkest Communion (Paranormal Romance, 18+)
Waiting a Lifetime (Contemporary Romance, Mystical)
Hiring John (Romantic Comedy 18+)

Foreign Language Translations
Il faut retrouver Emma (La serie des Bérets verts: Tome 1)

www.ingramcontent.com/pod-product-compliance
Lightning Source LLC
Chambersburg PA
CBHW071502110726
47908CB00003B/697